S0-BIJ-033

NUCLEAR NIGHTMARE

James J. Collins

iUniverse, Inc.
New York   Bloomington

NEW HANOVER COUNTY
PUBLIC LIBRARY
201 CHESTNUT STREET
WILMINGTON, NC 28401

Nuclear Nightmare

Copyright © 2009 by James J. Collins, Jr

All rights reserved. No part of this book may be used or reproduced by any means, graphic, electronic, or mechanical, including photocopying, recording, taping or by any information storage retrieval system without the written permission of the publisher except in the case of brief quotations embodied in critical articles and reviews.

iUniverse books may be ordered through booksellers or by contacting:

iUniverse
1663 Liberty Drive
Bloomington, IN 47403
www.iuniverse.com
1-800-Authors (1-800-288-4677)

Because of the dynamic nature of the Internet, any Web addresses or links contained in this book may have changed since publication and may no longer be valid. The views expressed in this work are solely those of the author and do not necessarily refl ect the views of the publisher, and the publisher hereby disclaims any responsibility for them.

This is a work of fiction. All of the characters, names, incidents, organizations, and dialogue in this novel are either the products of the author's imagination or are used fictitiously.

ISBN: 0-595-50834-0 (pbk)
ISBN: 0-595-50087-0(cloth)
ISBN: 0-595-61670-4 (ebk)

Printed in the United States of America

ACKNOWLEDGMENTS

The author appreciates the contributions of Jason Frye, Paul Keaton, and Rebecca McDiarmid. Jason reviewed multiple drafts of the book and helped to make the whole thing happen. Paul provided valuable technical advice and reviewed the first draft of the book. Rebecca, with her excellent reader's eye, helped to keep it real. Everything else is the author's fault.

This book is dedicated to the memory of my brother, Gerald Paul Collins.

Contents

1. Banishment　　　　　　　　　　　　　1

2. Echoes　　　　　　　　　　　　　　13

3. Replay　　　　　　　　　　　　　　20

4. Rejuvenation　　　　　　　　　　　　34

5. Reactivation　　　　　　　　　　　　46

6. Springboard Begins　　　　　　　　　59

7. Over There　　　　　　　　　　　　76

8. The Hunt Begins　　　　　　　　　　95

9. Scrambling　　　　　　　　　　　　109

10. Interrogation　　　　　　　　　　　123

11. Worry　　　　　　　　　　　　　133

12. Planning　　　　　　　　　　　　141

13. Reinforcements　　　　　　　　　　147

14. More Questioning　　　　　　　　　158

15. Moving Forward　　　　　　　　　164

16. Loose Ends　　　　　　　　　　　175

17. Collaboration　　　　　　　　　　189

18. Discovery　　　　　　　　　　　　212

19. Recovery　　　　　　　　　　　　240

20. In Hospital　　　　　　　　　　　254

21. At Home　　　　　　　　　　　　276

22. Interrogation　　　　　　　　　　281

23. Epilogue　　　　　　　　　　　　307

1

Banishment

It was an early fall day on the waters of Carolina Beach Inlet. The sun was warm on Jerry Paul's face; there was a slight breeze, and the marsh grass on Masonboro Island looked like burnished gold. The water temperature was sixty-eight, and the tide would be peaking in about an hour. Conditions for fishing were optimal, and there was no competition from other fishermen. Jerry's was the only boat at this spot. He had caught flounder here in the past.

Jerry set the anchor and opened his large tackle box. He smiled at its contents. He had fishing hooks of all sizes: barbed, unbarbed, rounded, different leader lengths. *There must be a hundred of them,* he thought. The numerous compartments had a variety of lures: yellow, orange, pink, black, green; some had spinners, some feathers, others were unadorned. There were spools of different weight fishing line, different weight sinkers, a knife, a fish scaler, a tape measure, fishing reel lubricant, and other stuff that he had never used. *You might think you are a professional fisherman,* he thought to himself, *not someone who fishes occasionally.* But he was a sucker for fishing tackle stores. He couldn't pass one by and couldn't leave one without buying something. Now that he was retired, he might actually use some of the stuff.

He selected a flounder rig, tied it onto his line, baited it with a minnow, and dropped it to the bottom. He was in about eight feet of water.

As he sat on the rear transom of the nineteen-foot skiff, fishing pole in hand, Jerry expected a bite at any moment. But time passed with no action, and his mind drifted to the problem that often troubled him when he was not occupied—a problem he had left behind when he was forced to leave the CIA. If a terrorist group were to get their hands on the missing Plutonium-239, it would be disastrous.

As much as Jerry disliked Vice President Cheney's policies generally, the vice president had stated a useful concept when he formulated the "One Percent Doctrine." Cheney's idea was that if there was a 1 percent chance that a catastrophic terrorism event would come to pass, the government should act as if it was a certainty. No resources should be spared in the face of discovering and counteracting terrorism risks, including the acquisition of weapons-grade nuclear material by terrorists. This policy was being ignored, mostly because other priorities had risen above it and resources were strained.

A slight bump to Jerry's fishing rod brought him out of his reverie. His full attention was immediately focused on the end of the rod while he held the line loosely between his right thumb and index finger. It felt like his brown minnow bait had attracted the interest of a flounder. He waited motionless. After a few seconds, he felt movement—more protracted this time. This was the hard part; he restrained his impulse to jerk the rod upward. It was like the spy business; setting the hook needed to occur at the right moment. In another few seconds, he detected additional movement in the line, made himself wait two more seconds, and jerked upward. Immediately he felt the weight of the fish.

The flounder was medium sized, about three and a half pounds. Even if he caught no additional fish, it would be enough for him and Kathleen to enjoy for dinner. He put the fish into his live well to keep it fresh.

Jerry rebaited his hook with a fresh minnow and dropped his line. His attention to fishing stayed acute for a few minutes, but with no further action, he began to think again of the plutonium problem he had left behind when he was forced to retire. His frustration seemed irresolvable. He no longer had access to CIA agency resources, and no current staff believed the risk was grave enough to reopen the case. Pursuing the case was impossible without agency cooperation and resources.

Jerry caught one more flounder about the same size as the first one. He eventually tired of the lack of action and motored back to his boat slip about a half mile away. He washed down the boat, flushed the seventy-horsepower four-stroke with fresh water, stowed his fishing gear, and filleted the two flounders at the fish cleaning setup. He walked back to his house a block away. It was only three o'clock and Kathleen was still out and about.

Jerry and Kathleen had retired to their home on the Intracoastal Waterway at the southeast end of North Carolina about a year earlier. Living on the water had helped to heal Jerry's psyche. Looking at the water, sitting on it in his boat, just being near it, had helped him come to grips with his forced retirement. But the move was bittersweet, too. Neither of them had been ready to retire. Jerry's retirement "execution" scene sometimes replayed itself in his head.

After the 2004 Federal legislation that combined all U.S. intelligence operations into a single agency, the new agency head and his political appointees managed operations with a slash-and-burn style. Jerry's boss—a long-term, highly productive intelligence official—complained publicly and was fired. This left Jerry exposed and isolated. While at work, he had often planned to discuss something with his boss before he remembered his friend was gone.

In an internal reorganization, Jerry was moved from his job managing several ongoing operations in the Mideast. When he had been undercover in the field, he had recruited two of the foreign agents he was now managing from headquarters. The new position was a supervisory job in a new unit that analyzed agents' field reports from Africa. The job was a promotion; he had a secretary and a staff of twenty two. But now Jerry was handling a lot of administrative and personnel matters—and he was working on an area of the world that was new to him. His focus had always been the Soviet Union, Eastern Europe, and the Mideast. He was bored in the new job and wrote a memo asking for a transfer. He waited a month and heard nothing about his request. When he made a personal inquiry, he was told a change was not possible at that time and was asked to consider withdrawing his request.

Instead of withdrawing his request, Jerry requested a meeting with the deputy CIA director in his chain of command. When he arrived at the meeting ten days later, he found the deputy Hal Bolton and two others—an official of the CIA Human Resources Office and an agency attorney. The atmosphere was grim. He had the strange thought that he was about to be court-martialed. Jerry shook Hal Bolton's hand and shook hands with the others. He took the empty chair in front of Hal's desk.

With his eyes looking out over Jerry's head, Hal began, "Jerry, you have been one of the agency's most valuable assets for many years. Your record is impressive; your annual reviews are all positive; there are no negative reports in your file. I noticed the agency has awarded you three superior performance medals. Most do not know how important you have been to our intelligence operations, but I do. I want to express my personal gratitude and that of your government."

Hal continued to look past Jerry, who felt tempted to turn to find what he was looking at. Jerry felt a knot growing in his stomach. Hal sounded like he was delivering a eulogy. Jerry's breathing became shallow.

"Thank you, sir," he said.

Hal continued, "We are disappointed that you are dissatisfied with your promotion. We gave you additional and more important responsibilities. As you know, the intelligence world is changing."

"I recognize that, sir, but as I indicated in my memo, I feel my skills are being underutilized. My past experience and operative contacts are not in

Africa. I usually accept agency decision making without question, but I think my expertise in Eastern Europe, the Mideast, and specifically with the terror threat are barely relevant in my current job."

"We considered your background and skills before we assigned you to the new position," said Hal.

Jerry chose not to respond. He was beginning to sense that decisions had already been made, that nothing he said would influence the decisions, and that expressing his rising anger would make things worse. He waited, trying to calm his mind and control his breathing. He found himself looking at Hal's neck. It was not heavily muscled. He could snap it easily.

Hal continued, "I asked our personnel and legal folks to look for a solution that would be optimal for you." He turned to the Human Resources officer and said, "Ted, would you discuss the options that you have put together?"

"Certainly. I'd be glad to."

Jerry was having trouble staying calm and was only dimly aware as Ted Weiss began talking about Jerry's retirement benefits. As Ted's description of benefits, options, amounts of money, and procedures droned on, Jerry's composure began to return. He had become aware that Ted had been discussing dollars and cents a few minutes previously, but Jerry had not been able to process the details.

"Excuse me," said Jerry. "I haven't quite caught up with you. Would you go over those last few points again?"

"Certainly," said Ted. "We will put all this in writing eventually, but the essential points are that you are eligible for full retirement now. This eligibility also means that the government will pay for your medical insurance and that of your wife until both of you become eligible for Medicare, at which point the government's health insurance remains in effect, but it becomes secondary to Medicare. Deputy Bolton and the director have agreed to two retirement plan enhancements to increase your retirement income. We will add five years of service to your total and classify you at the next highest salary grade if you retire now. This will add almost a thousand dollars a month to your retirement income and likely add hundreds of thousand of dollars over your lifespan. Agency attorneys have reviewed this plan and confirm the enhancements meet agency legal requirements."

Hal interrupted, "We realize we are throwing a lot at you, Jerry. We don't expect you to make a decision this morning. You will have opportunities to ask questions later. We'll give you time to think things over."

"What are my options?" asked Jerry.

"Well, you can take advantage of the plan that Ted has been describing. Or you can, of course, continue in your present position."

Jerry hesitated. One of the skills he had fine-tuned during his espionage career was detecting subtext. The subtext was clear: he was going to be forced out of the CIA. It could be slow or fast; the circumstances might vary. But he was a goner! The reality of his situation began wrapping itself around him. He continued to worry that his composure would desert him.

"How much time do I have to decide?" he asked.

"Oh, I don't think we have to press you for a decision, Jerry. Do you think a month is enough time?"

Jerry realized he needed to get out of Hal's office.

"A month is probably okay," said Jerry, "but can I think about the entire matter and get back to you next week?"

"Sure," said Hal. "Is there anything else we have to discuss now?" Hal asked, looking at Ted and the attorney.

Both shook their heads.

Hal looked at Jerry. "Do you have anything else right now?"

"Nothing right now," said Jerry.

They stood, shook hands all around, and Jerry left the room.

Jerry felt he was in another reality. The universe had shifted under him in a half hour. They were going to end his career. He hurried to the elevator, took it down to the fifth floor, went immediately into the men's bathroom, and entered a stall. Without unbuckling his belt, he sat down on the toilet. He sat stunned for a time, and then heard himself sobbing. He regained control quickly; leaving the stall, he splashed cold water on his face, dried it, went to his office, and wrote a short e-mail indicating he was taking personal leave for the rest of the day. He sent it to the e-mail distribution list for his division, and within five minutes he was in his car headed home.

Kathleen was not at home. Jerry felt lost, like he had entered a new world. He wandered from room to room. He knew he could not concentrate enough to read and turned the television on, but could not register what was being said there, either. He turned the TV off, reclined his La-Z-Boy and closed his eyes. The emotions rolled back and forth over him: rage, sadness, guilt, disbelief, fear, confusion, and rage again. He went and poured several ounces of scotch over ice and got back into his recliner. He continued on the emotional roller coaster, finished his drink, and quickly fell asleep exhausted.

Jerry woke up when he heard the garage door open. Kathleen was home. He waited for her at the door from the garage. Kathleen was surprised and startled to find him standing there when she came into the house.

"What's wrong?" she asked.

Jerry could not talk. He put his arms around her and began to sob.

Kathleen let him cry for a few seconds, and then drew back.

"Jerry, what's wrong? Tell me what's wrong."

Jerry tried to get control, but had difficulty speaking.

"Has something happened to one of the children?" she asked.

Jerry shook his head, took her hand, went into the living room, and they sat down on the couch.

Kathleen waited as Jerry gathered himself.

Finally, he said, "They're forcing me out. The agency…they're going to force me to retire."

"What?" said Kathleen. "They can't do that—can they?"

"Well, as a practical matter, they can."

"You need to tell me more."

"I had that meeting with Hal this morning."

"I thought that meeting was about transferring back to your previous job."

"So did I," said Jerry. "But when I got to the meeting, Hal had a human resources rep and one of the agency's lawyers there. Hal told me what a great asset I had been for the agency and then laid out a supercharged retirement plan for me."

"But you don't have to retire, right?"

"No, I can keep working in my current job. The possibility of a job change within the agency was not even mentioned. It's pretty clear. I can keep my current job or retire."

"Those bastards! Those sleazy, motherfucking bastards! Who the hell is Hal? A fat-assed son of a bitch who sits behind a desk. I'll bet he doesn't have the medals they've given you."

Jerry's funk was lifted. He looked at Kathleen and started laughing. "I love you, Kathleen. You really know how to cut to the chase. And, as usual, you're right. They are bastards. But they're powerful bastards. And the new regime doesn't give a shit about me."

"That son of a bitch," she said.

"Thank you, Kathleen. I feel better. The shock of that meeting is passing. I'm still stunned and pissed and a little scared. But I think I'll live."

"Do you know what you're going to do?"

"No—and I'm not going to think about it right now. Let's go out and get something to eat," said Jerry.

At dinner, Jerry and Kathleen were able to make a decision: Jerry would not stay at the CIA in his current job. He recognized that he could not tolerate this job for the long term. It would not be good for him *or* the agency. But he was determined that he would not let the agency fully dictate his options.

Jerry went to work the next day as usual. As soon as his computer booted up, he sent an e-mail to Hal.

Mr. Bolton:

At our meeting yesterday we agreed that I could give you my response to the alternatives we discussed within 30 days. After thinking about it, I believe it would be difficult to fully consider matters in 30 days. As you know, important decisions are involved. Please consider my request for 90 days to make a decision about the options you suggested.

In the meantime, I will continue doing my current job at as high a level as I am capable.

Jerry Paul

Before the end of the day, Jerry got Hal's response.

I approve 90 days for your decision.

Jerry did several other things: he consulted a high powered attorney who specialized in employee matters; he had a financial consultant analyze his situation, and he initiated informal inquiries with a few colleagues at other places in the intelligence bureaucracy. He quickly found that finding a good spot elsewhere in the intelligence world was not feasible. In the end, Jerry cleaned out his desk a few months later and left feeling he had not let the agency victimize him. His lawyer had turned out to be a terrific asset. He negotiated additional financial enhancements to his retirement income, got the agency to pay for the financial analysis that Jerry had arranged, and essentially wrote the letter that the agency signed and made a permanent part of Jerry's personnel file. The letter stated that Jerry had been a major agency asset, had served his entire career without blemish, and was being retired reluctantly and without prejudice due to "extraordinary" agency circumstances.

The analysis of Jerry's financial situation had been reassuring. His monthly income was substantially more than he needed. In addition, his contributions to the government's supplementary retirement plan had been invested in the stock market for more than twenty years and had grown to seven figures. His home in northern Virginia had tripled in value over the years. Retirement would not impose a financial hardship.

2

Echoes

JERRY STRIPPED FOR A SHOWER to get rid of the salt water and smell of bait and fish. He checked his naked image in the bathroom mirror. He was proud to have kept his youthful physique and worked hard to maintain it with running and strengthening exercises five days a week. He was just under six feet tall and at 185 pounds weighed only ten pounds more than when he played basketball in college. Jerry had thick black hair that was turning gray on the sides. One of Kathleen's friends had captured his appearance years ago: she said he was "quietly handsome."

Kathleen was not home yet, so he got a cold lager and sat down at his computer. His e-mail volume had steadily decreased since retirement. It was now mostly from old friends, his children, and junk that he could not figure how to eliminate without also eliminating an occasional message that was important. As his eye scanned the half-dozen e-mails in his inbox, one from an old contact from the agency days caught his attention. He opened that one first.

Hi Jerry:

Have you gotten lazy and soft yet? Probably not. You're probably still pissed off at the CIA and trying to maintain your fighting weight in case you have a chance to show us up. I don't blame you. I had a call from an old friend of yours the other day—Yuli Karpov. He tried to get in touch with you and spoke to me when he figured out you were no longer here. He would not tell me why he wanted to talk to you, but said it was important and you would understand. Give me a call when you have a chance.

Scott

Jerry was immediately excited. He suspected Yuli's contact and his secrecy with Scott meant it was probably about the missing plutonium. Yuli was the one who first alerted Jerry about the missing plutonium. He went immediately to the telephone, called Scott, and found him in his office. After exchanging pleasantries, Scott asked Jerry if he knew why Yuli was calling.

"I think I do," said Jerry.

"Can you tell me?" asked Scott.

"If it's what I think it is, we should discuss it in person."

"Does it qualify as *official?*" asked Scott.

"Yes, it already has a file and case number, but the case has been inactive for some time."

"Okay," said Scott. "I'll tell you what makes sense. I have a business trip to Fort Bragg in Fayetteville next week. Fayetteville is about a hundred miles from Wilmington, right?"

"Right," said Jerry.

"Would you like to get together for dinner next Tuesday or Wednesday night?"

"Good idea," said Jerry. He suggested they meet at a small restaurant on Route 401 just outside Fayetteville.

Scott suggested Tuesday night at seven o'clock, and Jerry accepted.

Jerry had worked occasionally with Scott Regan in the 1990s. They had initially become friendly because they both had spent their youth in Philadelphia. They had not known each other when they were young, but they had common experiences and were both Eagles and Phillies fans. They developed an easy rapport at work and discovered they also had a lot in common personally and politically.

Jerry and Scott worked well together. Scott had an easy demeanor that folks found comfortable, and he was good at encouraging people to share information by letting people draw their own conclusions while gently guiding them in the direction he wanted them to go. Scott was just as intense and goal-driven as Jerry, but it was not apparent. Jerry was open and friendly, but if there was something important on his mind, his face betrayed it. As a result people tended to be more guarded with him when he was "working."

Jerry went to the kitchen to begin dinner preparations. He was looking forward to the fresh flounder, and as he began preparing a green salad, he heard the garage door open. Kathleen was back. He felt a smile on his face; he was almost always delighted to see Kathleen, even after short absences. But he felt apprehension, hoping that she had had some success in her attempts to get some consulting work. He worried about her reaction to his plan to meet with Scott. The garage door closed, and Jerry waited for Kathleen to come into the house. He could not read anything in her face as they greeted each other with a kiss.

"How was the fishing?" she asked.

"Okay. Good enough to supply fresh flounder for dinner," he replied.

"How did your day go?" Jerry asked.

"It's hard to say," replied Kathleen. "I had appointments: one with the human resources manager at Corning and one with one of the partners at a construction company over in Leland. They both seemed interested in my ideas, but I didn't seen to generate any real enthusiasm. Frankly, I'm worried that there's not a niche for me down here."

From the late-1980s until she left the firm to move to Wilmington, Kathleen had developed a good professional reputation helping companies analyze and develop strategies for their personnel policies and practices. Kathleen was drawn to the employment equity area—focusing on companies' hiring, promotion, and pay policies. There were plenty of opportunities for this kind of consulting work in the Washington area, but similar opportunities were limited in Wilmington.

Kathleen was a quick learner who was good at problem solving, and she had an instinct for resolving conflicts. Jerry said she had a "playground sense of justice," and this basic sense of fairness helped her to design agreements that both parties in a dispute could accept. But Wilmington, North Carolina was much smaller than Washington, DC, had many fewer businesses, and a very different mix of business types.

Kathleen went back to the bedroom to change into what she had started to call her "beach-house costume"—loose, knee-length shorts, a loose top with no bra, and sandals. She came back out to join Jerry in the kitchen.

"What can I do to help?" asked Kathleen.

"I've got the flounder ready to broil and planned to bake a couple potatoes in the microwave. I've started a green salad."

"I'll finish the salad," said Kathleen.

"It's still early," Jerry said. "Would you like a gin and tonic before dinner?"

"That would be nice."

"Why don't you sit on the porch, and I'll bring our drinks out in a minute."

Kathleen got the newspaper and took it out to the screened porch overlooking the Waterway while Jerry mixed the drinks, finishing each off with a thick piece of lime.

When Jerry settled into his chair on the porch, he said, "I heard from Scott Regan today."

"Scott from the agency?"

"Yes," said Jerry

Kathleen waited.

"I'm going to meet him for dinner next Tuesday night in Fayetteville."

"What's it about?" Kathleen asked, trying to hide the concern in her voice.

"Yuli Karpov has been in touch with the agency. You remember him don't you? We had him over for dinner a couple times."

"Yes, I remember, but what's this about?"

"Yuli wouldn't tell Scott specifically. He wants me to get in touch with him."

"I don't like the sound of this Jerry. You're retired."

"I know, Kathleen. But it is important to find out why Yuli has come to us. He wouldn't do that unless it was important. He's probably sticking his neck out, too. The Russians don't like their people talking to us directly."

"But why can't someone else meet with him?"

"He would only talk to me. I expect it's because of all the turmoil and changes that have taken place at the agency in the last few years. Yuli no longer knows who is responsible for what at the CIA, and doesn't know who is trustworthy."

"You can help him identify the right person to contact, Jerry. You don't have to get involved directly."

"I think the important issue for Yuli is trust. There's plenty of reason for distrust and skepticism about CIA among the Russians. I suspect he'll want to take it slowly, to check things out before sharing any sensitive information. Yuli developed confidence in me over the years. I think he believes he can trust me, at least with some initial information. I also have a hunch that Yuli's contact could be about that missing plutonium case I worked on for several years."

"I have an uncomfortable feeling about this Jerry. I can see you being drawn back into this thing further than I think you should go."

"I'll be careful, Kathleen. I'm beginning to enjoy fishing, and especially being able to spend so much time with you."

"I know you, Jerry. If new information looks important or interesting, you won't be able to forgo getting involved. Be honest with me. If it looks like there may be a real opportunity for locating the missing plutonium, will you be able to resist?"

"I'm not sure I can, Kathleen. You know how important the case is. One hundred kilograms of Plutonium-239 can produce six or more nuclear weapons within months. If I can help, I think I have to try."

"You don't owe those bastards anything, Jerry. They treated you badly. The son of a bitch deputy director that forced you out should be shot!"

"You're right, Kathleen. I don't owe the agency anything. They got the best I could give for a long time. But at the risk of sounding corny, I'd like to make things safer for you and me and our kids and hopefully our grandkids some day, and our neighbors and their kids and grandkids, and …"

Jerry was uncomfortable talking out loud in this way.

Kathleen was silent. She understood it would be difficult to prevent Jerry's involvement in the case if promising information about the plutonium came to him. She began to think about how she might limit his involvement or reduce its risk, at the same time acknowledging silently to herself that she was unlikely to be able to exert much influence over the momentum of events. It wasn't until Jerry retired that she came to understand how much his job worried her. The murder of those CIA employees at Langley in 1994 had unsettled her, and the risks had only seemed to increase since then.

"I'm hungry," said Kathleen. "Let's get dinner ready."

3

Replay

JERRY LEFT AT FOUR O'CLOCK the following Tuesday for his seven o'clock dinner with Scott. Jerry got onto I-40, set his speed control at seventy-five, and settled into the half-hour drive before he got off at Route 24 toward Fayetteville. He began to wonder about Yuli's information. It must involve the missing plutonium. He could think of no other reason for Yuli's attempt to contact him. They had cordial professional relationship years before and had socialized on a few occasions, but they had had no recent contact with each other. If it wasn't about the plutonium, Jerry could not imagine what it could be. The history of the case still fascinated him. It had been an important historical moment.

The CIA did not understand, but the Soviet Union was beginning to come apart in the mid-1980s. Ronald Reagan had begun to exchange letters with the Soviet premier Andropov in 1984, but Andropov died after only a year in office. There was a short period after Andropov when Chernenko took over, but Mikhail Gorbachev came to power in '85 or '86. It wasn't long before we began to recognize the real possibility of change under Gorbachev. Our diplomats sensed new openness and flexibility in talking with their people. The CIA's own agents and sources also began to recognize change was afoot. National Security Agency intercepts were indicating the same thing.

After the first George Bush was elected, even before he took the oath of office, he began having discussions with Gorbachev. The first cracks in the Soviet Union were becoming visible. Hungary and other Soviet states were beginning to act independently, and, of course, the Berlin Wall came down in 1989. And there was the attempted coup against Gorbachev in August of '91.

Bush and Gorbachev met in Malta for a couple days in late-1989. Most folks, including the two presidents themselves, did not understand it at the time, but the Cold War was essentially over at the end of that summit. Bush was accommodating and offered Gorbachev substantial financial aid. So when Gorbachev announced the breakup of the Soviet Union on Christmas Day two years later in 1991, there was not nearly the shock and turmoil that might have resulted if there had not been the dialogue and cooperation between us and the Soviets.

After the breakup of the Soviet Union in 1991, when the initial exhilaration about victory in the Cold War passed, lots of people in the U.S. began worrying about the thousands of nuclear weapons spread around the former Soviet Union. Russian scientists and officials were concerned too, and a joint effort by Russia and U. S. officials was undertaken. Both countries tried hard to get control of the nuclear weapons and material scattered across the former Soviet Union. They worked together at weapons sites, signed agreements, and tried in a variety of ways to secure the weapons. Their efforts had a lot of success, but the recordkeeping on the Russian side was such that no one was confident that every nuclear weapon and all the fissile material had been secured. In fact, Jerry was aware of the details of one instance where a substantial amount of plutonium had gone missing. He was sure this was why Yuli had tried to get in touch with him.

Jerry arrived at the restaurant parking lot about twenty minutes early. There were half a dozen vehicles in the gravel lot—three pickups, a Town Car, and two SUV's. He was pretty sure none of these belonged to Scott; he would be driving a rental car—probably a midsize GM or Ford model. He waited in his car. A couple more cars pulled in while he was waiting, and just before seven, a gray Taurus pulled in. It was Scott. They met at the door to the restaurant and shook hands.

Scott was about ten years younger than Jerry and currently worked for the National Counterterrorism Center (NCTC). Scott had joined the NCTC in 1989 after he had been with the agency for about two years. In recent years, NCTC had grown in size and responsibility, working to deal with real risks to the country and its allies. Scott was smart and resourceful, could read and speak Arabic, and knew how to work the intelligence bureaucracy. He had quickly risen to be the youngest deputy director of NCTC.

Jerry and Scott first worked with each other in 1992. After the breakup of the Soviet Union, the agency had formed a working group with personnel from the NCTC, the directorate of Science and Technology, and Jerry's

Soviet/East Europe unit. Scott was a junior member of the ten-person working group, and Jerry was one of three senior people. The group stayed active until the Nuclear Nonproliferation Agreement was signed with Russia. Jerry had liked working with Scott and could tell he would move up in the agency over time. He was hardworking, smart, and politically savvy. He knew when to inject an observation or idea into the process and when to keep his head down.

Jerry had been right. Scott was now one of three senior people in NCTC. When U.S. intelligence operations were reorganized by Congress, the Counterterrorism Center had been placed prominently in the Office of the Director of National Intelligence. Counterterrorism was currently a high priority and a very visible focus of U.S. intelligence. Scott had come to Fort Bragg today for two days of meetings with the Special Forces Command.

The restaurant was at a rural intersection. The one-floor wood building was unimpressive, but the food was first-rate "Southern"—pork barbecue, lots of fried chicken and fish dishes, sweet iced tea, and hush puppies. There was a large bar separated from the restaurant area by a wood partition. The jukebox in the corner of the bar glowed rainbow neon. Willie Nelson was winding up the last few lines of "The Highwayman" as they sat down. There were only a few people sitting quietly at the bar. A half-dozen tables in the restaurant were occupied. The kitchen smell was sweet and warm.

Old Hollywood pictures hung on the restaurant walls. Jerry and Scott took a table on the far wall under a picture of Humphrey Bogart in *Casablanca*.

"So how is retirement, old man?" asked Scott.

"How about you drop the old man part? I'm still ready to go."

"I know," said Scott smiling. "I could not resist the chance to comment on your retirement."

"Thanks a lot, Scott."

"More seriously, Jerry, I never got the chance to talk to you when you were leaving the agency. I hope you understand that a lot of folks miss you and understand you were treated badly. Seems like the agency spent half its time looking for inside scapegoats for a couple years."

"Thanks," said Jerry. "I got a good separation deal, but I wish I could get over being pissed off about it. Has it gotten any better recently?"

"Well, it's quieter and counterterrorism is being allowed to do our work without much interference. And they're throwing more resources at us than we can use. Congress thinks the answer to just about everything is more resources. The director and congressional liaison people never say no to more money, so we're constantly hiring new staff."

"I know what you mean. Too much money can be almost as challenging as too little in our business. But how are things going for you and your group?"

"I'm pretty happy," said Scott. "I think you know my group is focusing on the Middle East. I have a few very good operational folks who spend most of their time out in the field, and two of them are fluent Arabic speakers. My office staff has been pretty stable and productive. Several of them are fluent in Arabic and a mix of dialects. My major problem is finding folks who speak and read the languages, or waiting for new language analysts to be trained. There is such a demand for Arabic speakers that I have a big turnover among these staff. There are a lot of opportunities for Arab speakers in both public and private sectors."

"It's nice that you're satisfied and feel like you can get some real work done." Jerry stopped talking, and waited for Scott to say something.

"Let's order," said Scott. "Then you can tell me why Yuli called."

Scott ordered the large barbecue plate. "That's my standard order whenever I come to North Carolina," he said. "I love barbecue."

Jerry ordered white meat fried chicken. They both had sweet iced tea to drink.

Scott started, "You remember Yuli Karpov, right?"

"Of course. He was a big help to us when we were trying to locate all those nuclear weapons and get control of the fissile material. Without him and his boss, we would have been lost. Yuli and I became friends, too. He visited Kathleen and me a couple times at home, and I took him to a couple college basketball games. He loves basketball. I was also able to help him get his son into Drexel University in Philadelphia."

"That's where you went to school, isn't it?" asked Scott.

"Yes. I graduated from Drexel in 1972."

"Well, I heard from Yuli about a week ago. He tried to contact you at the agency and asked for me when he figured out you were no longer there. He apparently remembered me from our work with the nonproliferation working group that we had in the early '90s. He asked that I call him back at a specific time two days later and gave me a number. I checked the number out before I called. The number was for a hotel room in Tallinn, Estonia."

"Really," said Jerry. "I thought Yuli was still working for the Russian government and living outside Moscow."

"I think he still lives outside Moscow, but he told me he works for the Yukos Oil Company. We had a fairly short conversation. The thing he wanted to be sure I told you was that 'Ryecatcher was loose.' He would not say more, and when I asked if CIA could help, he said he would not talk to anyone but you. Do you know what he's talking about?"

"I do," said Jerry. "Do you remember the operation we put together with the Russians in Kazakhstan in 1993?"

"I think so," said Scott. "Isn't that the operation where you and several of our nuclear scientists from the Department of Energy gathered up a bunch of nuclear weapons and weapons-grade nuclear material with the help of the Russian scientists and the KGB?"

"Yes. That's the operation. It was a major step in getting control of the nuclear weapons and fissile material that the Soviets had kept in Kazakhstan during the Cold War."

The waitress brought their food.

"Man, I love that northeastern North Carolina barbecue," said Scott as he put a large forkful into his mouth. "They just don't know how to make this stuff north of Virginia. Pass me that barbecue sauce."

"It's the pork fat," said Jerry.

"And these hush puppies are delicious. My wife tried to make them a couple times, and they just didn't turn out right."

"It's the grease," said Jerry.

Jerry started working on his fried chicken, and they ate in silence for a while. When they finished eating, Jerry continued giving Scott the background.

"I don't remember if you were in many of those early-1992 meetings at the agency, but many of us were really worried. A few thought the end of the Soviet Union was going to bring the nuclear holocaust that we had feared since the Soviets exploded their first bomb in 1948."

"I was still fairly new at the agency at that time. I didn't sit in on the meetings, but I remember the talk around the office. I know there were a lot of worried people."

Jerry continued, "Ukraine, Kazakhstan, and Belarus inherited thousands of nuclear weapons when the Soviet Union collapsed. And we worried about the hundreds of newly unemployed soviet nuclear scientists. But, as you know, after a few years, we were able to get a fairly good handle on the problem. We courted and reassured the Soviet nuclear science community, and Russia was also determined to get control of the nuclear weapons problem and was very helpful."

"Good thing," said Scott.

Jerry continued, "Now we come to the problem I think Yuli has contacted you about. You remember when Robert Gates elevated the CIA's Nonproliferation Center to be a unit under the Director, right?"

"Yes, that was about the same time as the Soviet breakup."

"You probably also remember the meeting Gates and Ambassador Robert Strauss had with the KGB in October '92."

"I remember."

"One of the priority projects identified at that meeting was the large stockpiles of nuclear weapons and material in Kazakhstan. The security of that stuff was really shaky, and the risk of these materials being stolen or sold by staff or others who knew about them was high."

Scott commented, "I remember writing a report about the shortage of money to pay Russian security staff, the staff attrition, and the facilities themselves were deteriorating."

"It was a very dangerous situation," said Jerry. "We developed a joint initiative with the Russians to secure the weapons and fissile material. One of the final outcomes was that the U.S. Air Force flew in with a C-5 aircraft in November 1994 and removed a half ton of weapons and weapons-grade uranium and plutonium, flew it to the U.S, and trucked it to storage at the Lawrence Livermore National Laboratory. As far as I know, the material is still at Livermore."

"That's amazing," said Scott.

The waitress came to remove their empty dinner plates and leave their banana pudding desert.

"About a year later, I ran into Yuli at a meeting in Geneva. He asked to have dinner one evening and told me he thought that about one hundred kilograms of Plutonium-239 had not made it out of that Kazakhstan facility. He had no idea where it was, but was convinced it was missing."

"Why did Yuli think it was missing?"

"There was about a twenty-page manifest listing all the weapons and fissile material that was being removed from the Kazakhstan facility. It was prepared jointly by us and the Russians. Each individual weapon and container of fissile material was listed separately by category. Yuli was examining the manifest for some other reason a few months after the removal and noticed an inconsistency in the Plutonium-239 section. The total amount of the Plutonium-239 shown and the individual amounts in each container were inconsistent."

"I'm not sure I follow you," said Scott.

"If you added the weights shown for each individual container, it comes to one hundred kilograms less than the total amount shown."

"Could it be a simple addition error?"

"Yuli believes that it's not possible because he was in charge of the plutonium aspect of the work. Each container was weighed two or three times; there were fourteen containers. The weight was marked on each container, and the total came to a little more than 1,000 kilograms. At this point in the process, the final plutonium manifest was prepared."

"Seems like a pretty careful process," said Scott.

"It was, but the plutonium was not loaded onto the airplane until the next day, and this is where it appears the problem occurred. Best he can figure, someone removed a small amount of plutonium from about half of the containers and changed the amount shown on these containers to the reduced amount."

"How could that have happened?"

"The plutonium containers were near the back of the warehouse, and the security guard was either not alert or part of the theft plan. It was a fairly simple matter to cut the metal fasteners on the containers, remove the plutonium, replace the fasteners, and affix a new label with the reduced weight."

"Didn't anyone check again before the containers were loaded?"

"They did weigh the containers again before they were put on the aircraft, but the labels accurately reflected the individual container's weight. Apparently no one checked to see that the individual weights were consistent with the total shown on the manifest. We guess that whoever took the plutonium was involved in the final checking."

"Wow. Didn't they pick it up at Lawrence Livermore?"

"No…and I'm not sure why. The checks that were used at Livermore when the shipment arrived were not documented. We assume that they may have simply weighed the containers and not added the individual container totals to see if they were consistent with the total shown on the manifest. We definitely dropped the ball there."

"I assume you had that checked out."

"Definitely. As soon as I got back from Geneva, I sent a memo to DCI about Yuli's belief. He got in touch with the Lawrence Livermore director and had them check it out. Yuli was right. There is a one hundred kilogram shortage."

"That's not good. Do we have any idea where it is?"

"No. Probably in Russia or one of the former Soviet states, assuming it has not already been sold."

"That's scary," said Scott.

"It haunts me," said Jerry. "Did Yuli tell you how I was to contact him?"

"Yes, I have an e-mail address. But you are to use a computer from an Internet café or public library when you communicate with him—not a computer that could be identified with you or the agency. It seems clear that the e-mail address that he has given me is also in some public location. Yuli will be at a computer with access to that e-mail address between nine and ten a.m. East Coast time next Tuesday. He hopes to hear from you during that hour."

"I can arrange to do that, but the contact will not be productive unless I can tell him what I can do—what agency assets we are willing to commit to help."

"I cleared our meeting here tonight with my boss," said Scott.

"That was smart," said Jerry with a smile. "I know what happens when your boss thinks you are acting independently."

"Tell me about it," said Scott. "Our new management has made things unpleasant in a lot of ways. And you won't be surprised to hear that they are not happy that Yuli has forced them to involve you."

"I'm not surprised," said Jerry. "They were happy to see me go, were miffed that I drove a hard bargain, and can't be pleased that I am back in their world with some leverage. They hate not fully controlling everyone in their orbit. And the missing plutonium is a problem they can't ignore."

"I agree," said Scott. "But you understand they will try to keep you on a short leash."

"Yes, but if Yuli has promising information and will only deal with me, I'll have the leverage I need to get the agency support and resources I need to work the case. I won't rub their noses in it. I want to make it easy for them so that we have the best chance to recover the plutonium. If I can help get control of it, I'll be very happy; I'll sleep better at night."

"No question it will eliminate a major threat if we can manage it," said Scott. "In the end, I think the agency will support your involvement."

"Where do we go from here?" asked Jerry.

"Here's the initial plan. I will be your contact at the agency, at least for now. You communicate with Yuli as he directed. If his information sounds solid and you assess that there is some possibility of locating the missing plutonium, call me to set up a meeting at the agency."

"Sounds good. I'll call you right after I have the e-mail exchange with Yuli."

Scott lowered his voice. "Can I say something off the record?"

"Sure," said Jerry, "just between you and me."

"If the agency agrees to put you back to work, I'm sure it will be under a consulting contract."

"That makes sense," said Jerry.

"Ask for a $700 or $800 a day consulting fee—plus travel, per diem, and other expenses."

"Really?" asked Jerry. "Do you think they would pay me that much?"

"Maybe not," said Scott. "But I bet they'd agree to at least $600 a day without any trouble."

"Thanks for the advice, Scott," said Jerry.

Jerry and Scott finished their banana pudding, talked about the recent underperformance of the Philadelphia Eagles football team, and were on their separate ways by 8:30. Jerry's mind raced on the drive back to Wilmington.

He usually used times like these to listen to music. Recently, he had discovered the singer-songwriter Guy Clark's material and had already accumulated four of Clark's CDs. Jerry had played a couple of them on the way to Fayetteville and normally would have done the same on the way home. But he could not help puzzling about what might be going on with the missing plutonium. He turned the music off.

4

Rejuvenation

JERRY AND YULI HAD WORKED together regularly on nonproliferation matters and had discovered they had a lot in common. Yuli was a few years younger than Jerry, but they had similar personalities. Each man was serious and hardworking, with a strong commitment to his profession. Yuli was primarily a scientist and thought like one. He had been trained in the Soviet Union as a physicist and had done graduate work in physics at the University of California. He completed all the work for a Ph.D. in physics at Cal, except the dissertation. The Soviet government was unwilling to provide the time and financial support Yuli needed to research and write a dissertation. Yuli was perpetually disappointed that he had not completed the Ph.D. The degree would have enhanced his professional opportunities and stature. He told Jerry that the experience left him with a vague sense of personal failure.

Yuli took pride in finishing things he started. Jerry and Yuli were a lot alike in that way.

Driving in the dark, Jerry started planning his next steps. He was excited about the opportunity to work the plutonium case again. He'd been forced by CIA management to move the case to an inactive status in the late 1990s because no new information about the case had developed for some time. But the case had never gone inactive in Jerry's head. With modest technical expertise, converting the Plutonium-239 into multiple nuclear weapons was within reach of a government or terrorist organization like Al Qaeda.

Jerry smiled about his likely role as an agency consultant. He would have a level of independence that he never had as a CIA employee. But he quickly realized he was getting ahead of himself. It was not yet clear that Yuli had new information. Even if Yuli's information was compelling, the Counterterrorism Center might resist Jerry's involvement, or at least try to minimize it. The agency was always reluctant to have outsiders working directly on cases, and Jerry had become an outsider as soon as he retired—especially because he had been forced out. Bringing him back might look like the agency had erred in letting him go. Jerry was concerned that Hal Bolton had a defensive mindset that would make it difficult for him to allow Jerry to come back—even as a consultant.

On the other hand, he was sure that if Yuli had new information that could be followed up, the agency would accept his involvement. Jerry recognized he would be smart to be on his best behavior when he sat down with the agency's decision makers. His old boss Hal Bolton was still in place.

He had to be careful not to appear to have any interest in payback for the way he had been treated.

Jerry was almost at the end of I-40 and only a mile or so from entering the city of Wilmington. At this time of night, there was no traffic. He would be home in about twenty minutes. His thoughts turned to what he would say to Kathleen. She would know a few minutes into their conversation that he had already been drawn back into nuclear espionage.

Jerry pulled into his garage at about 11:15. He hoped Kathleen was asleep. He was tired and did not want to have a discussion about his meeting with Scott. Better to talk about it after a night's sleep. But when he came up the steps from the garage, he could see the light in the bedroom was still on. She had waited up for him.

"Hi, baby," he said.

Kathleen put down her book and reached for a hug.

They hugged silently.

"Tell me about the meeting," she said.

Jerry summarized his discussion with Scott.

"So when do you contact Yuli?"

"Next Tuesday morning," said Jerry.

"And then what? You go meet with the agency assholes?"

"Yes—probably," he said.

"And strike a deal with the devil!" she said, tears welling up in her eyes.

"They will not dictate to me this time," said Jerry firmly. "If I decide to get involved, I'll have a lot of influence over what I do; I'll be an independent contractor."

"What are you likely to be doing?" Kathleen asked.

"I really don't know. It all depends on what information Yuli has."

"You won't be traveling overseas, will you?"

"I just don't know Kathleen," he said—knowing he probably would have to travel outside the country. Kathleen did not like his overseas trips. They were usually lengthy, and he was sometimes out of touch for days at a time.

Jerry took Kathleen's hand and leaned over to kiss her expecting it would be a perfunctory goodnight kiss, but Kathleen put her arms around his neck and drew him into a long embrace. Jerry kicked his shoes off and lay down beside her. Kathleen turned to face him. They kissed again—longer this time. Jerry felt a long sigh leave his chest. They lay quietly in an embrace for a time. Jerry reached under Kathleen's nightgown to stroke her thigh. His mouth found her breast. Soon they were both fully aroused.

Jerry stood up to remove his clothes; it took some twisting to get his trousers over his erect penis. Kathleen watched him. When his clothes lay in a pile on the floor, Jerry reached over and took Kathleen's nightgown off over her head. She lay back, and Jerry stood for a minute looking at her naked body. As usual his eyes were drawn to her legs, the same legs he first was drawn to years ago on the basketball court. He reached down with both hands and grasped her right thigh, massaged it gently for a few seconds, and lay down beside her.

Jerry and Kathleen's lovemaking was one of the best parts of their life together—sometimes predictable but always pleasurable. Kathleen was more adventurous than Jerry and often surprised him. Jerry was attentive to Kathleen's nonverbal preferences. It was rare when they were not mutually satisfied. Recently their encounters had slowed and taken on a sweetness that gave them new pleasure. Tonight was one of those nights. Neither of them was in a hurry; they savored the trip. When their bodies relaxed, they fell asleep without speaking.

Jerry was at the main library in downtown Wilmington just after it opened the following Tuesday. The library was two blocks from the Cape Fear River, clearly visible from the street corner outside. The river's current was running swiftly north. There were several free computers on the first floor; he selected one where the monitor faced a blank wall, opened the e-mail software, and entered Yuli's e-mail address.

Yuli:

Scott Regan told me to contact you about Ryecatcher, so I assume you have new information. I would like to help. I believe the agency will cooperate. Final approval will depend on additional information I provide from you, but I am optimistic.

I will wait at this computer for two hours (until 1008 EST) today. If I do not hear from you by then, I will return to the same computer tomorrow at 0800 EST and wait two hours. You can also contact me by phone at 910-764-1836 (L) or 910-866-7795 (C).

Jerry

Jerry sent the e-mail, went to the stacks, selected a reference volume at random, and returned to the computer. He smiled when he noticed the reference book was a listing of zoos in countries around the world. As he browsed through the volume, he remembered the tragedy of the Baghdad Zoo after the U.S. invasion of Iraq in 2003. He flipped to the section on the Baghdad Zoo, last updated in 1999, and read about the zoo's holdings. The holdings were not world class but seemed equivalent to smaller zoos he and Kathleen had visited with their children. He wondered how many of the animals were still alive. He was pretty sure the zoo was no longer operating. Iraq's infrastructure problems were so extensive that the zoo would be a low priority.

Jerry checked the inbox. Yuli had responded.

Jerry:

Good to hear from you. Can you tell me something about yourself?

Yuli

Jerry understood. Yuli wanted to be certain he was communicating with the real Jerry Paul.

Yuli:

I went to Drexel. Captain of the basketball team in 1971–72. Best point guard in Philadelphia that year. Kathleen, Jerry Jr., and Erin are all well. I think the score of the game you and I attended in College Park in about 1996 was Terps 79, AMU 62.

Jerry

Jerry sent his response. He had a response from Yuli in a few minutes.

Jerry:

Wonderful to hear from you. Are you sure you were the best point guard in Philadelphia college basketball in 1972? I'll have to verify that.

My information about Ryecatcher is vague and troubling. I am traveling quite a bit in my job with Yukos Oil and ran across a former physicist colleague at a meeting. He told me he had been asked to verify the authenticity of a substantial volume of plutonium that was being offered for sale. The man seeking verification is not a scientist; he is a known weapons trafficker. Rumor has it that he was involved in helping to divert oil to Sadaam after the Iraq oil embargo was implemented in the 1990s. It is likely this trafficker does not have the material in hand yet. My physicist friend was noncommittal, but left the door open.

The thing that really got my attention was mention of the name of the Russian who was the facilities manager at the location of that operation where Ryecatcher went missing. He is living in Estonia or Finland now and apparently has some role in the possible transaction. This man is one of those who could have managed the "inventory shrinkage" we verified.

I am not sure of the next best step, but it might make sense to have you come over to meet with my physicist friend and me to plan. What do you think?

Yuli

Jerry responded right away.

Yuli:

I trust your judgment. A meeting probably makes sense. But can you give me a little more information? I am retired. A new regime is in charge, and I have to convince them to reopen the case and commit resources.

Jerry

Yuli's response took a little longer.

Jerry:

My physicist friend was a Soviet nuclear scientist; he is employed at Yukos, but is also a technical advisor to the Russian Security Service. I cannot give you his name. Apparently the material in question is now physically located somewhere close to Estonia. Please do everything you can to keep my name secret. Although I no longer work for the Russian government, the relationship between Yukos and the government is very close. My job or worse could be jeopardized if my role became known.

Yuli

Jerry wrote back.

Yuli:

I will meet with my people late this week or early next. How about we communicate by e-mail again on Wednesday, one week from tomorrow (eight days) at 0800 EST. You can also call me at home or at my home e-mail: jerrypaul@colony.net.

Jerry

Jerry started to e-mail Scott at the agency to share Yuli's e-mails and to set up a meeting. But he reconsidered and closed the software. He thought it better to keep his communication with Yuli private for now. When he got home, he sat down at his computer and e-mailed Scott requesting a meeting at the agency.

Late in the day, Jerry got an e-mail from Scott confirming a meeting at headquarters in northern Virginia the following Tuesday at 9:00. A meeting agenda and list of attendees was included.

Meeting Time: October 23, 2007, 0900

Place: 8ᵗʰ floor conference room

Topic: Nonproliferation

Attendees: Hal Bolton, Deputy Director; Scott Regan, David Greenberg, National Counterterrorism Center; Charles Sparks, Science & Technology; Ted Weiss, Human Resources; Liam Hunter, Legal Affairs; Jerry Paul, Consultant.

AGENDA

Specifics of the problem

Proposed approach

Staff and other resource needs

Reporting

Agency support systems

Jerry read the memo carefully and placed a call to Scott.

"Hi, Scott."

"I guess you got my e-mail," replied Scott.

"I did," said Jerry. "But I'd like some help reading between the lines. Do you have a few minutes to talk?"

"I have a meeting in about twenty minutes, but go ahead," said Scott.

"First, can you tell me a little about some of the meeting attendees? I don't know David Greenberg or Charles Sparks."

"David works for me in counterterrorism. If we go forward with an operation, he will probably be your day-to-day contact; he'll be easier to reach than me. I don't know Charlie Sparks very well; he's a techie. I understand he's creative and easy to work with. I assume Hal is having him attend the meeting so that the technical folks can arrange secure communications for you. Charlie will also probably be your liaison with our science people in case there is a need to get nuclear expertise from their staff or our stable of consultants. Depending on how it goes, we may also want to involve the Department of Energy."

"I'm impressed," said Jerry. "From the attendees and their expertise, it seems that Hal is taking things seriously—like he is leaning toward a full-fledged operation."

"I wouldn't go that far yet," said Scott. "I had something to do with who is coming to the meeting. Hal was planning a meeting with just you, me, and him. I convinced him that it would save time if we had all the key offices involved from the beginning—in case he decides to move forward. I think he still has reservations. I think there's a part of him that would like this problem to go away. He is coming to the issue late, and I don't think he is convinced that the risk is a grave one. One of your jobs next week is to convince him that the missing plutonium is a real threat and that there is some hope of finding it and getting control of it. Hal was probably not even aware of this case until very recently."

"Okay," said Jerry. "I will plan to give the full background of the case. Does he have the case file?"

"Yes, he has the file, but I'm not sure he's read it yet. He has been up to his ass in alligators recently. I think he spends most of his days talking to congressional, Defense Department, and White House staff about the various terrorism threats. He is called to brief Congress, the White House, or the Pentagon several times a week. I actually feel sorry for him sometimes. I do think he will read the case file before our meeting though."

"I hope I can stifle my anger with Hal for our meeting. My limited contact with him was pretty negative. He's the one responsible for forcing me out."

"I know. You have reason to be pissed, but try not to take it personally. One of the things they were determined to do after the intelligence reorganization was to force people to line up shoulder-to-shoulder and follow directions. Your new job assignment did not make sense, and in a different time the agency would have corrected their mistake. But, at the time you requested reassignment, agency management was in a 'slap-down' mode. They had decided on a zero tolerance for dissent, and they made you an example."

"I'm sure you're right, Scott," said Jerry. "And I know I have to find a way to ignore my personal feelings for Hal if we are to get this case reactivated. Have things gotten any better at the agency?"

"Yes, they have," said Scott. "Folks are pretty much taking care of business. But the agency is still in the political crosshairs."

"I'll try to work up some sympathy and understanding for Hal," said Jerry. "But if you have a few more minutes, I'd like to ask you some questions about the meeting agenda."

"Go ahead."

"Am I correct in assuming that I should be prepared to discuss the first three agenda items: specifics of the problem, agenda, and staff and resource needs?"

"Definitely," said Scott. "You should view Hal as somewhat skeptical. So make a strong case for the certainty that the plutonium went missing, that Yuli's new information is reliable, and that your involvement is needed. I'm sure Hal will have thoughts of his own that will become apparent during the meeting. Hopefully, we can all leave the meeting with a general plan…and with Hal's agreement to provide whatever agency resources are needed."

"That would be a great outcome," said Jerry.

"I've got to get to my meeting," said Scott. "Give me another call before the meeting if you have other questions. If not, I'll see you next week. I'll be at the meeting and provide whatever support I can."

"Thanks," said Jerry.

5

Reactivation

JERRY SPENT TWO DAYS PREPARING for his meeting. He refreshed his memory about the details and circumstances under which the plutonium disappeared. He called Scott and got information from the agency's case files to document Yuli's bona fides. He decided against a PowerPoint presentation as being a little too formal under the circumstances and prepared handouts for the meeting. He left plenty of opportunity in his presentation for input from Hal and others at the meeting so that he didn't appear to be making too many assumptions. The draft budget was contingent on decisions others would make, but he did request a daily consultant rate of $650 for himself, a laptop with the latest encryption software, and a substantial travel budget.

When Jerry boarded the early-morning airplane to Reagan National Airport in DC on Tuesday, he was feeling a little anxious, but excited and well prepared. He was in the Counterterrorism Center's conference room in Liberty Crossing, Virginia, by 8:45.

All the meeting attendees except Hal were in their seats by 8:55. Hal arrived at 9:07, took a seat at the head of the table, and started the meeting by asking those around the long narrow table to introduce themselves. After the introductions, he reminded people that their discussions were secret, and asked Jerry to provide the background of the inactive case that was being considered for reactivation. Jerry distributed his first handout—a bulleted list of the case's major developments with their dates. He spoke about each taking time to describe the security procedures in place to keep track of the plutonium, the confirmation by Lawrence Livermore that one hundred kilograms were missing, and the theory about how the material was probably stolen.

When Jerry finished his summary, he asked if there were any questions.

"Why was the case moved to inactive status?" asked Hal.

Jerry responded, "The case was kept in an active status for about five years, but we ran into a dead end. We were pretty sure the plutonium was still in Kazakhstan, Russia, or the vicinity, but we had no new leads for a couple years and no indication it was being offered for sale."

"How would we know it was on the market?" asked Hal.

"We checked all our sources in nuclear countries and those aspiring to nuclear weapons and could find no indication that plutonium was on the market. We checked our sources in Pakistan—given their history of proliferation—and as best we could in Lebanon, North Korea, and Iran. The International Atomic Energy Agency could not find any hint of plutonium being offered for sale either. As you know, uranium is more commonly processed for nuclear fuel, not plutonium. We had a high level of confidence that the plutonium was not actively being marketed at that point. I thought the case should remain open, but I understood the agency's point of view in moving it to an inactive status."

"So tell me why you think we should reopen the case now," said Hal.

"A reliable Russian nuclear scientist who we know well has been told by a colleague that a substantial amount of Plutonium-239 is on the market. This guy worked with us on the original Kazakhstan operation. I know him well and have confidence in his integrity and judgment. His informant is also a nuclear scientist who has been asked by a weapons trafficker to verify the authenticity of a plutonium supply. It sounds like the trafficker does not have possession of the plutonium, but is considering buying it and wants to be sure it is the real thing."

"Do we know who the scientist that has been asked to assess the plutonium is?"

"Yuli would not give me that information. I could not assure him that the agency would help," said Jerry.

"What is the scientist's motivation?"

"We'll have to test him to be sure we're not being sandbagged, but I think he is concerned about the plutonium getting into the wrong hands. In a worst-case scenario, it could cause millions of deaths. It is most likely that the plutonium is in or near his neighborhood. Russia is still embroiled in Chechnya and Chechen fighters have demonstrated their willingness to fight with any weapon they can procure. And Russia's neighborhood is filed with a large number of radical Islamic groups. I think Yuli has a genuine concern about his own people and a potential nuclear catastrophe in that part of the world."

"Okay, what do you think the next step should be?"

"Yuli suggested that I come to a meeting with him and his nuclear scientist friend in Estonia."

"Why don't we assign one of our people to meet with him?"

Scott spoke up. "When Yuli first contacted us, we tried to engage him in a discussion. He would only talk to Jerry. Jerry and Yuli have a long history. They worked the Kazakhstan project together. And frankly, I think he may be a little wary of the agency given all the changes we have had in recent times. Yuli's life and livelihood could be at risk if he were discovered cooperating with us."

Jerry added, "When the plutonium first went missing, Yuli was on the short list of suspects. Those suspicions could be reignited if he is not careful."

"Okay," said Hal. "Let's assume for the moment that we can arrange your involvement, Jerry. How do you propose to proceed?"

Jerry had expected this question and was ready to respond. "I think the first step is to arrange a meeting with Yuli Karpov, perhaps including the nuclear scientist who has been approached to authenticate the plutonium. I believe Yuli will want this meeting to happen in Estonia. The major purpose of the meeting will be to see if this guy—lets call him Boris—is willing to help us and to make a plan to examine the purported plutonium."

"Why do you think Yuli wants to meet in Estonia?" asked Hal.

"He travels regularly to Estonia on business. Meeting there will appear normal and keep his involvement with us secret. I trust his belief that his life could be in danger."

"His life! That sounds exaggerated," said Hal.

"Maybe, but since the breakup of the Soviet Union, the old rules have been tossed out the window. Because of his involvement in the Soviet nuclear program, Yuli had a top-secret clearance and was an insider with the KGB over the years. He was both privileged and protected. Today in Russia, the old relationships between government, the intelligence services, and the business world—especially the oil and natural gas industries—are chaotic and dangerous. A new order has emerged, but it is not a stable order. Struggles between the old communist hierarchy and the new economic and political orders are ongoing. And within competing factions of the intelligence and political bureaucracies and the oil business, the competition and struggle is especially vicious. The Russian government has decided to use oil and gas as a weapon in the international political arena. If Yuli was thought to be acting against those interests, he could lose his job…or worse."

"But why Estonia?" asked Hal.

"I'm not sure, except that I know he travels there on business. Estonia has become a major place for East-West business contacts since the Soviet breakup."

"What do you know about the guy—Boris—I mean? Who does he work for?"

"I don't know," said Jerry. "All that Yuli would tell me is that he is a nuclear scientist that Yuli knows from the past. My guess is that, like Yuli, he is currently working in the private sector. But that's just a guess. I will learn more if I meet with him and Yuli."

Hal was silent, obviously thinking about the scenario Jerry had described. The conference room was silent. Everyone waited for Hal to say more. Finally, after a long minute, Hal said, "Let's take a ten minute break. When we come back, I'd like to have a further discussion with Scott and Jerry. The rest of you need not come back. If we decide to reactivate the case, each of you will be advised, and there will be further discussions about operational details. Thank you all for coming."

David Greenberg, the counterterrorism staffer, and the three others from science and technology, legal affairs, and human resources dispersed to their respective offices. Hal Bolton headed to his office at the end of the corridor, and Jerry and Scott went to the men's room and returned to the conference room in a few minutes. As they waited for Hal to return, Jerry said to Scott, "What do you think?"

"I think Hal is getting some advice from his boss and maybe even someone from the national security staff at the White House before he makes any commitment to reopen the case. I think your involvement is a 'red flag.' Bringing a consultant on board for such a potentially important case is not something he is willing to do without checking it out above his pay grade."

"I guess that makes sense," said Jerry.

"On the other hand, I'm sure Hal recognizes that he cannot ignore the information you've gotten from Yuli. The possibility of nuclear material in the hands of an enemy state or terrorist group is a big deal—at the top of the list of our government's worst fears."

Jerry and Scott chatted for about forty minutes before Hal came back into the room and took his seat at the head of the table.

"Okay," he said. "Here's how we'll proceed. I am recommending that we reopen the case. I'll write a memo to the key agency staff advising that the case is being reopened, and that the case is to have the highest security classification. The case will be referred to as *Springboard*. Information about the case is to be shared only on a need-to-know basis. Our legal and human resources folks do not need to know anything further about the case at this time. Science and Technology will be involved to set up our communications system for the case. At some point we will involve our nuclear experts at the Lawrence Livermore or Los Alamos labs or the Department of Energy. But not now. Scott, you will have the lead on the case; you will report directly to me. Jerry you will report to Scott. Limit the involvement of your staff, Scott—only one person if that is feasible."

"Okay," said Scott. "If you approve I will assign David Greenberg. He's smart, discrete, and speaks Russian."

"David sounds like a good choice," said Hal. "For now, I am not going to advise any of our stations in Eastern Europe that we have reopened the case. When things get a little further along and we can tell where we will be doing most of our work, I will probably alert the appropriate local clandestine service people."

"Okay," said Scott.

"Jerry, prepare a plan of action," said Hal. "I know you have limited details at this point, but give me as much as you can. Give me a cost estimate for your proposed daily fee, number of days you expect to work, travel, and other expenses. When you learn more in a few weeks, give us a revised plan and budget. Submit the initial and revised plans to Scott, and he will share them with me. Make sure any electronic communications between you and Scott and David are encrypted. Get the latest secure telephone too. I understand we now have a satellite telephone that scrambles the voice signal."

Scott said, "Jerry and I will start to develop the details right away, but I anticipate we will need to involve the Science and Technology people for communications between Jerry and us, his identity papers, and the hardware, software, and encryption plan."

"Go ahead and do that," said Hal. "But limit their knowledge of the details of the case as best you can."

"Will do," said Scott.

"Do we need to discuss anything further now?" asked Hal.

"I can't think of anything," said Scott. "How about you, Jerry?"

"Nothing for now," said Jerry.

Hall stood up, shook Scott's and Jerry's hands, and left the room.

"Let's go to my office," said Scott.

Jerry and Scott took the elevator in silence to Scott's office. Scott closed his office door and motioned Jerry to a seat at his small conference table.

"Wow," said Jerry. "Just like that!"

"While we were waiting for Hal to come back to the conference room, I'm sure he talked to the director, and I wouldn't be surprised if they both didn't talk to the national security folks. He obviously got clearance to go full speed ahead."

"Hal's uncertainty was gone when he came back into the room," said Jerry.

"For sure," said Scott. "Here are my initial thoughts. Get right to work on the plan Hal asked for. He'll be anxious to see it and to share it with others. I know you can't say much about where the plan will take you until after you meet with Yuli, but be a little creative. Make your best guess about next steps after you meet with Yuli. I'm sure the specifics will change, but give us something to chew on. Hal will feel better if he thinks we know more than we do at this point. He will be okay when we have to revise the specifics. And don't worry too much about accurate cost estimates. I don't think they will get much scrutiny. No one is worried about the cost of Springboard right now. If we eventually do locate the plutonium and get control of it, the cost could be in the millions. And spending millions—if that's what it takes—will not be a problem. So be generous in the budget."

"Okay, I'll start work on the plan as soon as I get home. I can probably have something to you in an encrypted e-mail in a couple days."

"Let's talk about a couple other things while you're here," said Scott. "I think you should travel under your own name and passport. If you operate under an assumed name and someone starts to scrutinize you, it would raise all kinds of red flags. We will create a position for you as a representative to a fictional U.S. oil company doing some marketing. If someone contacts the fake company, it will appear legitimate. A secretary will answer the phone and take messages. Regular mail and e-mail will be monitored and responded to as necessary. This will also provide some cover in case your contacts with Yuli are observed."

"Sounds sensible," said Jerry. "Yuli is in the oil business, so it would make sense that I am working in the same business as him."

"I'll get that lined up, and we can discuss the specifics next time we meet. Now, about your operational contact with my staff. As I indicated to Hal, I am going to assign David Greenberg to be your contact. You met him at the meeting earlier. He's young, but good. He works hard, has good judgment, and speaks Russian. I think you'll like him."

"David sounds just right," said Jerry.

"What do you think about carrying a weapon in your travels?" asked Scott.

"I hadn't thought about it," said Jerry. "I worked with one during most of my career in the field, but I often left it in my hotel room. I thought carrying a gun could focus suspicion on me and make me less safe, not more."

"Think about it," said Scott. "I recommend that you have a handgun and maybe a stun gun and one of those stilettos you can strap to your wrist. Conditions in Russia and the former Soviet states have gotten a little like the Wild West. Violence is a lot more frequent. It's your call, but I think you'd be safer with weapons."

Jerry had two immediate thoughts: he would not tell Kathleen he was carrying weapons, and he would need to practice on the firing range. He had not fired a gun for several years and wanted to ensure his accuracy was sharp.

Jerry caught the early evening flight back to Wilmington and got home about 8:30. Kathleen was watching the comedy channel; she liked the edgy and vulgar humor of many of the young comedians.

"I'm going to have a scotch," said Jerry. "Do you want a drink?"

"Yes," said Kathleen. "I'll have a light one with some lemon."

When Jerry came into the living room and sat down, Kathleen turned the TV off.

Jerry got right to the point. "I met with Hal, Scott, and some others at the Counterterrorism Center. Hal approved reopening the plutonium case and my taking the point on it. I think he checked his decision out at a high level before he approved, and it sounds like they will not spare any resources. I will report to Scott and one of his staffers named David Greenberg. Hal has agreed to the use of other agency resources, too."

"What will you be doing?" asked Kathleen.

"My first task is to develop a plan and budget. It will likely involve a trip to Estonia, meeting with Yuli, and hopefully following leads to locate the plutonium."

"Why Estonia?" asked Kathleen.

"Yuli does not want his involvement with the agency known. He is afraid it would compromise his position with Yukos. He travels regularly to Tallinn, Estonia, on business so we can arrange to meet there without attracting attention. There is also the possibility that the missing plutonium is located in one of the Baltic States so it makes sense to go there for that reason too."

"When do you go?" Kathleen asked coolly.

"I don't know yet," said Jerry. "I know you're not happy about this, Kathleen. I'm sorry. But this is potentially a big deal. I don't want to be dramatic, but it is not an exaggeration to say that a lot of lives could be at stake. One hundred kilograms of weapons-grade plutonium could be made into six or more nuclear weapons, and we have learned the hard lesson that today's terrorist groups would have no reluctance to use a nuclear weapon to kill indiscriminately."

"It has got to be dangerous, Jerry."

"It could be," said Jerry. "But I believe I will have the full resources of the agency at my disposal."

"I don't trust the agency—and I think you have good reason not to trust them either," said Kathleen.

"I agree they treated me badly, Kathleen. But this is not a routine personnel matter. This case may be an important national security matter. I believe the agency will do the right thing."

"But the right thing for the agency may not be good for you…or for me," said Kathleen.

"The agency has an interest in protecting me. I am their best chance to locate the plutonium. I think they will take that seriously."

"I'm not as confident as you are," said Kathleen.

Jerry and Kathleen sipped their drinks silently in their separate chairs. After a few minutes, they talked about the need for rain and a plan for getting together with their children over the Thanksgiving holiday. Jerry hoped silently that he would be home for Thanksgiving.

It took only a short time for Jerry to develop the plan and budget Hal Bolton had requested. So much remained unknown that the plan had to be general and flexible. But he also recalled Scott's advice to use his imagination. Jerry did so by assuming that he would get a firm lead for the location of the plutonium through Yuli and Boris. This allowed him to develop a plan and resource requirements to search for the plutonium overseas. He checked with Scott to verify that he did not need to estimate the time or costs of CIA agency personnel and resources as part of his plan. This too facilitated his work.

Jerry developed the draft plan in less than an hour and sent an encrypted e-mail to David Greenberg. David called Jerry two days later to tell him Hal had approved the plan and that Jerry should start implementing it as soon as possible.

6

Springboard Begins

ON HIS FLIGHT TO REAGAN National Airport two days later, Jerry was troubled by how he and Kathleen had said goodbye. They had gone out to dinner the previous evening and had a delicious seafood dinner at a restaurant overlooking the Intracoastal Waterway. It had been a beautiful, cool night, and they sat at an outside table. They dined at this restaurant on special occasions, but at home there was tension between them and conversation was strained. Kathleen did not seem angry; Jerry thought she seemed sad. Later in bed, their lovemaking was restrained. Jerry felt sadness mixed with anticipation.

Long ago Jerry and Kathleen had developed their own way to say goodbye when Jerry was leaving for a trip. Neither of them liked to say goodbye in public at the airport. They said their goodbyes at home, and Jerry took a cab to the airport. This morning, their farewell embrace was unlike any that Jerry remembered. It was long, tight, and silent. When they released each other, both were in tears. As he looked out the window during takeoff, Jerry felt tears on his cheeks again.

Jerry took a cab from National Airport to the Liberty Crossing Building and went to Scott's office. Scott and David were waiting for him.

As they shook hands, Scott asked, "How was your flight?"

"Easy," said Jerry. "I like short, direct flights."

"Great," said Scott. "I think you remember David Greenberg. He was in our meeting with Hal last week. David will be your routine contact here."

"I remember," said Jerry as he shook hands with David.

Scott continued. "I thought we would first go over your plan for Springboard and then discuss how you and David will communicate. We have also set up a meeting for you with the Science and Technology people this afternoon. I noticed from your plan that you will practice tomorrow with a nine-millimeter handgun. I think your decision to be armed for this job is a good one. As I mentioned the other day, the old expectations for dealing with the Soviets are out the window. Often we don't even know who's who nowadays. And this case is even more uncertain because it seems like we're dealing with a wildcat arms dealer. Those guys have no rules except to make their deals and kill anyone who gets in their way."

"Thanks a lot," Jerry laughed. "That makes me feel real safe."

"I'm not trying to scare you," said Scott. "I just want to be sure you understand the risks."

"I do," said Jerry. "I haven't been retired that long, so I remember how the Soviet breakup and sale of state assets scrambled the picture and increased the uncertainty."

"There are lots of independent operators nowadays," said Scott. "Don't take the weapons with you on your flight. It could attract attention even in your checked luggage. David will arrange to have them delivered to you at your hotel once you get there."

"Okay," said Jerry. "I was also wondering about the radiation detection instruments I included in my budget. I am not sure they're all that I need. I know this technology has advanced a lot."

"I'm not sure either," said Scott. "See what advice the Science and Technology folks have when you talk to them. That's also equipment we should ship to you when the need arises."

Scott continued, "You should be aware that, at this point, we are not telling our local CIA offices in the Baltic about your operation. This will help keep your operation secret. We don't have any reason to think our Baltic operation doesn't keep secrets, but leaks are always possible. Later, depending on how things go, we may bring them in. I suspect that if you are able to locate the plutonium, you'll need help to secure and transport it. Also, in an emergency, we will involve them immediately."

"That makes sense," said Jerry. "So my contacts will be directly with headquarters?"

"Right," said Scott. "Lets talk about how that will work. All non-emergency contacts will be with David by encrypted e-mail. His e-mail address will appear to be at the straw firm you are supposed to be working for. David will go over those details with you later today. Be in touch by e-mail with him every day, preferably around noon our time. In your e-mail messages, misspell words in the second and fourth lines of the e-mail—misspell any word and change the words you misspell from day to day. This way, David will know it's you who is communicating with him."

Jerry asked, "Our technical people were developing a way to block interception of laptop keystrokes by eavesdroppers just before I left the agency. How is that going?"

"I think we can now do that," said Scott and turned to David. "Didn't we hear that they are just about operational with that technology?"

"Yes," said David. "I'm pretty sure we can equip Jerry's laptop with that capability. I'll go with Jerry to his meeting with the Science and Technology folks to make sure they include it on his laptop. I need to know more about it myself."

"Good," said Scott. "Please don't forget that daily e-mail Jerry. If we don't hear from you within thirty-six hours, we are going to assume that something has gone wrong and start running around. And when our folks start running around, they attract a lot of attention. We want to reserve satellite telephone communications for real emergencies because we haven't yet figured out how to block satellite phone signals. We can scramble the voice communications, but we can't block the signal."

"I won't use the phone unless I have to," said Jerry.

"David, tell Jerry about the GPS plan," said Scott.

"We are going to arrange for you to have two GPS's. The first one is a regular handheld GPS loaded with the mapping software for the Baltic area, including Russia. This will help you get around and will be useful when you begin to search for the plutonium. The second GPS is one that is modified to be simply a location beacon. It cannot download signals; it only sends a signal—a signal that has a unique marker. This will be useful for marking your locations and hopefully the location of the plutonium when you find it. This GPS is small and disguised to look like a digital alarm clock. Our technical folks will monitor the location of this beacon. At some point, you may want to place it at a critical location."

"Great," said Jerry. "Both of those devices will be useful."

Scott got up from his chair. "I have to go meet with the bureaucratic nitpickers upstairs. Why don't you guys continue your meeting in David's office?"

Jerry and David moved a few offices down the hallway to David's office. Right away, Jerry noticed the basketball paraphernalia in David's office. There was a William and Mary team picture with David seated in the front row holding a basketball.

"You played basketball for William and Mary, I see," said Jerry.

"I did," said David. "We didn't have a great team, but we had a winning record my last two years."

"I love college basketball," said Jerry. "William and Mary is in the Colonial Athletic Association, right?" said Jerry.

"Right," said David.

"So you played Drexel every year," said Jerry.

"Right," said David. "I think we played Drexel twice every year when I was on the team. If we didn't play them twice in the regular season, we ended up playing them in the CAA playoffs."

"How did you do against them?" asked Jerry.

"I'd have to check, but I think we about broke even against them. Our record against Drexel was probably four and four or three and five. Did you go to Drexel?"

"I did," said Jerry. "Played basketball for them, too."

"Really!" said David. "I didn't know that. What years did you play?"

"I played from '72 to '76. Drexel didn't play William and Mary back then. It was before the Colonial Athletic Association was formed. What years did you play?"

"I played from 2000 to 2004."

David was slightly shorter than Jerry. "You look like you were probably a guard," said Jerry.

"I was," said David. "I usually played shooting guard. I had a decent three-point shot."

"I was a point guard," said Jerry. "There was no three-point shot when I was playing—it wouldn't have done me much good anyway. My strengths were playmaking and driving to the basket."

"It's a different game nowadays," said David. "My father has been a lifelong college basketball fan. He's always telling me how much more fun the old game was to play and watch."

"I agree it's a lot different," said Jerry. "I still enjoy watching it, but I have to admit I focus on the guard play and compare it to my time."

"I guess we should get to work," said David.

"Good idea," said Jerry. "Would you mind telling me a little about what you've been doing recently for the agency?"

"Not at all," said David. "As you know, I work for Scott in the Counterterrorism Center. I have been focusing on Islamic terrorism activities in the former Soviet states—especially Georgia, Uzbekistan, Kazakhstan, Chechnya, and Turkmenistan. This experience is probably why they have assigned me to work with you. I speak and read Russian pretty well. I haven't worked out in the field much yet, but I am hoping to develop in that direction. I don't want to spend my career as an office-bound analyst."

"I think you're smart to work overseas and develop agents of your own," said Jerry. "My most satisfying times professionally were when I was out in the field running agents. Has there been any recent evidence that Islamic terrorists are trying to get nuclear material?"

"Yes," said David. "There is a lot of evidence in that regard. We have no reason to believe that any of the terrorist groups have succeeded so far, but they are trying. We think they want nuclear material to construct dirty bombs. As you know, the technical knowledge required to make a dirty bomb is much simpler than for building a real nuclear weapon. Nuclear weapons technology is probably beyond the technical and financial reach of most terrorist groups."

Jerry changed the subject. "Are you married?"

"No. I have a girlfriend, but we don't have marriage plans."

"That does make your professional life a little easier."

"I guess so. I'd like to get married eventually, but I'm not sure my current girlfriend is the one."

"You'll probably know when you meet Ms. Right."

"You're married, aren't you?"

"Yes, I've got a great wife and two grown children—a boy and a girl."

"I hope to have kids someday."

"Getting back to business," Jerry said, "I think you know that the first step in our project will be a trip to Estonia. But after that, I don't know where we'll be searching. The plutonium went missing in Kazakhstan during our operation with Russian and Kazakhstan authorities to move the material to a secure location in the U.S. There's no telling where it is now…although my guess is that it is probably somewhere in the former Soviet empire."

"Can we talk about some details?" asked David.

"Sure," said Jerry. "You've seen a copy of the plan I sent Scott, haven't you?"

"Yes, but I have some questions."

"Okay, I'll try to answer them," said Jerry.

"How reliable is Yuli?" asked David.

"Very reliable," answered Jerry. "I have known and dealt with Yuli for a long time. Even when he was an adversary before the Cold War ended, he was a straight shooter. He was tough but open minded. He was the lead Russian nuclear scientist in the operation to remove the missing plutonium from Kazakhstan. He was as disturbed as any of us when that stuff went missing. I believe he has a genuine concern about the danger it poses. I think he feels some responsibility, too, because he had an oversight obligation during the removal operation. Also, I think I will know if Yuli is not playing it straight with us."

"Why is he being secretive? Why wouldn't he talk to Scott or tell us who his source is?"

"Yuli works for Yukos Oil, and I take him at his word that he could be at risk if it were known that he was cooperating with the U.S. I am not sure whether it is his Yukos job at risk or whether the danger for him is from Russians or others if they knew he was helping us find the plutonium. One of our challenges will be figuring out what the interests and affiliations of the various players are."

Jerry continued, "When the Soviet Empire was still intact, we knew whose interests were at stake most of the time, and what the threats were to our people and those who were helping us. For example, if we were looking for this plutonium when the Soviet Empire still existed, we would understand we were working against Soviet interests. It would primarily be the KGB that we would have to worry about. In our current situation, we don't know who might be involved: the KGB successor, the Federal Security Service, Yukos Oil, the entity that is trying to sell the plutonium, whoever is considering buying the plutonium, or some other state or terrorist group. So I am not at all surprised that Yuli is being cautious. His life could be in danger. But until he gives us reason to think otherwise, I believe we can trust him."

"Okay," said David. "I trust your judgment on Yuli."

"In my daily e-mail to you, can I assume you do not want to know details of my activities, only significant developments?"

"Yes," said David. "It's not important that I know every action you take, but I would like to know where you are and what your overall daily plan is. I think Scott will be asking me for a report regularly. Remember, the laptop you get will have the new technology that will prevent anyone from intercepting your keyboard strokes. So you can be assured that only I am reading your e-mails. Your satellite phone emits a GPS signal, so even though you are only going to use it in an emergency, keep it with you so we can track where you are."

"Okay," said Jerry. "Now can we talk about my cover? I know I am traveling under my own name and passport, but I believe I will also be identified as representing a make-believe company."

"Yes," said David. "I am almost finished setting that up. You will have ID and supporting documentation as a marketing representative for the Steadfast Gas and Petroleum Service Company. We have a Houston address, telephone number, fax, and e-mail address. Communications to Steadfast will come to me through a secretary close to real time so that anyone who checks you out will get a response."

"Steadfast—I like that name," said Jerry.

David smiled. "I like to be a little creative with this phony stuff; helps reduce the boredom."

"I understand," said Jerry.

"We have also set up some marketing activities for you to do for Steadfast while you are in the Baltic. You will get a list of contacts in Estonia, Finland, Denmark, and Sweden. After you get over there, call these people and try to set up appointments to market them for Steadfast. We have also developed a little script for you to use when you call and some literature for you to send to 'prospects.' Don't worry about actually getting appointments. We are simply interested in creating a credible trail in case anyone checks you out. If someone does agree to see you in person, try to keep the appointment or at least postpone it if you are not going to keep it. If you do have to actually meet with someone in person, play it straight. Use the literature we create for your pitch."

"Good, maybe I can market my gas and oil sales experience and parlay it into a job when I get back."

David looked at Jerry with a puzzled look on his face.

"Just kidding," said Jerry.

"You're going to fly to Tallinn, Estonia, right?" said David.

"Yes," said Jerry. "I was hoping to leave this weekend."

"That's good," said David. "I hope we can give you approval to do that."

"Approval? I thought the operation was already approved."

"It is," said David. "But we've gotten an inquiry about our agreement with you from our contracts office. They have to sign off, and they usually do so without asking any questions. I think we are running into some bureaucratic caution. Recently Congress has been asking pointed questions about the size of the agency's expenditures for private contracts. Somebody over there noticed that we spend more than two-thirds of our budget with the private sector. Questions are being raised about the extent of this commitment. There was a congressional subcommittee recently on the topic of 'Potential Problems with the Privatization of U.S. Intelligence.' We think they are discussing how to respond to Congress and have held up on signing new contracts with private individuals and firms."

"Is that right? The agency spends two-thirds of its budget with the private sector!"

"I think so," said David. "I am told most of it goes for big technology contracts such as satellites and new technologies like the laptop you will use. But the contracts office is holding us up right now. I am going to see the contracts people tomorrow while you're on the firing range to try to break it loose. If I can do that, you will be able to leave for Tallinn on schedule."

"I'd almost forgotten what a pain in the ass the bureaucracy can be."

"Do you know what hotel you will be staying at in Tallinn?" asked David.

"I have made a reservation at the Hotel Schoessle in the Old Town section. I thought I would e-mail you with the details as soon as I get there."

"That works for me," said David. "I'll work on the contracts holdup and get back to you as soon as I resolve it. Where are you staying tonight?"

"The Crystal City Marriott," said Jerry.

"That's a convenient location," said David. "Let's get some lunch."

After lunch, Jerry and David met with Charles Sparks of the agency's Science and Technology office. His office had a quirky look. He had a variety of colorful posters on his walls from *Star Wars*, *Spider Man*, and other science fiction themes. A Rubik's cube and other small puzzles were scattered on his desk and conference table. A picture of Charles in a Superman costume was on a bookshelf.

"I like your décor," said Jerry.

"Thanks," said Charles, smiling.

Jerry got tutorials on the new laptop, telephone, and GPS's. He picked up his nine millimeter so that he could practice with it the next day. David and Jerry agreed that the gun and other weapons would be sent right away, and the nuclear detection equipment would be shipped to him when he needed it.

Jerry asked, "We need some basic information about the plutonium we're looking for—simple information like what will this stuff look like and how is it likely to be packed. We're spooks, not scientists, so we're not certain we'll know the stuff when we see it. We also need some advice about how to locate the material—assuming we get close to where it is."

"Okay," said Charles. "Let's start with a description of the stuff. The plutonium itself will be gray and will feel warm if you hold it in your hand. But it will almost certainly be stored in heavy metal containers. Do you remember what those old World War II metal ammunition containers looked like?"

"Yes, I remember," said Jerry.

"The plutonium is probably going to be stored in similar containers—except they may be cylindrical in shape. I'm guessing there's going to be about twelve to fifteen containers, each one containing six to nine kilograms of plutonium. The containers themselves are heavy; they are lined with lead to keep the radiation from escaping. Each one is going to be about twenty-five pounds when loaded with the plutonium. The container size can vary, of course, but a reasonable guess of their size is eighteen-inches high, eighteen inches deep, and six inches wide."

"So if they are all together, we could easily line them up beside each other on a regular size desk," said Jerry.

"That's reasonable," said Charles.

"Is it going to be dangerous to handle this stuff?" asked Jerry.

"No, as long as you are not exposed to it for an extended period, you're okay. You will get some radiation exposure, but not a dangerous dose. Probably not much more than you get from a chest X-ray."

"Let's be optimistic and assume we find the plutonium," said Jerry. "How do we handle it from there?"

"My office will assume that obligation with the help of some nuclear experts—probably from the Department of Energy. I think the best way for us to support your operation is to come over to the Baltic after you've found the material. We will come over to transport it and arrange for storage. The current job is detective work, not science. Your job is to find it and guard it until we get there."

"So you don't plan on coming over right away?" asked Jerry.

"We'll come over right away if you think it is important, but we've developed a plan that provides technical support from Washington and on-the-ground responsibility when the plutonium is found. You and I can talk on the phone or by e-mail as often as you think helpful, and then turn things over to us after you've found the material. We can also envision circumstances where we would need to come over before the plutonium is actually found, and we are willing to do that."

"So, we can call you and ask you to come if we think we are getting close?" asked Jerry.

"Right."

"Good," said Jerry. "Now what about the detection equipment?"

"We are going to send you two gamma detectors—a portable and a handheld. The portable will be a little larger than a laptop, and the handheld is a little larger than a Blackberry."

"Will it be obvious how to use them?" Jerry asked.

"Pretty much…but I need to tell you about their capabilities and limitations. First, I think we need to assume that the plutonium will be shielded—that means it will probably be in a container like the kind I described earlier. And like I said, the plutonium will probably be in metal containers. The containers reduce the gamma rays that the plutonium will emit."

"How close will we have to get to the stuff to detect it?" asked Jerry.

"It will depend on how much of the material there is and whether it is further shielded—such as inside a building or buried in the ground. If it does not have a secondary shield, you will probably detect it within four to eight feet."

"So we're going to have to get pretty close," said Jerry.

"Right. But there is something else about gamma-ray detection. The detectors will accumulate and register the gamma emissions over time. For example, if you walked past the plutonium inside a building with your gamma detector, it may not register. But if you left the detector outside the building for half an hour, the detector would probably register the plutonium's presence. In short, there are three major detection factors: the degree of shielding of the plutonium, your distance from it, and the amount of time your detector is exposed to the material."

"Interesting," said Jerry. "So we're going to have to get pretty close to the plutonium to detect it or leave a gamma-ray detector in place for a while near where it is."

"You got it. I have also copied some short technical papers for you about fissile material detection. You may want to read them."

"Thanks," said Jerry. "Can I ask you a few more questions?"

"Sure. I am not in any hurry."

"I was familiar with the potential for turning uranium and plutonium into weapons years ago, but I imagine things have changed. Can you give us a short lesson on the latest about that? I remember that years ago it would have been almost impossible for an unsophisticated terrorist group to make a nuclear bomb. Is that still the case?"

"That's pretty much still true—although some of today's terrorist organizations have the sophistication and resources to recruit the necessary technological help."

"What is the technical problem?" asked Jerry. "Why is it so difficult to make a nuclear bomb if you have the nuclear material?"

"It's the difficulty of creating a chain reaction. You don't get a nuclear explosion with its massive destructive capacity without setting up a chain reaction with the fissile material. That's the scientific challenge that's beyond the reach of today's terrorists and the reason why we think the major risk from terrorist nuclear attack currently is a dirty bomb."

"What does a dirty bomb do?" asked David.

"A dirty bomb spreads radioactive material around. It may not kill a lot of people at the site of the explosion, but it can kill thousands over time and would be a major public health and economic catastrophe. It might cost billions to clean up. And unfortunately, you can create a dirty bomb with conventional explosives and fissile material. You simply explode uranium or plutonium into the atmosphere with dynamite or plastic explosives, and you have a disaster."

"Thanks Charles," said Jerry. "I don't have any more questions. How about you, David?"

"I have no more questions," said David.

The next morning Jerry went to the agency's firing range. He was rusty initially, but by the time he left, he was placing most of his bullets in a nice cluster in the center of the target. He spent the afternoon at the mall picking up some travel things. He had in the back of his mind that when the general location of the plutonium was determined, its precise location might not be known immediately. If this happened, Jerry figured he might have to do some searching on foot, bicycle, or with all-terrain vehicle. So he bought a good pair of running shoes and some running and biking clothes. When he got back to his hotel, there was a message to call David. He called David and found that the contracts office had given its okay. He was approved to go anytime. Immediately, Jerry could feel his adrenaline level increase.

7

Over There

Jerry's flight arrived at the Tallinn airport in Estonia at about eight o'clock in the morning. He took a cab to the Hotel Schoessle in Tallinn's medieval Old Town a short distance from the Town Hall. The Schoessle was one of Tallinn's oldest hotels, built in a traditional style with open beam ceilings in the lobby. He had intentionally picked a European-style hotel in the hope that his American identity would be less obvious. The hotel also had an ideal location in the Old Town and was a fifteen-minute walk from the central business district where there were modern Western hotels.

Jerry got a room on the third floor at the back of the building and unpacked. He sent an e-mail to David confirming his arrival and giving his hotel and room number. He took a shower and lay down to rest. He had slept fitfully on the airplane and wanted to be sharp and clearheaded for his meeting with Yuli that evening. He slept about two hours before ordering breakfast and coffee from room service. He and Yuli had made arrangements to meet at a prearranged spot in Old Town, and Jerry wanted to check that location before the actual meeting. In mid-afternoon, he dressed and left the hotel.

Jerry had been in Tallinn's Old Town years before, but his memory of the place had faded. As directed by Yuli, he walked up the narrow, winding cobblestone streets of the Old Town to the highest point and found the spot he was sure Yuli wanted to meet. The view overlooked the city with the harbor in the far distance. It was a picturesque, high location with a 180-degree view out to the Gulf of Finland. The view below was crowded with red-roofed buildings and the occasional church spire. He could see cruise ships and commercial vessels tied up at the piers in the distance. It was a cloudless, cool, sunny day. Jerry checked the area closely to assure that he was at the right spot for the evening's meeting with Yuli. The jewelry shop that Yuli had referred to was right behind him, and the small black onion-domed church was at about a ten o'clock location as he looked out toward the harbor. He was sure it was the right location.

Jerry returned to his hotel and went to the hotel's health club for an hour's workout. He spent a half hour stretching and using the weight machines and a half hour running on the treadmill. After a shower and a short nap, Jerry ordered room service again and had a green salad and quiche. He felt rested and sharp as he prepared for his meeting.

When Jerry returned to the meeting place that evening, Yuli was already there, but he did not acknowledge Jerry. Yuli walked a short distance to the jewelry shop window and stopped to look. Jerry looked out over the Gulf of Finland and waited. In a few minutes, Yuli strolled off. Jerry waited a minute and followed. It was a steep downgrade, and the uneven cobblestones made walking tricky. After about a quarter-mile, Yuli turned abruptly into a narrow alley. Jerry followed, and in about a hundred feet he found Yuli waiting for him around a corner. Yuli motioned for Jerry to follow, and in about two minutes they entered a dimly lit bar, went up to the second floor, and sat at a small table.

A smiling Yuli put out his hand, and Jerry shook it vigorously. Yuli had gained a little weight, but still looked to be in good shape. His dark hair was mostly gray, but he looked the same otherwise. Jerry remembered how Yuli often looked friendly and tense at the same time; that demeanor was the same, too.

"It's nice to see you, Jerry'" said Yuli. His accent had gotten a little thicker —probably because he had not been speaking English regularly.

"It's great to see you too, Yuli. How have things been going?"

"Pretty well. I have been working with Yukos for about three years now. I went there directly from my Russian government job. It's interesting work; I'm developing advanced oil and gas extraction methods, and doing very well financially. My family is well. Anna seems happy. She enjoys teaching and having extra money to shop. My son finished at Drexel and went to work for Goldman Sachs in Hong Kong. They turned him into a capitalist! I hope you and your family are well, too."

"I am and they are," said Jerry. "Kathleen and I retired to southeastern North Carolina a little more than a year ago. I am enjoying fishing, reading, and piddling around the house for now. I wasn't really ready to retire, but for now it's fine. I might look for something productive to do down the road. Meanwhile, I appreciate the opportunity you have given me to get back into the game."

"What happened at the CIA?"

"Well, I'm sure you were aware of the reorganization of U.S. intelligence agencies in 2004."

"Generally," said Yuli.

"That went okay for a while, but my boss got into trouble for criticizing the activities of the new management and was fired, or as they said 'he resigned to spend more time with his family.' I was okay, but they gave me a new job. They called it a promotion, and I guess it was. But it was in a different section and involved too much paperwork for my taste. I asked for reassignment, and they refused. They offered me some retirement sweeteners, I took them, and we moved to the beach."

"That doesn't sound too bad," said Yuli. "They could've sent you to an American Siberia without sweeteners. And I understand you would not be happy sitting at a desk shuffling papers. You were out in the field working with agents and informers for most of your career, weren't you?"

"You're right on both counts," said Jerry. "I spent most of my career working in the field, but I did well financially at retirement. And now here I am in Estonia with you and back on the payroll as a consultant with my retirement income still flowing. Not bad."

"Let me tell you what I know about this plutonium," said Yuli. "It's not much at this point."

"I'm very curious," said Jerry. "By the way, we have been calling your friend 'Boris' just so we have a name for him."

"That's not his name, but it works for me, too. Boris and I have been professional acquaintances for years. He is a nuclear physicist like me. We both worked for the Soviet Nuclear Agency, although in different jobs. I was a pure technical type. Boris is a very competent physicist, but he is also a very good speaker and communicator. He had gradually moved into international jobs that involved going to meetings and talking to scientists and politicians from other countries. He has excellent political skills."

"That made him visible and I assume is one of the reasons someone approached him to verify the plutonium," said Jerry.

"Good point. But I am still unsure why Boris approached me at that Geneva meeting to tell me about being asked to examine the plutonium. As far as I knew, there was no reason why he would know about our missing plutonium."

"I see," said Jerry. "So he would not have been informed when the plutonium originally went missing?"

"Right, he would not have been in one of the 'need-to-know' groups," said Yuli. "But Boris knew about it and was aware of my role at the Kazakhstan operation. And here's something else: I think Boris would have guessed that I would contact you or someone in U.S. intelligence to help in the plutonium's recovery. He had to be careful not to expose himself, but he was definitely interested in seeing that the plutonium did not get into the wrong hands."

"Were you able to tell from Boris who was trying to buy the plutonium?"

"The arms dealer is Ivan Savinkov. He is a well-known weapons merchant who does business with a lot of different customers—some governments and some terrorist and paramilitary groups. He is nonpolitical himself; he'll sell to anyone. Boris was not aware of his ever having trafficked in nuclear material before this. The key question of course is who will eventually end up with the plutonium, and does Savinkov already have a customer in mind. Some of the potential customers are scary."

"What do we know about who has the plutonium now?" asked Jerry. "Do you think it has changed hands since it went missing in 1993?"

"That's unclear," said Yuli. "My guess is no. We have had no indication of any unexplained activity involving plutonium. All the nuclear material and weapons-development activity in recent years has involved uranium—not plutonium. I checked with the International Atomic Energy Agency. They are unaware of any plutonium-based weapons development or any offers to sell or buy weapons grade plutonium. IAEA has an excellent information network. It's hard to believe that this much plutonium could be in circulation without their knowledge."

"So you think whoever stole the plutonium initially probably still has it?" asked Jerry.

"That's my guess," said Yuli. "When we eventually became aware of the theft, the investigative activities were intense. Everyone involved in the Kazakhstan operation was interviewed by the KGB on multiple occasions. This was intimidating and could have forced the person or persons who had the plutonium to lay low. Who knows what has happened since? It would have been difficult and risky to attempt selling at that point."

"Well, some live person is trying to sell it now," said Jerry.

"Right," said Yuli. "I think Boris is going to inspect the material we suspect is the missing plutonium very soon. He is in Tallinn, and I am to meet with him tomorrow. He expects to have information for me then."

Jerry and Yuli spoke for a while longer and made arrangements to meet again.

Jerry was surprised when he got an early morning telephone call from Yuli at his hotel room. Yuli had previously avoided contacting him by phone. He answered the phone out of a deep sleep.

"Hello," said Jerry hoarsely.

"It's important that we talk," said Yuli without identifying himself.

"Just tell me when and where," said Jerry.

"Do you remember the time of day that we had our first communication on the current matter?"

Jerry struggled to awaken his sleeping brain and after a few seconds said, "Are you referring to our initial e-mail contact?"

"Yes," said Yuli. "I will let you know a location and day for our meeting at the same time as we started our e-mail discussion. Use local Estonian time."

Yuli broke the connection without waiting for Jerry's reply.

Jerry tried going back to sleep after Yuli's phone call, but he could not. He got out of bed and sent an encrypted e-mail to the e-mail address at CIA telling them of his upcoming meeting with Yuli. After he read the *Financial Times* for a while, he was able to go back to sleep. His dreams were disturbing. He was lost in a strange city without transportation or directions to his hotel.

He struggled with his luggage as he walked unfamiliar streets and looked for his hotel. He kept forgetting the hotel's name and location. He came to doors that were closed and locked. He knocked, but no one answered, and there was no sign of life inside. The hotel was familiar, but now seemed abandoned. The dream kept recycling itself. He finally awoke exhausted and relieved. Right away, he noticed the envelope that had been slipped under his door. An unsigned typewritten note said:

Tomorrow morning, walk along the Olympic Yacht basin at the right time. There is a bench across from the Soleil Coffee Shop. Sit and read a newspaper until you are sure you are not being observed. When you are sure you are not under observation, go into the coffee shop and sit at a table on the left. Order coffee and continue to read your newspaper. If no one joins you after a half hour, leave and return the next day using the same approach.

At 7:30 the next morning, Jerry shaved, showered, dressed, and had a light breakfast from room service. At 9:45, he took a cab to the yacht basin, found the bench across from the Soleil Coffee Shop and sat to read his newspaper. There was little pedestrian traffic, and he was satisfied he was not being observed after ten minutes. He entered the coffee shop and took a seat at a table on the left.

Twenty minutes passed. Jerry was beginning to think no one would join him. After twenty-eight minutes, he folded his newspaper and was about to leave when Yuli emerged from the restaurant's kitchen and took a seat at his table.

Yuli could manage only a weak smile and curt greeting.

"Our man has been killed," said Yuli.

"Who has been killed...your physicist friend?"

"Yes. He had gone to verify the plutonium. I was to meet with him at his hotel here in Tallinn. When he was late for our meeting, I went to his room. As soon as I got off the elevator, I found the hallway crowded with police. I walked past the room and left the hotel."

"How do you know he's dead?" asked Jerry.

"I have a friend in Tallinn's detective bureau. He told me the hotel maid found him when she entered to clean the room. He was shot twice in the head from close range. His belongings were in order, but someone had searched his billfold. His money was still there, but the billfold's contents were scattered on the dresser. As far as the police can tell, there is no other evidence. They will do ballistics studies, but they are not optimistic that any useful information will result. The gun is probably untraceable and would have been discarded after the killing. Boris's hotel room door had not been forced...although the security chain had been cut. Boris was in his bed and there was no sign of struggle, so the killer was apparently able to enter the room without alerting him. No one heard anything so the police think that the killer probably user a silencer on his weapon. The coroner has estimated the time of death at about midnight."

"Why would he be killed?" asked Jerry.

Yuli hesitated, "My guess is he was killed by the people who want to buy the plutonium...perhaps to prevent him from disclosing its location. There is also the possibility that someone knows he has spoken to me—that I am at risk."

"Do you think that's likely?" asked Jerry.

"No. I'm almost certain no one knew that Boris spoke with me. Boris knew how dangerous it would be to tell anyone he talked to me. We spoke only twice—both times briefly and in public. We have not communicated by telephone or e-mail. You are the only one I have spoken with about the plutonium, and I don't see how a third party could know about the contacts between us. My guess is that the plutonium buyers or sellers eliminated Boris so that he could not report the existence of the material…unless there is a leak on your end."

Jerry replied, "It's unlikely there is a leak from my people. We have no reason to give this information to anyone. It would make recovery more difficult."

"There could be a mole in your operation," said Yuli.

"I hate to admit it, but based on recent history, that's a possibility," said Jerry. "Our internal security has had some major failures in recent years. Aldrich Ames of the CIA and Robert Hanssen of the FBI compromised our operations for years before they were discovered."

"Well, I think we should assume that the sellers or buyers of the plutonium are aware of our efforts. I do think it's most likely that Boris was killed simply to eliminate the possibility that he would tell someone about the plutonium. But let's leave open the possibility that our operation could be leaking too."

"I will ask my people to limit sharing further details of our work within the agency," said Jerry. "And I'm sure you will take another look at your activities and do anything you can to reduce the risk of exposure."

"I will," said Yuli. "I'm also going to dig around to see what I can find out about Boris's recent activities. He was to be paid for the plutonium-assessment work. He did not tell me how much, but I believe it was a substantial amount. I am going to attempt to follow that trail. It may lead us to the killer and eventually to the plutonium. With Boris gone, we are really in the dark about where the plutonium is."

Jerry and Yuli made arrangements to meet again in two days and to communicate via e-mail in the interim. Yuli left the restaurant through the kitchen. Jerry went outside and took a cab back to his hotel.

When Jerry awoke the next day he realized he had forgotten to ask Yuli for Boris's real name. He went to the lobby, bought two newspapers, and looked for a story about a local murder. There was no information in the newspapers. Jerry wrote an e-mail to David Greenberg reporting Boris's murder and his meeting with Yuli. When he finished, he noticed a new note on the floor by his hotel room door. It was from Yuli. The instructions directed him to the coffee shop along the Olympic Yacht basin. Again Yuli joined him at his table after entering from the kitchen.

After a curt greeting, Yuli said, "I see no reason to continue referring to our man as Boris. His real name was Sergei Andromov."

"I remember him," said Jerry. "We started watching him in the late 1980s. It appeared that he was rising in the Soviet hierarchy. I don't think we ever developed much of a file on him. Your Union broke up a couple years later and the game changed."

"I'm not surprised your service was keeping track of Sergei," said Yuli. "He was gaining influence in those years. But back to the murder. I have gotten two pieces of information from Tallinn's detective bureau about Sergei's recent movements. I have been describing myself to the police as a colleague and family friend—both accurate descriptions of my relationship with Sergei. So, I don't think they are suspicious that I may have knowledge about the reason for the murder."

"On the day before he was killed, Sergei took the ferry from Tallinn to Helsinki. He bought a round-trip ticket, left at 0830 and returned to Tallinn the same day at 1645. The police are attempting to find out where he went in Helsinki. Subtracting ferry travel and waiting time, I estimate he had at most six hours in Helsinki. This suggests the plutonium is in the Helsinki area. The police have also found evidence that Sergei opened an account at Metalex, a Swiss precious-metals dealer several days before his trip, and that two kilos of gold bullion were deposited in that account the day before his Helsinki trip."

"That's useful information," said Jerry. "What are the chances that we can find out where Sergei traveled when he was in Helsinki?"

"I can't say at this point," said Yuli. "But the Tallinn detective bureau is going to send two men to Helsinki to try to find out where Sergei went when he was over there. There is a reasonable chance that they will get some useful information. The Tallinn and Helsinki police have a good relationship. Because of the ferry service between the two cities, they often cooperate. Fugitives flee in both directions, and there is illegal drug trafficking between the two cities."

"That's hopeful," said Jerry. "How soon do you expect to get information from Helsinki?"

"One or two days, I think," replied Yuli.

Jerry asked, "How promising is the Metalex lead?"

"That could be a difficult source to develop," said Yuli. "Swiss banks are hard to get information from; secrecy is one of their major assets. Swiss precious-metals firms are even more secretive. They facilitate financial transactions where there is a minimal transaction trail. I am not optimistic that the Tallinn police will have any success there. The Russian intelligence services could probably get information, but I think it unwise to involve them. I do not want my involvement known by any officials at this point. It might not be safe."

"Metalex might be a lead that our people can develop," said Jerry. "I will check and let you know. It would be very helpful to know who deposited that gold in Sergei's account. Two kilos of gold bullion are worth a lot of money."

"I don't follow the price of gold," said Yuli. "About how much would two kilos be worth?"

"Well, two kilos is about seventy ounces—and I think gold is currently selling for about $950 an ounce. That's about $66,000."

"Not bad for a day's work," said Yuli. "Too bad Sergei will not get to spend it."

"It is too bad," said Jerry. "Do you know anything about his family situation?"

"Sergei was hoping to retire soon. His three children are grown. He and his wife Stacia were planning to travel in Europe and Asia after he retired."

"I guess he was hoping to increase his retirement travel fund," said Jerry. "But he was doing business with ruthless people."

"I do not think the money was important for Sergei. He had made a significant amount of money in the oil business after our Union collapsed. He was not wealthy, but would have had enough to travel and live comfortably in retirement. He tried to help because he wanted the plutonium taken out of circulation. Like you and me, he knew just how dangerous the material would be in the wrong hands."

"We can't help Sergei now, but I hope those two kilos of gold go to his wife," said Jerry.

"That would be some small comfort to Stacia," said Yuli.

Jerry went back to his hotel and sent an e-mail to David asking him to find out what he could about Sergei's precious metals account—especially who had made the gold bullion deposit. He also suggested David look up the CIA file on Sergei. David replied almost immediately that he would check the Metalex connection and Sergei's file. He also advised Jerry that he had sent his package overnight. Jerry understood the package contained his nine-millimeter handgun, stun gun, and stiletto.

Reluctantly, Jerry started making phone calls to companies for Steadfast Oil to establish his commercial credentials. The agency had provided him a long list of companies that were potential prospects for Steadfast services. After two failed attempts to get trough to an appropriate person at two oil companies, he decided he needed to study the "marketing" material that David had provided. The material gave him some hints about what department in the companies he was calling would be a logical contact point; the literature suggested the production or development departments would be most likely to be receptive to his pitch. The material also gave him specific directions for how to present the straw firm's products, which were a bundle of production support and transportation services. Jerry started to feel more comfortable so he tried a few more phone calls.

Jerry got through to the appropriate department in two companies, but could not get the person who answered the phone to put him through to the person in charge. He knew his sales pitch sounded wooden. He could feel its awkwardness himself. But he was at least developing a list of companies he had contacted in case someone questioned why he was in the Baltic. On a lined yellow pad, he noted times of contact, who he spoke with and a "result." He would leave the pad on the desk in his room. He made a few more calls and began to feel more comfortable. He finally spoke to a few production managers and made arrangements to send literature to two firms with the promise that he would follow up with them again.

Jerry got a call from the front desk about a package addressed to him as representing Steadfast. He picked up the package, unwrapped it in his room, and placed the gun, silencer, and box of bullets and other weapons in the safe in his room.

The next day Jerry made some more Steadfast calls and smiled to himself as he began to sound as if he knew what he was talking about. He got e-mails from Yuli and David. Yuli wrote:

The Tallinn police found that Sergei rented a car in Helsinki. He picked the car up at 0940 and brought it back at 1535. He used a personal credit card to pay. There were 98 kilometers on the odometer when he returned the car. The car rental company does not know where Sergei traveled over there. The rental car was not equipped with a GPS.

The Tallinn detectives will stay in Helsinki another day in an attempt to find out where Sergei traveled while he was there.

Let me know what you learn from your contacts.

Jerry also heard from David.

I have been able to learn some things about Sergei. Regarding the gold deposit, our source in Switzerland was able to get information about his Metalex account. This precious-metals account had been opened the day before the gold bullion deposit was made.

The arms dealer Ivan Savinkov also has an account at Metalex. We acquired transaction records for this account; there are nine transactions in the last six months—seven into his account and two out, including the one for Sergei's bullion. Most interesting and worrisome is that the largest deposits (one seven-figure and three six-figure) into his account appear to be originating from Iran through a numbered Swiss account. We have not been able to acquire details, but will keep trying.

Sergei's CIA file had been inactive for several years, but had recent entries from one of our Eastern European operatives. The entries themselves are innocuous, but we are curious why he has recently been judged to be of interest to one of ours. I will check this out and get back to you. Meanwhile, try to find out more from Yuli about what Sergei has been doing.

Jerry began planning a trip to Helsinki. He went to a bookstore and bought a good map of Helsinki and its surrounding areas. He also bought a sightseeing book for Finland. Back in his hotel room, he reviewed the map and book. Sergei had put almost sixty miles on the rental car so Jerry reasoned that the site he visited was probably outside Helsinki proper. The map suggested at least two destinations within twenty-thirty miles of the Helsinki ferry dock—Tikkurila and Porvoo to the northeast and Kerava to the northwest. He hoped to get information from the Tallinn police through Yuli or from his own inquiries in Helsinki that would help him narrow his search further.

Jerry got an e-mail from Yuli late in the day.

I spoke with the Tallinn detectives. They got little information about Sergei's activities in Finland. Sergei did ask for directions heading north out of the city at the car rental company and took one of their maps. Otherwise they know nothing of his activities there.

My police contacts are getting suspicious of my inquiries. When I last spoke to them, they questioned me in a new way about Sergei, his connections, and activities. They also asked a number of questions about the relationship between Sergei and me. I think they sense a larger context for his murder, although I do not think they understand any specifics. I believe they will be looking into Sergei's situation further, and perhaps my own. I do not think I should contact them further.

Jerry wrote back.

I agree with your decision to avoid further contacts with the Tallinn detectives. I too am curious about Sergei. Please provide additional background on him. When did he know about the missing plutonium from the Kazakhstan operation? Who does he work for now? What are his duties? Has he ever been an intelligence operative? Do you think it is possible he was an active participant in the current operation—not just as an advisor? I will appreciate your reply as soon as possible.

I am planning a trip to Helsinki and may leave tomorrow. You will be able to reach me via e-mail. Please do not use my mobile phone except in an emergency.

Jerry decided that he might be watched and decided to resurrect some of his rusty tradecraft. He reminded himself to be attuned to any interest in him or his activities. He would carry his gun with him to Helsinki. Jerry had dinner in his room, watched the international news, a movie, and slept lightly during the night. He awoke several times in response to noises outside his room. He awoke in the morning in what he called his "game" state—mentally alert with his adrenal gland ready to fire.

There was an e-mail from Yuli.

I do not think Sergei was ever formally an intelligence operative, but as you know back in the 1980s and 1990s, there was not a clear distinction between the scientists and the spies. Sergei moved into a more prominent and public role in the late 1980s, so he would have had knowledge I do not have. He was not directly involved in the Kazakhstan operation, but could have become aware of the missing plutonium when it became known to the security service. The security investigation around that matter was intense and went on for a couple years. I think I was fully cleared, but something like that always leaves a hint of suspicion. Sergei would have been aware of the protracted investigation, but perhaps not of the details. I cannot be sure how much he knew.

Sergei was also a Yukos employee, although he and I worked in different capacities and did not have regular contact with each other. Sergei worked at the corporate level. He was involved in planning, finance, and I think was often included in boardroom discussions. Here too, there is some blurring of the line between his Yukos business responsibilities and perhaps some Russian government obligations. Yukos and the Russian state cannot be fully separated. Oil and politics mix in Russia.

Jerry responded to Yuli's e-mail.

Thank you. Is there any reason to think that Sergei and/or the Russian government might be involved in the situation we are working on?

Yuli replied:

I doubt it. I am almost certain that Sergei was not involved for profit in the sale of the material. I have no knowledge, but I guess it is possible he was involved in some "official" way to locate the material.

Jerry did not respond further to Yuli and put together an e-mail for David at the Counterterrorism Center. He sent copies of his own and Yuli's e-mails regarding Sergei. He told David of his plan to travel to Helsinki, make inquiries there, and probably travel to one or more of the areas outside Helsinki. Jerry asked David to let him know within eight hours if there was any problem with a trip to Helsinki. Jerry would let David know where he was staying in Finland and asked that he be ready to ship the gamma-ray detectors to him.

Jerry got a very brief e-mail from David within a couple hours: *Go for it!* Jerry knew they could track his movements with the GPS in his telephone and fake clock.

8

The Hunt Begins

EARLY THE NEXT MORNING, JERRY packed clothes for three days. He arranged his room to detect any search effort. Over the years, he had embellished the tradecraft he was taught at the CIA's training facility at The Farm. One unobtrusive method was to put something on top of an item a searcher might want to examine. He turned the yellow pad with his Steadfast notes upside down and placed a pen on top pointed clocklike to his departure time. He did similar things with his Steadfast marketing material and the book on his bedside table. He arranged his clothes in the drawer and closet so that it would be difficult to return them exactly to their original position. He wrote precise shorthand notes to himself indicating the clothing placement patterns and placed them in his wallet. Before he left the hotel, he called housekeeping and asked that they not service his room until further notice.

He made the same request at the front desk and told them he would be away for several days.

Jerry took a cab to the ferry terminal and got the 8:00 ferry to Helsinki. It was a chilly but sunny morning with little wind. The waters of the Gulf of Finland were smooth. Most of his fellow passengers appeared to be on their way to work. There were quite a few students; he wondered how often the Estonians and the Finns went to school in each other's countries. The coffee bar was busy, and he had to wait five minutes before getting served. The coffee was not worth the wait.

He was at the car rental agency before 9:00 and rented the same make, model, and color car that Sergei had rented. He hoped that having the same car type might stimulate the recall of those he would question about Sergei's movements four days earlier. He fired up his handheld GPS, entered the address of the ferry terminal, consulted his travel book, and entered the name of a hotel in Tikkurila. He left the car rental lot, navigated his way out of the congested surrounding area, and found his way on the road out of Helsinki to Tikkurila. Most of the Monday morning traffic was headed into Helsinki, and there were no traffic lights after he left the business area. He was in Tikkurila in less than twenty minutes having traveled only twenty-one kilometers. Sergei had traveled further than this; Tikkurila was not Sergei's destination. Jerry consulted his travel book again and entered the location of the old cathedral in Porvoo—one of the oldest stone churches in Finland dating to the thirteenth century, according to the guidebook. Back on the two-lane road, it was an easy and scenic drive to a very picturesque Porvoo located on a river. Jerry parked in a gravel parking lot just before an old stone bridge over the river. His odometer indicated he had traveled 44 kilometers—about five miles less than half of the distance Sergei had traveled. The Porvoo area may have been Sergei's destination.

Jerry drove around the area, noting its topography and land use. Porvoo was a small rural town with little commercial activity. Housing density was sparse. He again consulted the travel book and located the Mihkli Manor Hotel and Conference Center. The hotel was in a beautiful setting overlooking a long expanse of green meadow and old-growth forest. He parked and entered the hotel. The lobby was impeccably decorated in a traditional way with several large landscape paintings on the walls. The reception desk was shiny, well-polished oak. There was a large restaurant with white tablecloths on the tables. It was not yet open. A well-dressed woman was sitting at one of the tables outside the restaurant; she appeared to be writing on a menu.

Jerry approached the woman; she was an attractive woman in her early-thirties who did not smile as he approached her. "May I have a moment of your time?" he asked, taking note of the name Sonia Pernen on her name tag.

"Certainly," she said.

"My name is Jerry Paul, Ms. Pernen. I am trying to locate a Russian gentleman who had lunch here a few days ago. I had a conversation with him in the lobby just before he dined in your restaurant. He gave me his business card, and I was to call him. But I am embarrassed to say I have lost his card. I was hoping he may have made a reservation and you might have his name. I know he dined with at least one other person." With his most charming smile he asked, "Would it be possible for you to check your lunch reservations for last Wednesday to see if you had a reservation for a Russian gentleman and one or two others?"

"What is your business?" she asked.

Jerry gave her one of his Steadfast business cards and said, "I am in the oil business, and the gentleman I am trying to locate works for Yukos Oil."

She looked at his card, then at him and went to a desk in the lobby just outside the restaurant. She opened a large heavily bound book, turned a few pages, looked down the page, turned to another page, and scanned down. "I'm sorry. I had no reservation like you describe on that day."

"Thank you for looking," said Jerry. "The gentleman I am looking for would speak Russian or English with a Russian accent; he is older, but not elderly. He is a very friendly man. Do you recall anyone like that on that day?"

"No, I do not," she answered, clearly indicating the conversation was over.

"Thank you again," Jerry said, and left the lobby.

Out in the car, Jerry sat and considered his options. The Porvoo area fit almost exactly within the travel radius for Sergei's trip. He would need some time to survey the area and to ask questions. The Mihkli Manor Hotel would be a good location to work from. He went back into the lobby and inquired about a room. Yes, they had a vacancy. He booked a room for two nights, went out and got his bag from the car, and took the staircase to his second floor room. He left his bag and locked his gun in the safe.

Jerry called the car rental company from his room and asked for the manager. When the manager answered, Jerry identified himself as being from Yukos Oil.

"I know you have probably had a lot of inquiries in connection with your rental of a car to the man who was later killed in Tallinn. Do you know the situation I refer to?"

"Yes, a tragic case," said the manager.

"I think this will be the last time that we will have to bother you about it. We are simply trying to close our accounting books on the car rental transaction. Did Mr. Andromov put gas in the car before he returned it to you?"

"Yes, I believe he did. That information is shown on his bill."

"I am sure it was indicated on the bill," said Jerry. "But the receipt has been lost. Would you mind checking your records?"

"Hold on for a moment," said the manager, somewhat irritated. He returned a minute later. "The car was returned with a full tank of gasoline."

"Thank you," said Jerry. "Can you tell where the gasoline was purchased?"

"I do not have that information," said the manager. "But I assume it was near Helsinki or else the tank would not have been full when he brought the car back."

"Thank you for your help—goodbye."

Jerry went back out to his car and drove again to the parking lot where he had stopped earlier. He parked, walked across the stone bridge, and turned right up toward an area where there appeared to be some commercial activity.

About a quarter-mile up a stony walkway there was a courtyard. On the left there were tables and makeshift booths suggesting an outdoor market, but none was in use at the moment. To his right and in front of him were several retail stores. Most were open, but none appeared to have customers. He went into a bakery, browsed the pastry cases, and bought a large chocolate chip cookie. He asked the middle-aged woman who waited on him about the outdoor market.

"The flea market is only open on weekends," she said.

"What kinds of things do they sell?" asked Jerry.

"A variety of things: pottery, books, clothing, small electronics, kites, and other things."

"A Russian friend of mine was in the area a few days ago. He mentioned an outdoor market. I'll bet this is the place."

The woman did not respond.

"I am trying to find where my Russian friend told me about. He was here several days ago. Do you recall seeing a Russian man in his late middle age? He might have been with another Russian."

"We have a lot of people visit the area," said the woman. "I don't remember anyone like that."

"He would have been driving the same kind of car as I am driving," Jerry pressed.

"I don't know what kind of car you are driving. You parked at the bottom of the hill, didn't you? That's where most everyone parks."

Jerry lingered for another minute, said goodbye to the woman and left the bakery.

Jerry entered a small clothing store on the other side of the courtyard. The store sold T-shirts and colorful sportswear. They stocked a lot of children's clothes. He browsed the clothing racks. A young woman was folding shirts into neat piles on one of the tables.

"Let me know if I can help you," she said.

"Thank you," said Jerry. "A Russian friend of mine was in this area several days ago. He was probably with another man. He told me about some very nice little girls' shirts he saw in a shop. I am wondering if this is the shop he was referring to."

"We have a nice supply of girls' clothing. Most of it is on your left toward the back of the store."

Jerry walked to the back and looked at the girls' clothing.

"Do you recall seeing one or two Russian gentlemen in this area a few days ago?"

"I don't think so," said the girl. "We don't see many Russians shopping around here. I think I would remember him"

Jerry thanked the girl and left the shop. He walked back down the stone path toward the parking lot where his car was parked. Just before the left turn to the parking lot, he saw the sign for the Porvoo Cathedral on the right. He decided to walk up the long hill to the cathedral. When he got there, an old man was working in the garden outside. Jerry walked to greet him. The man was removing a dead plant from a well-kept bed on the path to the church door. He had a dozen containers of yellow chrysanthemums in his wheelbarrow.

Jerry stopped near the wheelbarrow.

"Those are beautiful plants," said Jerry. "What kind are they?"

"Mums," said the gardener.

"I guess you are going to plant them in that bed. They will look great there."

Jerry barely noticed the slight nod of the man's head. "Some Russian friends of mine visited this area a few days ago. They were very impressed by the grounds outside the cathedral. They said it's obvious someone takes a lot of care to keep the grounds looking good." Jerry got a more noticeable nod from the gardener. "Do you remember two Russian men visiting here a few days ago?"

The old gardener thought for a minute. "There were three men talking Russian over there in the corner of the garden not long ago. Don't think they paid any attention to the flowers. Don't think they even went into the cathedral. Didn't say anything to me."

Jerry's heart rate increased. "I understand," said Jerry. "Some tourists just don't appreciate what they are seeing."

The gardener agreed with a nod.

"What could they have been talking about that was more important than this old cathedral and your beautiful gardens?"

"Don't understand Russian," said the gardener. "Don't care for Russians for that matter."

"Did they stay long?" asked Jerry.

"Maybe ten minutes. They were talking really quietly. Went off down the hill. Left in two different cars."

"Did you notice which way they went?" asked Jerry.

"Headed back toward Helsinki looked like," he said.

"Was one of them driving a car like mine? Like that yellow one down there in the lot."

The gardener looked down into the lot. "Maybe," he said.

Jerry decided he ought to go into the cathedral before he left. He went in and sat in one of the pews. The building was much smaller than other European cathedrals he had seen, but it had a fifty- to sixty-foot high ceiling. The old building was only about twenty feet wide, but it had gorgeous stained glass windows. There were eight windows along the side walls and another four behind the altar, each about twenty feet high. The windows depicted a variety of religious figures in mostly dark red, blue, and purple colors interspersed with light greens and yellows.

Jerry felt like he had gone back in time; the church had the feel of the Middle Ages. Jerry stayed for fifteen minutes, admiring the windows and considering his conversation with the gardener. He believed he had turned up a promising lead. Sergei and Ivan the arms dealer may have spoken in the cathedral's garden a few days ago. He left the cathedral and waved to the gardener as he went down the path to the parking lot.

Jerry went back to his room at Mihkli Manor and sent an e-mail to David Greenberg reporting the day's activities, this time remembering to misspell words in the second and fourth lines. He had forgotten the misspelling in his last e-mail, and David had reminded him. Because of the gardener's promising report, he told David he would stay at least another day and try to develop additional leads. David confirmed receipt of Jerry's e-mail and told him the gamma-ray detectors were on their way, but would probably not arrive until the day after tomorrow.

Jerry went back out to explore the area further in his car. He was not sure what he was looking for and had trouble imagining where a likely hiding place for one hundred kilograms of plutonium might be. The area was picturesque and sparsely populated. The late-fall leaves on the trees were a mix of red, gold, and brown. The colors were breathtaking in spots. The river ran through the area, coming in and out of his view as he drove. The river gave a peaceful feel to the countryside. He wondered if he might be wise to get a bicycle so that he could reach areas not accessible by car. If he could be more certain that he was in the area that Sergei had visited on the day before his murder, a bicycle might be a sensible option. Tomorrow he would make additional inquiries.

Jerry drove back to his hotel in late afternoon, watched the evening news, and went down to the hotel dining room for dinner. The woman he had spoken with earlier in the day seated him without acknowledging their previous conversation. He found himself watching her move fluidly among the tables. She was a striking, shapely woman. After dinner, he walked on the expansive and luxurious hotel grounds for a half hour and went to his room. He was asleep by ten o'clock.

Early the next morning, Jerry sent David an e-mail indicating his plan for the day—to make further inquiries in the area to see if he could confirm Sergei's presence there and pinpoint it more precisely. He had breakfast in the hotel dinning room, noticing the familiar hostess and wondered when she did not work.

Jerry decided to wait until rush hour traffic had ended before driving toward Helsinki to check with gas stations. In the Porvoo area, he quickly discovered there was not much opportunity to question people who might have seen Sergei. There were few restaurants or retail establishments, and the few that he attempted to question about middle-aged Russian visitors were unproductive.

In the afternoon, he drove to the outskirts of Helsinki and started asking about Russian travelers. He did find one station where the attendant remembered a Russian man who had trouble getting the gasoline pump to read his credit card. The attendant had to assist the man, but he had no recollection of the type of car the man drove, nor could he describe him. He remembered only his Russian accent.

Feeling uncertain, Jerry decided to stay in the Porvoo area another day and drove into Helsinki. He bought a modestly priced ten-speed bicycle and a bicycle rack for the car. He drove back to Mihkli Manor and reported his progress, or lack of progress, to David. He then went out for a bike ride to get comfortable with the new bike. He biked to the Porvoo Cathedral. The gardener had apparently finished work for the day.

Jerry showered, watched the BBC news, and went down to the dining room for dinner again. Ms. Pernen seated him and may have recognized him with a slight smile. He was not sure. At about 10:30 that night, Jerry woke up with the television still on. He had fallen asleep watching an American basketball game. He turned the TV and bedside lamp off and went back to sleep.

Shortly after midnight, Jerry woke up. This was not typical for him; he usually slept through the night for at least six hours without interruption. He lay quietly in bed attuning his senses. After about five minutes, he could not detect anything unusual. It was a very quiet hotel. But he had learned to trust his instincts, and they told him to be alert.

He got out of bed quietly, went to the door, and listened. He heard nothing. He went to the safe, removed and loaded his handgun, being as quiet as he could. He took the extra pillow and blanket from the closet shelf and laid them on the floor on the side of the bed furthest from the door. He arranged the bed so that it appeared someone was still sleeping in it. Then he lay on the floor with the pillow and blanket, gun in hand.

He had been lying on the floor for some time and was beginning to feel a little silly. But he made himself stay where he was. He had begun to drift off to sleep when a sound brought him back. There was movement at the door. He could not see the door because the bed was in the way. Jerry waited. He remembered how Sergei's killer had gained access by cutting the security chain. Jerry felt a rush of air when the door opened. He lay motionless. Then he heard a metallic click—perhaps the sound of the chain being cut. There was no further sound for about thirty seconds, but then movement. Jerry could see a change in illumination as light from the hallway seeped into the room.

Jerry listened to the slow, deliberate movement of someone approaching the bed. In what seemed a long wait, he finally saw a man's upper body come into view. Then the arm was raised, and Jerry heard the sound of a gunshot muffled by a silencer. Jerry slowly raised his gun and fired. The shot was immediately followed by a gasp and the sound of a body collapsing to the floor. Jerry jumped up and quickly turned the light on. The man lay on his back. Jerry's bullet had entered his neck about where a necktie knot would be. The man's jaw was opening and closing as if he were trying to talk. Jerry watched him for a few seconds until he was satisfied that the man was no longer a threat.

The man's gun had fallen onto the bed. Jerry grasped the gun with bedspread in his hand and moved it to the top of the bed. He noticed the door to his room had not fully closed and went quickly to close it. He looked back at the man whose jaw was still moving up and down. A puddle of blood had begun to spread across the carpet underneath the man's head. Jerry stayed at the door and listened for sound in the hallway. He heard none. He heard a gurgling sound from the man on the floor and went to stand over him. The man's jaw had stopped moving. Jerry checked for a pulse and found none.

Jerry checked the man's pockets. There was nothing in the jacket's pockets; the shirt had no pocket. The labels had been removed from both the jacket and shirt. There was nothing in the trouser pockets. He removed the man's shoes. They were good quality walking shoes with the manufacturer's name cut out. He removed the man's brown leather belt. It had lettering imprinted that he did not recognize. The dead man looked to be in his mid-thirties, of medium height and weight, but obviously in good physical condition. His shoulders were broad, and his upper torso came to a neat V shape at the waist. Jerry's bullet had entered the man's throat at an upward angle. A chunk of the man's skull in the back of his head was gone.

There was still no indication that anyone in the hotel had been alerted by the two gunshots. The silencers had done their job. Jerry decided to leave the hotel immediately. He did not want to be involved in official questioning about the killing or his own activities. He did not try to remove his fingerprints from the room. Officials would quickly identify him; the hotel took his passport number when he registered. He packed quickly and did not touch the dead man or move his weapon. He put the man's belt in his suitcase. He hurried down the hotel staircase and exited through a door directly into the parking lot. The thought crossed his mind that he had killed a man less than twenty minutes ago.

Jerry was putting his suitcase into the trunk of his car when he heard someone approaching. There were two men. Jerry turned to run, but one of them tackled him. He struggled to get up, but the second man threw himself on top of him. One of them held a sweet-smelling rag over his face. He was unconscious within seconds.

9

Scrambling

DAVID GREENBERG PICKED UP THE phone and called Scott Regan.

"We have a problem. I haven't heard from Jerry, and there's a problem at his hotel. Can I come up to see you?"

"Sure, come on up. Do you have any details?"

"A few," answered David.

David came into Scott's office with a file folder, and both silently took a seat at Scott's conference table. David began. "I was hearing regularly from Jerry by e-mail, once, sometimes twice a day. The last I heard—the day before yesterday—he was in a little town called Porvoo about twenty-five miles outside Helsinki. He had gotten some information suggesting that the murdered physicist had been in the area the day before he was killed. When I didn't hear from Jerry, I called the hotel where he was staying in Porvoo.

The desk put me on hold for several minutes, and then someone came on the phone and asked who was calling. I did not identify myself; instead I asked who I was talking to. The man identified himself as Inspector Thor Roskil of Finland's Ministry of Justice. I gave him my fictional name and identified myself as representing Steadfast Oil, the fake firm Jerry is supposed to be working for."

"What's going on?" asked Scott.

"I'm not sure, but I think it's serious. The inspector would not tell me exactly what had happened, but he did say a violent crime had occurred. I asked if Jerry was hurt and he said he did not know that Jerry was not there. He asked if I knew how he could locate Jerry to talk to him. I told him I did not—that I had expected to hear from Jerry and called the hotel when he had not contacted me. He asked if Jerry had a mobile phone, and I said I thought he did but that I did not have the number. He would not give me any more information but took my number. If he calls, he will be connected to Steadfast Oil."

"Do you have any idea what is happening?" asked Scott.

"Nothing other than what I've told you. It seems clear Jerry is not at the hotel. I think Jerry had planned to stay in the area for at least another day—maybe longer. He was going to look around the area and told me he had bought a bicycle to allow him to get around easier. So it's clear something happened to change his mind. I shipped him the gamma-ray detectors; they should arrive at the hotel today. I'm sure the Finnish police will confiscate the package, but hopefully will not know what to make of the instruments."

Scott was silent for a minute. "How long ago did you talk to the Finnish inspector?"

"Less than an hour ago," said David. "And it's getting to be late afternoon over there."

"I'm wondering if we should wait a while before doing anything," said Scott. "Maybe Jerry will get in touch with us."

"My gut tells me that Jerry can't get in touch," said David. "Even if he couldn't use his laptop, I think he could have used his satellite phone to call me. At least for now, I think we should assume he's hurt or hunkered down or worse."

Scott hesitated. "Okay," he said. "We have some people at our embassy in Helsinki, don't we?"

"Yes," said David. "There are a few CIA people, and the State Department has a fully staffed operation."

"Get a hold of the CIA station chief as soon as you go back to your office. Wait, let's try to get him right now and do some problem solving. It's still business hours over there, isn't it?"

"Yes, the office should still be open. The CIA guy's name is Roy DeSantis; I have the number here in my file."

Scott dialed.

"I'll switch this to speaker as soon as I get someone. I think I've met Roy DeSantis somewhere along the way."

Scott waited for the call to go through, connected to a secretary first, and asked for Mr. DeSantis.

"Yes, it's urgent," he said. "This is Scott Regan of the National Counterterrorism Center in the Office of the Director of National Intelligence. Please ask Mr. DeSantis to come to the phone." Scott covered the mouthpiece, "He's in a meeting."

In about two minutes, Scott said, "Hello, Roy. Thanks for coming to the phone." He identified himself again and asked, "Can I put you on the speaker? David Greenberg of my office is here with me."

"Sure," said Roy.

Scott spoke. "Roy, we have a situation in your area. It's not clear what has happened, but it could be serious. I'm going to have David tell you about it."

"Hello, Roy," said David. "Jerry Paul, a retired CIA guy, has been doing some contract work for us in the Counterterrorism Center. We thought he would be working in Estonia so we did not alert you. But Jerry's work took him to Helsinki and Porvoo a couple days ago. He was staying at the Mihkli Manor Hotel…which I believe is in Porvoo."

"I know the place," said Jim. "It's a classy old place. They have a lot of conferences there. Beautiful, scenic setting."

David continued, "Less than two hours ago, I tried to reach Jerry at the hotel, but could not reach him. When the hotel heard who I was calling, they put a Finnish Ministry of Justice inspector on the phone. His name is Thor Roskil. The inspector said that a violent crime had occurred and that they were looking for Jerry. He wanted to know how to reach him. The inspector would not tell me anything further."

Scott continued to brief Roy. "Jerry is working on a potentially important matter for us. I don't want to go into the details now on the telephone, but it involves nuclear material. I'm somewhat undecided how to proceed at this moment. It is possible no major problem exists with Jerry, but we cannot assume that. We need to check it out. Is it possible to make a discrete inquiry to find out what is going on?"

"I'm not sure we can do anything discretely if the Finnish Ministry of Justice is involved in a violent crime investigation," said Roy. "Maybe the thing to do is have one of our diplomats make an inquiry to the Justice Ministry indicating that we are concerned about the welfare of an American citizen who may need help. One of these folks could simply call Inspector Roskil."

"Do you think that would work?" asked Scott.

"It's worth a try. Even if we don't get the information we need, their reaction to our inquiry will be informative."

"Good point," said Scott. "Do you need me to do anything on this end or can you arrange such an inquiry?"

"I can handle it," said Roy. "I'll get someone to make a call right away. You will be in the office for several more hours, right?"

"Yes. Call David when you have some information." David gave Roy his direct line number, and they ended the call.

David Greenberg got a call from Roy DeSantis in the late afternoon. "Our diplomat spoke with the police inspector. There is a serious problem. A man was found dead in our man's room at Mihkli Manor—killed by a single bullet to the neck. The dead man is not Jerry, but Jerry and all his stuff are gone. The police have checked the parking lot, and the car that Jerry was driving is gone, too. They have not yet been able to identify the dead man. A gun was found in the room, and the police are checking to see whether it is the gun that did the killing. A second shot was also fired; the bullet was imbedded in the pillow on the bed. As you can imagine, the police are very anxious to find Jerry."

"Damn!" said David. "That is worrisome. There's no indication where Jerry is?"

"None," said Roy. "They think they will find him if he's still in Finland, but they are concerned that he may have gotten the ferry across the Gulf. The guy was dead for hours before the hotel maid found him, so Jerry could have traveled a long way. The police have asked us for our assistance. I told them we would be glad to help in any way we can."

"That's the right answer," said David. "We certainly want to find Jerry. But helping the Finnish police could be tricky…given what Jerry was doing."

"I'd like more information about Jerry's work as soon as you can provide it."

"I understand," said David. "I'll check with Scott; I'm sure he'll tell me to provide that information. If Scott says it's okay, I'll send you an encrypted e-mail."

"There's one more thing," said Roy. "The police seized a package that arrived at the hotel for Jerry earlier today. You probably know it contained scientific instruments. The police have asked what the instruments are for.

Our man from the diplomatic staff was in the dark about this so it was easy for him to plead ignorance. But the police are very curious."

"I'll bet they are," said David. "We might have trouble coming up with an explanation that does not acknowledge what Jerry was up to."

"Do you think there is anything more I can do tonight?" asked Roy. "It's late here so I'll go home unless there is something else I can do tonight."

"Go home," said David. "I'm going to meet with Scott before we leave tonight. We have some decisions to make. Given the time difference, you will be back to work about the time we need to talk again."

David made a list of things for him and Scott to talk about:

•Notify Jerry's wife

•Provide Springboard information to Roy?

•How to search for Jerry—include CIA agency assets?

•Jerry's hotel room in Tallinn and what to tell the police?

•Contact Yuli?

•Brief Hal Bolton

He called to ask if Scott could see him. Scott told him to come up in a half hour.

When Scott and David were seated, David gave Scott a list of the topics they needed to discuss.

"We have a lot to talk about," said Scott. "Still no word from Jerry, I guess."

"None. I spoke to our technology people. They are working on Jerry's GPS and telephone signals to track his movements. They've been able to determine the handheld GPS and telephone are in one location, and the disguised GPS device is in a different place. If it's okay, I'll ask Roy DeSantis in Helsinki to check these locations."

"Go ahead," said Scott.

David continued with his discussion items. "No one has yet said anything about Jerry's time in Tallinn or his hotel there. I hope that means the police are unaware of this. I suggest we ask our local man to check Jerry's Tallinn hotel room; we may get some useful information."

"Good. Go ahead," said Scott.

"Is it time to call Jerry's wife?" asked David.

Scott took a deep breath. "I think we have to. And I should make that call even though I hate the thought of it. I know Kathleen. She's terrific, but she is going to be very upset. She also speaks her mind, and I know she is not happy with the agency. I'd like to wait until I have something concrete to tell her, but I don't think I should. I'll make that call as soon as we finish here."

"How about Yuli Karpov? Shall we get in touch with him?"

Scott thought for a while. "Has Yuli been involved in the operation since Jerry went over there?"

"Yes," said David. "He and Jerry met a couple times in Tallinn, and Yuli was the one who was our liaison with Sergei Andromov, the physicist who was killed. Yuli had not had a chance to meet with Sergei after his visit to Helsinki."

"It was also Yuli who first alerted us," said Scott. "We should get in touch with him. Do you know how to reach him?"

"I have an e-mail address for Yuli," said David. "I'll send him a message right away. I imagine you are going to brief Hal Bolton on things."

"I've made an appointment to see him as soon as we finish—another conversation I'm not looking forward to. I don't think he was crazy about this operation from the beginning—especially Jerry's involvement. I'll see him myself this time, but when we have a little more information, I'll ask you to join me for the next briefing. I know you'll enjoy it," said Scott with a smile.

"I'm sure I will," David answered, returning Scott's smile.

They discussed some steps they might take tomorrow, and David went back to his office.

Scott Regan took a deep breath, picked up the phone and dialed Kathleen's number in Wilmington. He took another deep breath while the phone rang. Kathleen answered on the fourth ring.

"Hello?"

"Hello, Kathleen. This is Scott Regan from Washington."

"Hi, Scott," she said, but quickly realized this might not be a pleasant phone call. "What's up?"

"I have some worrisome news."

"What is it?"

"We haven't heard from Jerry for a couple days. He had been staying in touch with David Greenberg here every day, but it has been about two and a half days since he last contacted David."

"Tell me more."

"I think you know he was in Tallinn, Estonia. A couple days ago, he went to Helsinki to check something out. He told David he had developed some interesting information the day before yesterday and was going to stay in Finland a little longer. When David did not hear from him, he called the hotel where Jerry was staying in Porvoo, a little town outside Helsinki. A Finnish police inspector took the call. He told David that Jerry was gone and his things were gone from his room, too."

"Oh, Jesus!" Kathleen was silent.

Scott waited. "Are you okay?" he asked.

"Of course I'm not okay," she said. "What are you doing to find Jerry?"

"We have our local people in Helsinki working on it, and we're working on some electronic locator information, too. Jerry had a few GPS devices that might help us locate him. I wanted to let you know right away, Kathleen. But we only became aware that Jerry was not where we thought he was recently, and we were hoping he would turn up back in Tallinn. I promise I will let you know as soon as we get any new information. Is there anything I can do?"

"Maybe I'll go over there."

"Please don't do that," said Scott. "Give us a little time."

"Okay," she said. "What's your telephone number, Scott?"

Scott gave Kathleen his office and mobile telephone numbers. "You may want to take David Greenberg's numbers, too," he said and gave her David's numbers.

Kathleen sat stunned. She walked from room to room. She opened the door to go out onto the porch, turned back and got the cordless phone, went out onto the porch, and sat down. It was cloudy and cool. Her mind raced. Several times she wiped tears from her cheeks. She prayed. She thought about calling someone, but she could not decide who to call or what she would say if she did call. It seemed like a long time passed. There was little boat traffic on the waterway. The summer crowds were long gone, and it was not a nice day to be on the water. She prayed more.

After some time, Kathleen could not estimate how long, she came back into the house having decided that she had to do what she found most difficult—wait. She decided to wait another day before calling anyone. She would give the agency people twenty-four hours and then call them if they had not called her. She knew it would be agonizing if she heard nothing further, wondered if she could tolerate it, and knew she would not be able fully to distract herself. She drove to the beach and took a long walk.

David Greenberg answered his phone; Roy DeSantis was on the line.

"We haven't had any luck locating our man so far," said Roy. "We checked the location of the GPS signals your technology guys received. You'll recall two were coming from the same location. Turns out they were coming from the shrubbery surrounding the parking lot at Mihkli Manor. Someone had thrown the telephone and the GPS into the bushes alongside the parking lot. The third signal was a few miles away in a gas station trash can. It looks like a digital clock, but we were able to follow its signal."

"That's disappointing," said David. "Jerry would not have discarded those devices. We had hoped that clock would stay with Jerry to allow us to keep track of where he went. It looks like someone figured that out. The device emits a signal that can be detected."

"It sounds like we're dealing with people who know what they're doing. It also looks like someone got physical control of Jerry at the hotel or in the parking lot and that he is not at or near the hotel any longer. The Finnish police searched the hotel grounds."

"Were you able to check out Jerry's hotel room in Tallinn?"

"The police were waiting for us when we got there. Apparently the Finnish police ran a check using Jerry's passport number and found he had a room in Tallinn. They know about the car he rented at the ferry dock in Helsinki, and I'm sure they asked the Tallinn police for help over there. It would have been pretty simple to find out where Jerry was staying in Tallinn. All the hotels collect their guests' passport numbers, and the information is stored electronically—making it easy to locate visitors."

"What did the police at the hotel in Tallinn have to say?" asked David.

"They were right nasty—knew there was a homicide involved. It took a little talking to stop them from taking me and my partner in for questioning. My diplomatic passport saved the day. But they are unhappy with us, and they have confiscated Jerry's stuff. I'm expecting some blowback in Finland and maybe in Estonia, too. You might want to alert the appropriate people at the State Department. Our diplomatic folks will be sending reports, but this can become a big deal. We have a missing U.S citizen who is a suspect in a murder."

"I'll pass that problem on to my boss," said David. "I'm going to keep my eye on the ball—which is finding Jerry. But I'm at a loss for what to do next. Do you have any suggestions?"

"Nothing, except basic detective work like searching for Jerry's rental car, checking the gas station where the GPS signal device was found, asking around the Helsinki-Tallinn ferry and stuff like that. We will need help from the local police. We just don't have the manpower over here to do the footwork."

"I understand, and if I follow you, the local Finnish and Estonian authorities are not real happy with us right now."

"That's right," said Roy. "I think we will have to tell them what Jerry was doing. I understand your concern about keeping the project quiet, but if we're going to get cooperation from the local authorities, we'll have to take them into our confidence. And from my point of view, that would be a good thing. I've been over here long enough to know that these folks are very competent and professional."

"I understand," said David. "I have not had a chance to send it yet, but my boss told me to send you a briefing memo on the project Jerry is working on. I'm going to stay late tonight and send you an encrypted e-mail report. It should be there for you in the morning."

"Great," said Roy.

"Something just occurred to me that could explain the Tallinn's police reaction to you," said David. "The reason Jerry went to Helsinki was to follow a lead for some missing nuclear material. The e-mail I'm going to send you will give you the background. The lead Jerry was following was from a Russian who had gone to Helsinki for the same reason two days before Jerry. This Russian was killed in his hotel room in Tallinn the night he came back from his Helsinki trip. Do you think the Estonian and Finnish police have connected the two?"

"Ah! That explains it," said Roy. "I was wondering why they were so aggressive with us, and why there were so many of them involved. Seemed like half the police force was involved in the case. I'll bet they have connected the two cases. That explains my strong sense that there will be some 'undiplomatic' diplomatic inquiries."

"I'm starting to feel like we will soon be getting pressure from several directions at once," said David.

"That's a good bet," said Roy. "I can't wait to see your e-mail."

10

Interrogation

As Jerry started to wake up, he struggled with confusion. He was lying still on a hard surface, and it was dark. He listened; there was no sound. After a few minutes, he started to remember: Mihkli Manor, his room, the man with the gun, his gun, the lifeless body. Gradually he remembered his own thinking: the decision to leave his hotel room, packing, his rental car, the two men, being tackled. His shoulder and knee were sore; he had a headache, but he was not seriously injured.

Jerry decided to organize his thinking before opening his eyes or moving from where he lay. He assumed he was being monitored and wanted time to analyze his situation. The people who attempted to kill him must be the same people who had killed Sergei. It must be related to the plutonium. *You're brilliant,* he thought to himself with a smile. But who are these people:

the arms dealer, those who had possession of the plutonium, someone else? After a while, he acknowledged that he did not have enough information to infer who the killers represented. But he remembered the Iranian connection to Sergei's gold bullion account.

He decided to concentrate on his own situation. He assumed he would be questioned, so he planned a story. At least initially, he would stick to the Steadfast Oil creation. He would describe his marketing activities. He tried to remember the names of companies he had called a few days ago. Jerry realized that if his interrogator was experienced, his Steadfast story would collapse. What then? He considered alternatives to the truth, but he realized that if his Steadfast story was exposed, it would be clear that he was serving some intelligence function. He thought about trying to identify himself as working for a private company in industrial espionage, but he did not think he could pull that off.

Jerry decided on a sanitized version of the truth. He would try to keep Yuli out of the account. He would claim that Sergei was working with American intelligence and had reported the request that he verify the authenticity of some weapons-grade plutonium to the CIA. Jerry had previously worked on nuclear disarmament so he was selected to interview Sergei. Sergei was killed before Jerry could interview him. Sergei had told Jerry he was going to Helsinki; Jerry had come to Helsinki to try to determine where Sergei had traveled. Jerry thought he might be able to sustain and defend that story in an interrogation. He hoped it would keep him alive. He was sure his colleagues knew by now that he was missing and they should know generally where he was. He wondered if his GPS alarm clock was nearby.

Jerry decided to explore his surroundings. He sat up and then stood; his left knee was sore. It was black dark. He looked around the room at floor level, hoping to see light under a door. There was no light of any kind. He looked around the room at eye level hoping to see the outline of a window. None was perceptible. He started moving slowly forward, arms extended. After seven short steps, he found a smooth wall. He put his hands on the wall and moved to his right hoping to find a light switch. After a few steps, he came to a corner and turned right. After eight or ten steps, his foot hit something movable on the floor. He reached down and felt metal, then a handle. It was a bucket.

Jerry continued to circle the room and found a light switch after his second right turn. He tried it several times, but nothing happened. There was a wooden door a step after the light switch. The door handle would not turn. It was solid, too; there was no give when he tried to move it. He encountered nothing else. As far as he could tell, it was only him and the bucket. He went around the room again, estimating its size. The room was rectangular about fifteen feet by twenty feet. He found the bucket and relieved himself in it. He went and sat on the floor a few feet from the door with his back against the wall.

It wasn't long before Jerry saw a streak of light at the bottom of the door, and in a few seconds he heard a voice at the door. The Voice, with a slight hint of an accent, called loudly, "Are you awake, Mr. Paul?"

"Yes."

"Move away from the door. When you are ten feet away with your back to the door, tell me."

Jerry rose, took several steps away from the door, and turned away from it. "I am away from the door with my back turned."

Jerry heard a bolt move out of its casing. A florescent light in the ceiling came on. The Voice, no longer encumbered by the door, said, "Keep your back turned. When you hear the door close, look behind you and you will find a mask I have thrown on the floor. Put the mask on and tell me when it is in place covering your eyes."

When the door closed, Jerry turned, retrieved the mask, and put it on. It covered from the top of his forehead to his upper lip. The mask was heavy cotton with a thick elastic band. It seemed homemade. "The mask is in place."

The door opened and closed, and Jerry heard what sounded like a plastic chair being placed on the floor. "You may turn around," said The Voice.

Jerry turned, but said nothing.

"You've gotten yourself into a bad place, Mr. Paul. You may live to tell about it, but only if you provide every detail of your activities and mission. I already know a great deal. You arrived last week and are staying at the Hotel Schoessle in Tallinn; you have met with Yuli Karpov of Yukos Oil; you came to Helsinki three days ago, rented a car drove to Porvoo, and are staying at Mihkli Manor. You have been asking questions around the area. You proved yourself adept and killed an assassin before he killed you. The bicycle and rack on your rental car made it awkward to dispose of it. And by the way, your GPS, telephone, and that clever alarm clock device have been disposed of. The likelihood that anyone can find you here is remote."

Jerry remained silent. His sore knee was making it difficult to stand steadily. The mask was disorienting, too.

The Voice continued, "I know quite a lot about your personal and professional life, too. You spent almost thirty years with the CIA, retiring less than two years ago. You and your beautiful wife Kathleen live in Wilmington, North Carolina. But I think I have told you enough to demonstrate you will be wasting your time and your life if you lie to me."

Jerry said nothing.

"I require that you confirm that you understand what I have told you. Do you understand?"

"I understand," said Jerry.

"Do you understand that I will kill you if you do not give me all the information that I require?"

"Yes, I understand."

"Good. Here is what you must tell me. I have made a list. I need to know the history of the case you are working on—a full and detailed history. I need to know what element of American intelligence you are working for. I want to know what your orders are in connection with this initiative. And I want to know all of your findings so far, including your conversations with Yuli and any information you were able to get from the interviews you conducted in Helsinki and Porvoo. Is all that clear?"

"Yes, it is clear."

The Voice continued. "Some of the information I have asked for, I already know. That part is a test. If you do not provide full and accurate information, I will kill you."

The Voice made Jerry repeat all the elements of information he was demanding—case history, who he was working for, and case results. Then The Voice continued.

"I have given you a lot to consider, so I am going to leave you to think about things. I will come back in a day or two. I do not have time for a protracted interrogation; that is why I am making the demands that I am. I have no time to waste. When I come back, we will take all the time that we need to get through the information you are going to provide. But there will be only one interview. If you fail to satisfy my information needs, you will die. If you satisfy me, you will be free a short time after I leave. Understood?"

"Yes," said Jerry.

"Now turn around again and do not remove your mask. I am going to put some food and water inside the door and then leave."

Jerry turned away from the door and heard some activity behind him. The door closed and the bolt was slipped into place. The light remained on.

Jerry waited about thirty seconds and removed the mask. Just inside the door was a tray with fruit, cheese, a small loaf of bread, and a liter of water. He was too preoccupied to eat at that moment.

Jerry wondered about The Voice's words. The man knew so much, he might have been walking around in Jerry's shoes. He decided that he should believe The Voice's threat to kill him. There would be no protracted interrogation, and he would be killed if he did not satisfy the man's demands. The Steadfast story was not a credible option. The man already knew about Yuli, although he identified him as being with Yukos Oil. Jerry wondered if

The Voice knew of Yuli's Soviet background. The Voice's slight accent was difficult to identify. It did not sound Russian or Iranian.

Jerry had a strange feeling of relief. His biggest fear during his espionage career was that he would be caught and tortured to extract information. Jerry wondered if he could withstand torture. He worried that he might give up secrets—especially secrets that would result in the deaths of his countrymen or U.S agents. The treasons of the CIA's Aldrich Ames and the FBI's Robert Hanssen had resulted in the deaths of many who worked for the Americans. The thought that he might be responsible for the deaths of others horrified and disgusted him.

If The Voice was being honest—a big "if" Jerry realized—he would not be tortured. He had a simple decision to make. He could provide the information demanded or refuse to do so. If he refused, he would die, but presumably the death would be quick—like an execution. His first thought was that he simply had to decide to talk or not. But as he considered his situation further, he wondered if there might be a middle ground—to withhold some information and still live.

Jerry went and got the food and water, sat on the floor, ate heartily, and drank almost half of the water. Later he fell asleep on the hard floor wondering who The Voice was and who it was affiliated with.

David and Scott met in Scott's office to go over developments and do some planning. David briefed Scott about what was happening in Finland. The GPS devices that they had hoped would help to locate Jerry had been discarded. Jerry's rental car had not been found although a bicycle and bicycle rack had been found abandoned behind a gas station outside Helsinki. The authorities were checking to see if these were the items Jerry had purchased. It had been determined that the gun found in Jerry's room was not the weapon used to kill the still-unidentified corpse, and Jerry was still being sought as a murder suspect. The Estonian police had confiscated Jerry's belongings from his room in Tallinn. There was reason to think the Finnish and Estonian police had connected the killing of Sergei in Tallinn and the one in Jerry's room in Porvoo. The Finnish and Estonian authorities were being unfriendly to the U.S. diplomats seeking information and reported no success or leads in the search for Jerry. The airports, train stations, and car rental companies in both countries had been alerted to watch for Jerry. It was being assumed Jerry was still in Finland or that he had been able to flee the area entirely.

David spoke, "Roy DeSantis, our man in Helsinki, thinks it might help if we share information about Jerry's mission with the local police. It's clear to us that Jerry is probably a victim, but the police see him as an offender. Both the Finnish and Estonian police are suspicious about the entire affair. The killing has the features of professional work, and the gamma-ray detectors have them wondering what the hell is going on. Gamma rays usually mean radioactive material is involved. If we tell them what we are trying to do, they might be more helpful."

"That's probably right," said Scott. "But I don't think we can disclose the details of the operation. There is still a large amount of weapons-grade plutonium floating around eastern Finland. Or we have to assume that until we determine otherwise. If we give that information out to the police, I don't think they could keep a lid on it. Next thing we know, it would be in the newspapers, and any chance we have to get our hands on it would be out the window. It might go underground again for years."

Scott's phone rang. He looked at the display on his telephone and said to David, "It's Hal; I'll have to take his call."

"Do you want me to leave?" asked David.

"No, stay," said Scott as he answered the telephone.

"Hello, Hal. What's up?" Scott listened intently for a full minute before speaking. "David Greenberg is in my office right now. We were going over developments in Finland. Bottom line is we have no idea where Jerry is. I'm not surprised the State Department has gotten involved. David has been telling me the Finnish and Estonian police are suspicious that the killing in Jerry's room in Porvoo and that of the nuclear physicist in Tallinn are connected. I assume they got their Foreign Affairs people involved, and that they contacted our diplomatic people."

Scott listened more. David could hear only Scott's part of the conversation. Finally Scott responded, "I don't think we should simply release full information about our Springboard project. That could ruin our efforts to recover the plutonium, and I think that is still a high priority."

Scott listened again and responded, "Okay, how about if David and I talk to our CIA man in Helsinki, develop some alternatives, and come up to see you. Give us a couple hours. We'll come up to see you at 1530."

Looking stressed Scott told David, "Apparently the Finnish police got their Foreign Ministry to contact our diplomats over there, and our suits there in turn contacted the State Department over here, and someone from State called the Director of National Intelligence Office. As these things go, our director's office called Hal to ask what the hell was going on, and as we both know 'shit flows downhill.'"

David smiled. "And we're the shit stoppers, right?"

"Right. We have a diplomatic fire to put out, but we have to try doing it without compromising Springboard. Someone who knows the case is going to have to brief the Finnish authorities in a way that allows us to protect critical case information. Let's discuss some options and take them to Hal in two hours."

11

Worry

KATHLEEN PAUL HAD NOT SLEPT much. She called Scott's office. Scott took the call as he and David were developing options for Hal.

"Hello, Kathleen. I was going to call you. I wish I had some progress to report. We haven't located Jerry, but the Finnish police are still looking intensively, and our office is considering what else we can do."

"What has the Counterterrorism Center been doing?" asked Kathleen.

"We've had our local diplomats and CIA people working the case in Finland, and we're considering additional efforts. I hope that by the end of today additional actions will be underway."

Kathleen repeated, "What has your office been doing so far?"

"As I said, at this point it is mostly coordinating with our people in Finland."

"It doesn't sound like much," said Kathleen. "Don't you usually call out all the troops when one of your folks is missing in action?"

"Yes, we do, Kathleen. The problem has been that there are hardly any leads to follow, but I promise you we will not spare any effort."

"Tell me straight," said Kathleen. "What do you think happened?"

Scott hesitated, looked at David and said, "Hold on for a moment, Kathleen; I'm going to get someone else on the line…"

Scott turned the telephone microphone off so that Kathleen could not hear and spoke to David. "I'm going to turn the speaker on so you can join my conversation with Kathleen. Let's give her more information, but don't tell her about the guy Jerry killed."

Scott turned the telephone's microphone back on and spoke to Kathleen. "I'm going to put my phone on speaker. David Greenberg is here in my office; he has been Jerry's daily contact so you can hear what he has to say, too." Scott pushed the speaker button.

"Hello, Mrs. Paul," said David.

Scott continued, "Some of what I will say has not been firmly established, but we'll give you our best information and inferences. David, interrupt me whenever you like to add your observations. Some of this you already know, Kathleen, but I'll start from when Jerry arrived in Tallinn." Scott summarized Jerry's arrival, his activities in Tallinn, and his trip to Helsinki. He told her where Jerry was staying in Porvoo and what little he knew about Jerry's activities there. "Why don't you take it from here, David?"

David continued the summary. "Our understanding of what happened after Jerry left the hotel is uncertain. Initially, we thought Jerry might simply be lying low to avoid questioning by the local authorities, so that he could avoid having to discuss the plutonium case. We no longer think this likely because we discovered the electronic devices that Jerry carried to identify where he was had been discarded."

"Jerry wouldn't do that," said Kathleen. "So it means someone else did it after they did something to Jerry."

Scott and David looked at each other, and David continued. "I'm sure you are right that Jerry would not throw the location devices away. But we have no evidence that Jerry has been hurt."

"But he is missing and obviously not missing voluntarily," said Kathleen.

"That is a reasonable conclusion," said Scott.

"What are you going to do next?" asked Kathleen.

"We are going to continue looking very hard for Jerry," said Scott.

"That hasn't worked so far," said Kathleen. "What things are you going to do differently?"

"We are developing new ideas right now," said Scott. "That's what David and I are discussing. In another hour or so we are going to meet with Hal Bolton to discuss options and make a plan."

"He's the guy who fired Jerry, isn't he?"

"Mr. Bolton is our boss, and, yes, it was he who forced retirement for Jerry."

"That's not reassuring," said Kathleen.

"I promise you, Kathleen, we will do everything we can to find Jerry. And between you and me, if Mr. Bolton seems to be doing less than he could to find Jerry, I will call him on it. There is no higher priority for us right now."

"I trust you, Scott, but I also know an individual's power to move a bureaucratic organization like you work for is limited. Will you keep me informed every day?"

"Yes, either David or I will be in touch daily."

"Thank you," said Kathleen. "I'm sorry to say this to you, Scott, and I do not mean it as a personal criticism, but I will not be quiet if I think too little is being done. I'm not sure what I'll do, but it will be noisy."

"I understand," said Scott.

An idea had occurred to Kathleen during her telephone conversation with Scott and David. There had been no mention of Yuli Karpov during their conversation, and she knew that Yuli had been the stimulus for reopening the plutonium case. He and Jerry went back a long way too. Kathleen decided she would try to reach Yuli.

Yuli had returned to his Yukos office in Moscow after his meeting with Jerry in Tallinn. He had checked his secret e-mail account several times expecting to have a message from Jerry. It had been several days, and he was concerned. He had e-mailed Jerry, but got no response. He hoped nothing had gone wrong—that Jerry was simply preoccupied with his search.

Finally, five days after he returned to Moscow, he had a message.

Mr. Karpov:

I am writing in connection with the project you and Mr. Paul were working on. You may know he traveled to Helsinki several days ago. There have been problematic developments, and we have been unable to locate Mr. Paul. Please call me in the U.S at Steadfast Oil 703-801-1887 and confirm that you have gotten this e-mail.

David Greenberg

Yuli decided to return David's call from a public phone during American business hours the next day.

When Yuli arrived at his home about twenty one kilometers outside Moscow that evening, his wife Anna had news for him. She had gotten a telephone call from Kathleen Paul. Kathleen asked that Yuli call her urgently and had left her telephone number.

Yuli and his wife had become comfortable having uninhibited conversations at home in their new apartment in recent years. During the Soviet years when Yuli worked in the Soviet's nuclear program, they worried about implanted microphones. This had been a burden to them—always wondering if their conversations were being recorded or listened to. They often went away on weekends just to experience the luxury of personal privacy, especially in the bedroom. Now they had a new apartment, and the most intrusive Soviet intelligence operations had been discontinued. They enjoyed a spontaneity at home that gave them ongoing pleasure.

Yuli was still suspicious about the telephone and was uncertain if their telephone line was private. After dinner, Yuli walked a half mile to an appliance market that had a public telephone and called Kathleen. She answered almost immediately.

"Hello, Kathleen, this Yuli Karpov. I got your message."

"Oh, thank you for calling, Yuli. Did you know that Jerry is missing?"

"I did have an e-mail message from David Greenberg that I have not responded to yet, but I do not know anything specific."

Kathleen told Yuli what she knew from her conversation with Scott and David.

"Do you know what may have happened or who might be responsible for Jerry's disappearance? He must be hurt or is being held by someone," said Kathleen.

"No," said Yuli. "Jerry went to Helsinki because we think the plutonium is in that area. Do you know about the killing of Sergei Andromov in Tallinn?"

"No! Who is Sergei Andromov?"

Almost immediately, Yuli understood he should not have mentioned Sergei's murder. The information would surely add to Kathleen's anxiety. Yuli tried to minimize Sergei's killing. "It is probably just a coincidence. Andromov was one of our people, and he was involved in some extracurricular activities that probably caused his death."

"Then why did you mention it here?"

"He was a colleague of mine, and I am still upset by his death. Now Jerry is missing. I guess…"

"Did Jerry know Mr. Andromov?"

"No. Jerry never met him and did not know him."

Kathleen was silent. After a long pause, she asked, "Do you have any idea who has the missing plutonium?"

"It seems clear that the plutonium was initially stolen by someone connected with the joint Russian-U.S. project in Kazakhstan. In that operation, a large number of nuclear weapons and fissile material were moved to secure storage. I am suspicious of a warehouse manager who handled the logistics of the Kazakhstan operation. I believe that warehouse manager lives in a Baltic country today."

"Has anyone looked for him?" asked Kathleen.

"Not that I know of," said Yuli.

"I'm at a loss, Yuli," said Kathleen. "I'm convinced that something bad has happened to Jerry, but I don't know what to do. I'm going crazy just sitting down here in Wilmington. I haven't said anything to our children yet, but I think I will do that today. I was hoping to be able to give them some positive news."

"I'm sure the American authorities will do all they can," said Yuli.

"I'm not so confident," said Kathleen. "I was not reassured much by my conversations with the National Counterterrorism Center. Since we underwent that massive reorganization of our intelligence bureaucracies several years ago, things have gotten even more bureaucratic. They may not be as nimble or as quick to act as they used to be."

"I hope you're wrong," said Yuli. "But that does happen."

"Do you have any suggestions?" asked Kathleen.

"I've been thinking about what I can do," said Yuli. "I am going to call David Greenberg early tomorrow to see what he has to say, but my thinking now is that I can be most useful making inquiries where I am in Russia. I might also be able to develop some information in connection with the original disappearance of the plutonium such as identifying the most likely suspect and his current whereabouts. If I can determine this, it may get us closer to Jerry. I want you to know, Kathleen, that you can count on my help. If you can think of anything I can do, let me know."

"Thank you, Yuli. Your current action plan sounds right to me. Will you let me know as soon as any new information develops?"

"Yes, Kathleen. I will keep you informed."

12

Planning

SCOTT AND DAVID WENT TO meet with Hal Bolton in his office.

When they were seated, Hal asked, "Why do you think the diplomats have stuck their noses into this business?"

Scott answered, "We've been holding our cards close to our chests. We've not yet briefed our own CIA guy in the embassy in Helsinki about Springboard. We are in process of preparing a background memo for him, but we have been careful not to let anyone over there know there could be a substantial load of weapons-grade nuclear material in their backyard. It would be hard to keep a lid on information like that. But the police are also aware that something significant is behind what's happened. They have one dead guy in a hotel room in Porvoo, apparently killed by our man Jerry, another dead guy who had just visited Helsinki in a different hotel room in Tallinn, and their chief suspect is missing. The missing suspect also had gamma-ray detectors delivered to him. The Finnish police and diplomats know there is something significant going on in their country, and they are aggressively pursuing information.

"I think the police believe we are withholding information, and they are right, of course. David and I are going to recommend that we reach out to the Finnish and Estonian authorities and take them into our confidence. We think we can do that without compromising the Springboard project—at least for a little while. If possible, we don't want to warn the people who are trying to sell and buy the plutonium and push them underground again."

Hal asked, "What shall I tell our director? I think the Finnish authorities have complained to our State Department about a lack of cooperation in their homicide case."

Scott answered, "I recommend that we send David over there to meet with the police and the diplomats. I don't think our CIA guy on the ground has enough information or background to satisfy them, and if we send someone over from Washington, that in itself suggests we are taking their concerns seriously."

"How can we take them into our confidence without telling them the full story—which as you said would probably blow things open?" asked Hal.

"Here's our initial plan," said Scott. "David goes over there as soon as he can get there. First he meets with Roy DeSantis, and then the two of them meet with the police. We'll request that the police meeting include only the senior police people. We'll tell them all we can, but frankly acknowledge that there is some information we are withholding. We'll ask for a limited time to keep our secrets and at the same time offer our resources to find Jerry."

Hal interrupted, "That sounds tricky. Do you think they'll buy it?"

"I'm optimistic. It will be in their interest, and our guy in Helsinki says they are solid professional folks."

"It'll be a challenge," responded Hal.

"I agree, but we can offer to assign investigative resources, too. We were hoping you will contact the FBI and ask them to commit agents over there to the search for Jerry. Then we'll work day and night to find Jerry and the plutonium."

"I do think we need to send someone over there," Hal said. "But I think maybe you should both go. It sounds like the natives are restless, and I think the two of you would give us the best chance for success. Is there anything you are doing here, Scott, that cannot be put on hold?"

"I guess I could go," said Scott. "Having two of us over there is probably a good idea."

"Good, let's do that," said Hal.

"What do you think about FBI support?" asked Scott.

"I think that's a good idea," said Hal. "I'll call the FBI deputy director right after we finish here. He probably has some folks already over there that he can commit to the project."

"One more thing," said Hal.

"Yes?"

"Remember our first priority is to locate that plutonium. We want to find Jerry, too, of course, but the most important thing is the plutonium."

David had just sat down at his desk when the phone rang. It was Yuli.

"I got your e-mail, David. I'm sorry to hear Jerry is missing."

"Thank you," said David. "I was hoping you could give us some help in that regard."

"I'll do anything I can, but I left Tallinn the day Jerry went to Helsinki. I am back at Yukos in Moscow. I was wondering why I had not heard from Jerry."

"So you knew Jerry was going to Helsinki, but have not spoken to him since?"

"Right. Jerry and I met after I discovered Sergei was killed, and I was able to find out from the Tallinn police that Sergei had gone to Helsinki, rented a car there, but came back the same day. Jerry decided that he would go to Helsinki to see if he could retrace Sergei's steps and try to locate the plutonium."

"So you can't shed any light on what happened with Jerry in Helsinki?"

"No," answered Yuli.

"You may not even know Jerry had centered his activities on Porvoo, not far from Helsinki. He must have found some information that caused him to focus there. He disappeared from a hotel in Porvoo."

"What is the name of the Porvoo hotel?" asked Yuli.

"Mihkli Manor," answered David.

Yuli did not respond for several seconds. "That's interesting," he said finally.

"Why do you say that?" asked David.

"I am not sure," said Yuli. "Except I think there is some connection between Mihkli Manor and the warehouse manager from the original project in Kazakhstan where the plutonium went missing."

"That could be important," said David. "Will you check further?"

"I will," said Yuli. "I have been giving these recent developments some thought, too. I think I might be able to develop some new information here in Russia. I think you know I work for Yukos Oil. Sergei worked for Yukos, too."

"Do you think Yukos is involved in the plutonium situation?"

"I have no evidence of that," said Yuli. "But I have a feeling it makes sense to find out more about what Sergei has been doing. I am also going to make some discrete inquiries about the original Kazakhstan project just in case it turns up some useful information. I'll have to be careful here."

"They sound like good ideas," said David. "Let's keep in touch. Scott Regan and I are going to Helsinki within the next day, but let me give you an e-mail address where you can reach me."

"Why are you going to Helsinki?" asked Yuli.

"A diplomatic problem has flared up. The Finnish police apparently do not think we are being as helpful as we could be in locating Jerry. We are also going to try to keep the plutonium search on track during what the police over there think may be just a murder investigation."

"Good luck," said Yuli. "One more thing. I had a call from Kathleen Paul yesterday. Jerry and I go way back, and Kathleen and Jerry and my wife and I have socialized a few times when I was stationed in Washington."

"What did Kathleen want?"

"She very concerned about Jerry—as you can imagine—and wondered if I could help. I also sensed that she is uncertain you guys are doing all you can to find him."

"I understand where she is coming from," said David. "Things don't look like they are moving quickly. But I can assure you that Scott Regan and I will make certain that the search for Jerry is the highest priority."

"Good," said Yuli. "I'll be in touch soon."

13

Reinforcements

SCOTT AND DAVID ARRIVED IN Helsinki in mid-morning. It was a cool, breezy day. David, who had never been to Helsinki, was impressed with the modernity and cleanliness of the city. The traffic and busy-looking people on the streets impressed him. Helsinki seemed like a twenty-first-century-city with purpose. The onion domes on top of the Helsinki Cathedral contrasted with the modern skyline to add old-world charm to the city.

Scott and David had considered taking rooms at Mihkli Manor in Porvoo, but had decided it would be better to stay in Helsinki to make their visit less visible. Roy DeSantis had reserved rooms for them at the Crowne Plaza Hotel, close to his office at the embassy. Scott arranged a visit with Roy for that afternoon. He and David showered and shaved, rested for a couple hours, had something to eat at the hotel restaurant, and took a short cab ride to Roy's office.

Roy met them in the lobby. His appearance was a contradiction to the image that David had unconsciously created in his mind. David had envisioned him as an average-sized man who dressed conservatively. Instead, Roy was six feet, two inches tall and thin; he looked like he weighed less than 180 pounds. His gray pinstriped suit looked custom made, and he wore a bright yellow necktie with large dots against a pale violet shirt. He looked like he worked in the entertainment business. They shook hands in the lobby, and David had to suppress a smile as they walked back to his office.

When they were seated, Roy looked at David and said, "Thank you for the briefing paper on the Springboard project. It was very helpful. I had no idea there might be a mother lode of weapons-grade plutonium right under our noses around here. It helps me understand why you were reluctant to provide much information on the telephone, and it also explains why there is no hesitancy to kill people to get control of that much nuclear material. If you are interested in profit, it must be worth millions; if you are interested in developing nuclear weapons, it is a bonanza. If we can get control of it, we will make millions of people safer."

"I agree," David said. "Having the full picture makes the importance of this case obvious."

Scott asked, "What's the latest on the Finnish police investigation into the search for Jerry?"

"I spoke with Inspector Roskil of the Ministry of Justice this morning. They have not made much progress. They have no clue where Jerry is and think he is still in the country because they can find no evidence that he has left and the rental car has not turned up. They did establish that the bicycle and bicycle rack they found a couple days ago were the ones purchased by Jerry the day after he arrived. I told them you two were arriving today and that we will meet with them tomorrow. As you know, they believe we have not informed them fully about the case."

Scott asked, "Who will we meet with?"

"They are insisting that we meet at the Ministry of Justice. I tried to get them to come here, but they would not agree, and I thought it best not to antagonize them further."

"I understand," said Scott. "Do we know who will be at the meeting?"

"Not exactly," said Roy. "And I'm afraid they may have more people at the meeting than we prefer. The Inspector said representatives of the Ministries of Interior and Foreign Affairs want to attend."

"Really?" said Scott. "That's not good. We're trying to limit the number of people who know about the plutonium. Our chances of recovery are much better if we can hold that information close."

"I understand," said Roy. "But I think we're stuck. Even our own diplomats are a little miffed about our stinginess with information."

David spoke up. "Maybe we should try to do some diplomatic damage control."

"What do you have in mind?" asked Scott.

"I'm not sure exactly, but maybe we could start with our own diplomats— meet with one or two of them here today. We could brief them generally— tell them generally there may be a substantial amount of fissile material in the area. But tell them that there are still a lot of unknowns and we will appreciate their help in keeping a lid on."

"That could help," said Roy. "I think part of the problem is the simple feeling that we are arbitrarily withholding information just because we are arrogant spooks."

"How about if we have two levels of briefing," said David—especially tomorrow if a bunch of people show up for our meeting. In the first level, we could pledge our cooperation and apologize for our slow initial reaction. Try to smooth ruffled feathers. Then we could ask that we meet with just a few selected people to give the full briefing. We could tell these folks generally about the possibility of nuclear material in the area, and emphasize the need for secrecy. I'm guessing most of them would accept the need to limit information after they know the story."

Scott and Roy were quiet.

Finally Scott said, "I think that's worth a try. Could you try to set up a meeting with our own diplomatic folks this afternoon, Roy?"

"I think so," said Roy. "In fact, it might be best if we meet with just the deputy. He has been the one involved in dealing with the Finnish authorities and the one who has complained to me about the absence of information. If we satisfy him, I think our problem here is solved. It will be trickier with the Finns, but the problem under our own roof is easily solved."

Scott, David, and Roy met with the deputy chief of mission a short time later and told him about Springboard. As expected, when he heard the story, he was satisfied and supported the plan for moving forward. He offered to attend the meeting with the Finnish authorities the next day, but Scott thanked him and declined his offer.

Roy drove Scott and David to Porvoo after the meeting with the deputy. Scott and David were interested to see the Porvoo area and Mihkli Manor where Jerry had stayed. Roy showed them where he had discovered the discarded telephone and GPS. They drove over to the area where Jerry had questioned the bakery and clothing store clerks, and walked up the hill to the Porvoo cathedral. It was late in the day, and there were no tourists. The gardener was not visible on the grounds.

On the way back to their hotel, Roy pointed out some of Helsinki's sights—the Olympic stadium where the 1952 Olympics were held, the old underground Rock Church, and the new Opera House. They had dinner at a downtown café and returned to their hotel. Scott and David had a nightcap in the hotel bar and discussed the briefing they would give the next day. They identified the information they would provide, the information they would not share, and how they could set a positive general tone for the briefing.

The next morning Roy picked Scott and David up at their hotel and drove to the Finnish Ministry of Justice. A young woman was waiting for them at the reception desk and escorted them up a wide marble staircase to a large conference room on the second floor. The room had carved dark wood paneling on its walls, long rectangular windows high on the walls near the ceiling, delicate looking gold lamps spaced every eight feet on the walls, and a large oriental rug under the conference table. The conference table itself was impressive. It was heavy mahogany, about thirty feet long. A half dozen reading lamps were spaced along the center of the table, and delicate looking microphones were at each seat. The high-backed wooden chairs had crimson cushioned seats. A lectern, also with a thin microphone, was on the table at far end. David almost gasped at the number of people already seated; he guessed twenty-five.

Scott, David, and Roy were directed to chairs at the head of the table to the left of the podium. Almost immediately after they were seated, a door behind them opened and a short, balding, impeccably dressed man in his fifties walked to the podium. He did not introduce himself. He had no notes. He spoke in slightly accented English.

"Good morning, ladies and gentlemen. Thank you all for coming. I would like to extend a special welcome to our American guests. They have come a long way to meet with us and we appreciate that.

"As we all know, there was a tragic and mysterious death at Mihkli Manor in Porvoo several days ago. A few days before that, there was a killing in a hotel room in Tallinn that may be related to the one at Mihkli Manor. The victim in the Tallinn killing had visited Helsinki the day before he was killed. Mr. Jerry Paul, an American who had booked the room at Mihkli Manor where the killing took place, has disappeared. Our police have been unable to locate Mr. Paul or the car he was driving.

"We are having some communication difficulties, perhaps a result of the distance between us and the agency that employed Mr. Paul in the U.S. Our police have felt frustrated at the absence of information about Mr. Paul and his mission. It is possible that Mr. Paul is a victim of an attack or kidnapping, but it appears likely that Mr. Paul is the person who killed the man at Mihkli Manor. Our police must talk to Mr. Paul.

"We have asked our American guests to help and have invited them here this morning for a discussion. I am confident that once we have a full and frank discussion, our confusion and concern will disappear.

"Mr. Regan, would you like to begin that discussion? If so, please come to the podium."

Scott went to the podium.

"Good morning, ladies and gentlemen. Thank you for inviting us here today. I, too, am confident that once we have had a chance to discuss the situation, you will be satisfied with the result.

"First, let me tell you who I am and who I work for. My name is Scott Regan, a U.S. government employee. I am employed by the National Counterterrorism Center in the Office of the Director of National Intelligence. As many of you already know, the U.S. reorganized its intelligence functions in 2004. Many of you, like me, might be a little confused by the result. Joining me today are Roy DeSantis of our embassy staff here in Helsinki and David Greenberg who works with me at the Counterterrorism Center.

"For reasons that are fairly obvious, the primary focus of our intelligence operations since September 2001 is the collection of information about terrorism to reduce the ranks, capabilities, and threat of terrorists to the U.S. and its interests. Jerry Paul, the U.S citizen who is currently missing, was working on an assignment for the Counterterrorism Center. Jerry worked with the Central Intelligence Agency, the U.S. intelligence agency most of you are probably familiar with, until a year or so ago, at which time he retired after almost thirty years with the agency. He was a highly skilled and dedicated employee who had an impeccable record for his entire career. He was brought back to work on his current assignment for the Counterterrorism Center because he had a history of working on the case for several years before his retirement. He has knowledge about the case that no one else has.

"I want to say two more things and then answer your questions. First, I am confident that Mr. Paul is not missing voluntarily. We have been unable to contact him ourselves since the night of the killing in his room at Mihkli Manor. I hope he is alive; it would be a real tragedy if he is not. I am also highly confident that if Jerry killed the man in his room, he did so in self defense. This remains to be demonstrated to your satisfaction, of course, but I have known Jerry for years and am familiar with his entire CIA career. Any other explanation is inconsistent with all that I know about him.

"Second, and this may be the explanation for your feeling that we are not fully cooperating with your investigation, Jerry is involved in a highly secret case, and that case is now at a critical moment. I hope you will understand that I cannot provide much information about the details of that case. I can assure you that the case is of the highest priority and potentially involves massive loss of life. Your own country may be at risk, too. I hope you will allow us to keep the details of that case secret for a little longer. I think we are talking about days or at most a few weeks until we can judge whether our focus on the Helsinki area is justified.

"I would like to propose something, if I may. When I finish speaking in just a minute, I will answer your questions. But I may not be able to answer some of your questions due to the need for secrecy surrounding our project. But I would also like to offer that, after meeting with all of you, we meet with a small group, perhaps two, of your investigators. In this meeting, I am confident I can provide more information relevant to your investigation. As I said, I want to be of as much help as I can. Thank you for your attention."

Scott took his seat, and the gentleman who introduced the meeting went to the podium and asked for questions. There were a number of hands raised immediately. A number of the questions were hostile ones. The first questioner asked, "Who in the Finnish government did you notify before you began your operation here?" Another asked, "Is Mr. Paul still in our country?"—implying that Jerry's whereabouts were known by the Americans." Someone else asked, "Was the U.S. diplomatic mission aware of the operation you had begun here?"

Scott answered these and other questions as diplomatically as he could, given the reality that target countries are never notified of impending or ongoing espionage operations on their soil, and given that he could not provide details about Jerry's mission. Gradually the hostility of the questions decreased. The Finnish minister let the questioning run its course, and when that happened, he told Scott that he would accept his offer to give a briefing to the Finnish police. When Scott agreed, the minister asked if the meeting could take place immediately if the minister designated two officers. Scott agreed.

The large meeting adjourned, and they moved to the Justice Minister's office for the smaller briefing. The minister selected Inspector Thor Roskil, the inspector the U.S diplomats had already spoken to, and a second inspector named Paavo Hassi. The Justice Minister remained in the room to hear the briefing.

Scott gave a detailed history of Springboard, including as much as was known about recent developments in Estonia and Finland. The Finns were stunned that a substantial stockpile of weapons-grade plutonium might be stored in their area. After Scott and David responded forthrightly to their questions about Jerry and his activities, their skepticism was replaced by a desire to help in the search for Jerry and the plutonium. Scott, David, Roy, and Inspectors Roskil and Hassi began developing a collaborative plan of action. Scott and David left the meeting feeling positive about their search for Jerry and the plutonium. The Finns, at least in the short term, were going to be assets in their effort. All agreed the meeting had been a success.

When David checked his e-mail at the hotel he found a message from Yuli.

David:

My questions about Sergei here at Yukos have turned up important information. Sergei was working the plutonium case with the knowledge of Russian intelligence, perhaps even under their direction. This was a big surprise to me. I am trying to determine details. I am also trying to access the records of the case from its origin in Kazakhstan. This case file may contain information to assist our current search.

Yuli

David immediately called Scott's hotel room. "I just got an e-mail from Yuli. He tells me that Sergei Andromov was working for Russian intelligence when he was killed."

"What?" exclaimed Scott. "The Russians are hunting for the plutonium too? What does that mean? Wasn't it Yuli who told Jerry it was important to keep this thing quiet? I assumed he meant keep it quiet from the Russians. The Russians could be responsible for Jerry's disappearance."

"Those are all important questions," said David. "Yuli said he is checking further."

"Damn! We can't wait for Yuli to get information for us. I'm going to call Hal. Someone above me in our own bureaucracy needs to find out what's going on. Hal will have to decide what he wants to do, but if I were him, I think I would ask our director to call their top guy. We need to know what the Russians are doing. Christ, they might be the ones to lead us to Jerry."

"I agree," said David. "What should I do right now?"

"Well, Inspectors Roskil and Hassi are coming over here to pick us up soon, right?"

"Yes," said David. "They will be here in about twenty minutes."

"Why don't you go with them? Tell them about this new development. They might have some channels to the Russians they can check. I was going to suggest that we go back to the Porvoo Cathedral and try to talk to the gardener. He seems to be the only source that Jerry spoke to who may be able to confirm that there was a meeting between Sergei and the weapons dealer. The Finns may be able to get more information from the gardener than Jerry could. While you guys continue hunting, I'm going to call Hal and get some inquiries underway at a higher level. I am also going to call Kathleen to bring her up to date."

"Okay," said David. "Good luck with Hal."

14

More Questioning

JERRY'S CONFINEMENT WAS BEGINNING TO agitate him. He did a lot of calisthenics and walked back and forth in his small room constantly. His ability to sleep had diminished even when his muscles were exhausted from exercise. His food and water were gone. He could not estimate how long it had been since he and The Voice had talked. It took all his powers of concentration to keep his mind focused. He found himself longing for a visit from The Voice.

Jerry spent a lot of his time in a twilight zone—especially in his thoughts and dreams about Kathleen and his children. To elevate his mood, he had focused his mind on some of his life's more pleasant times. At one point, he called up his memory of the first time he saw Kathleen. It was in high school and he was a spectator at a girls' basketball game in a small gymnasium.

The girls were wearing those heavy cotton half-skirts that were the required uniforms for girls in the 1960s. He remembered how his eyes were drawn to Kathleen as soon as the game started. She was constantly in motion—especially when playing defense.

Jerry attempted to recall the details of that day. One thing he clearly remembered was Kathleen's legs. He thought they were perfectly formed. But sometime during his recollections, he fell asleep and it morphed into a nightmare. He noticed a cloud beginning to form over the basketball court and soon recognized it was a mushroom cloud. He looked around. The other spectators continued to watch the game, not noticing the mushroom cloud formation. Suddenly the players began to be sucked up into the cloud, and still no one noticed. Kathleen disappeared. Jerry tried to get down to the court to find Kathleen, but he could not. It seemed he spent an hour looking for her until he finally woke up sweating. It took him some time to realize he had been dreaming.

After more calisthenics and walking, Jerry fell asleep exhausted. He had no idea how long he slept before he was startled awake by pounding on the door. He was confused for several seconds until he remembered where he was. He heard The Voice.

"Put your mask on, Mr. Paul, and face away from the door. You know my expectations."

Jerry got up stiffly, found the mask, and stood facing away from the door. The Voice entered with his plastic chair.

"Okay, let's begin. I assume you recall my demands."

"Yes," said Jerry. "I am to tell you everything I know about the missing nuclear material and my recent activities."

"Good," said The Voice. "If I believe that you are being fully cooperative in your responses, I will allow you to sit. Begin with 1993, with the joint Soviet-American project to remove nuclear weapons and material from Kazakhstan."

Jerry described the operation from start to finish as best he could recall it. The Voice did not interrupt him. When he finished, The Voice asked, "Was there any indication at the conclusion of the operation that one hundred kilograms of plutonium was missing?"

"None," said Jerry. "It was many months later that Yuli Karpov told me about the discrepancies in the plutonium manifest."

"Why didn't your people at Lawrence Livermore discover the discrepancy?"

"I don't know," said Jerry. "Apparently they made the same mistake as your people made. They verified the amounts on each plutonium container, but never checked to verify that the total and individual container amounts were consistent."

"Tell me about your investigation after it was discovered that one hundred kilograms of plutonium was missing?"

"We began an active investigation, but we could never develop specific information to guide a search for the plutonium. The case remained open for several years, but when we were unable to develop fresh leads after a couple years, the CIA moved the case to an inactive status. There was no indication that the plutonium was in the U.S. or at risk of being transported there, so the risk seemed minimal to us."

"What is the current status of the case in the U.S.? Why is it active again?"

"Someone at the International Atomic Energy Agency informed the CIA that Plutonium-239 was being offered for sale. The case was returned to active status and I was engaged to begin working it again."

"When was that?" asked The Voice.

"Less than a month ago."

"Good," said The Voice. "I sense you are being cooperative. Turn around, and I will get you a chair to make you more comfortable. But do not remove your mask."

The Voice brought a chair into the room, and Jerry sat. Jerry had been paying close attention to each word spoken by The Voice, straining to detect the nature of his accent. He decided that The Voice was most likely a native Russian speaker. He had developed generic-sounding English, but there was an occasional hint of a hard Russian syllable in his speech. Jerry did not know what to make of a Russian who was obviously well connected but not coordinating with his own people. Perhaps The Voice was part of whoever was marketing the plutonium.

The Voice spoke again, "Now I want you to describe your work plan with the CIA, who you report to, and all the activities you have been engaged in since you started your work."

Jerry corrected The Voice by informing him that he was working for the National Counterterrorism Center, not the CIA. He then had to give The

Voice a short primer on the new structure of U.S. intelligence agencies since the 2004 reorganization. Essentially he gave The Voice a description of the publicly available U.S. intelligence organization chart, not in his judgment providing any information that was not easily available in public documents or online. Having to do this in itself gave Jerry a hint about The Voice's affiliation. It suggested to Jerry that The Voice was not a part of the Russian intelligence apparatus; he would have been aware of the new U.S. intelligence structure if he was in Russian intelligence.

The Voice made Jerry go over his plan and activities since starting to work on Springboard several times. He was especially interested in what Jerry knew about Sergei's killing and what he had discovered since coming to Helsinki. He made Jerry go over the results of his questioning of the Mihkli Manor staff, the store clerks, and the gardener again and again. Jerry was able to report all this consistently and truthfully with the exception of his conversation with the gardener. He avoided acknowledging that the gardener had provided information that Sergei had met with some Russian speakers at the old cathedral. Jerry insisted that the gardener saw nothing and that his conversations with the gardener were largely about flowers. The Voice seemed satisfied with Jerry's responses.

Finally, after what seemed several hours of answering his questions, The Voice said, "I appreciate the information you have provided, Mr. Paul. I have decided to let you live. This is what we are going to do. I have here two small pills. You are going to take these pills. They will put you to sleep, but they are harmless. When you wake up in several hours, you may have a little hangover, but you will be fine otherwise. The door will be unlocked and you will be free to go. I am sure you will find a way to go wherever you wish."

"Where am I?" Jerry asked, feeling deeply skeptical about the safety of the pills.

"You do not need to know where you are," said The Voice.

"Okay," said Jerry. "But I would prefer not to take your pills. I often have severe reactions to medication. I will wait here as long as you say after you leave."

"That is unacceptable," said The Voice. "Your choice is to take these pills. Otherwise I will put a bullet in your brain. What is your choice?"

"I will take the pills," said Jerry.

"Hold out your hand."

Jerry held out his hand for the pills and accepted a plastic bottle of water in the other hand.

"Now take the pills and do not try to avoid their ingestion. I will wait until you are unconscious before I leave. If you are not unconscious shortly, I will shoot you."

Jerry took the pills and a long drink of water. Within a few minutes, he felt his head getting light and then nothing.

15

Moving Forward

DAVID RETURNED TO THE HOTEL in the early evening. He called Scott's room as soon as he entered his own.

"Hello, Scott. I have some things to report."

"Good. I do as well. I spoke with Hal and Kathleen. Why don't you come up and we'll talk. Have you eaten dinner?"

"No, and I'm starved," said David.

"I'm hungry too," said Scott. "Come up and we'll order room service and discuss where we are."

David got his laptop and went to Scott's room.

Scott said, "I spoke to Hal at headquarters and convinced him that we needed a high level contact from us to Russian intelligence. He is going to ask our director Mike McCarthy to call the Russian director of the Federal

Security Service; they know each other. If Mike does make that call, I think we'll get some information we can use."

"I'm impressed," said David. "The Director of National Intelligence does some case work."

"I hear Mike is a pretty good guy—not afraid to get his hands dirty. He was a very creative intelligence officer years ago. They say he ran successful undercover operations in Lebanon and the Middle East about twenty years ago. He accomplished something few have been able to do; he collaborated with the Israeli Mossad without getting ripped off."

"If the Director is going work a case, what better situation to get involved in than one where one of our guys is missing," observed David.

"I hope it works," said Scott. "We should know something within a day or two. I spoke to Kathleen Paul too."

"How is Kathleen doing?" asked David.

"She's doing okay, but is obviously worried and frustrated about Jerry's disappearance. She still seems skeptical that we are doing all we can. She doesn't trust Hal to commit all possible resources. She didn't make any threats, but she is a woman who craves action. I'm not going to be surprised if we hear from her congressman or some other muckety-muck."

"Did Hal say anything about FBI support? He was going to check to see if they could give us some help on the ground over here. The reason I ask is the Finnish Justice Ministry has a negative reaction to the idea. We didn't mention it yesterday during our briefing, so I brought it up today when we were out in Porvoo. I was surprised at the inspectors' immediate negative reactions."

"Hal said that we can have some FBI assets, and I have a name of someone to call. But I'm not surprised the Finns don't like the idea," said Scott. "Police agencies like to think they can take care of things themselves, and the FBI has a reputation for being heavy-handed—wanting to take over a case whenever they are involved. At least for now, I don't think it's a problem. Our problem isn't manpower. Our problem is workable leads to follow."

Room service knocked on the door and Scott and David took a break to eat. Scott found ESPN on the television, and they watched the results of the latest weekend of National Football League action. Scott and David both followed the Redskins, but they were disappointed again. Six weeks into the season, the Redskins were only three and three.

After they finished eating, David began. "I had an interesting day with the Finnish police. We went out to Porvoo and visited Mihkli Manor and the cathedral. The gardener at the cathedral confirmed what Jerry had already told us. He did observe a conversation between three men speaking Russian in the cathedral's garden on the day Sergei visited. He didn't add any other useful information though. We also spoke with the Mihkli Manor manager. I don't think he gave the inspectors any new information."

"Have they identified the dead guy in Jerry's room?"

"No," answered David. "They have checked his fingerprints and come up blank. They're sure he was not local and don't think he was a Finn either."

"What makes them think he wasn't a Finn?"

"Two things," said David. "His clothes appeared foreign, and they did some DNA testing."

"DNA testing? Do they keep DNA data for their population?"

"Not exactly," said David. "They have a guy at the university who specializes in studying the DNA features of the Finnish population. I don't really understand it, but he has identified the historical DNA ancestral origins of most Finns, and this guy had a different distant maternal ancestor than most Finns."

"Are the Finns that homogenous that they had a common maternal ancestor?"

"No, and they're not making a lot out of the DNA thing. It's just one of the reasons why they think the guy who tried to kill Jerry was a foreigner. His fingerprints were not in the Finnish, Estonian, or Interpol databases, he was wearing clothes not typically sold in the Baltic, and his DNA suggested a Middle Eastern origin."

"Middle Eastern—really?"

"Yes, the dead guy had a Middle Eastern mama in his gene pool thousands of years ago," said David.

"Doesn't sound like very solid evidence to me," said Scott.

"It's not," said David. "There was lots of population movement over the centuries of course, and even today there are immigrants to Finland from other parts of the world. The dead guy's DNA is just one suggestive piece of information."

"I'm not sure we can make any more headway tonight," said Scott. "But let's check our e-mail to see if there is anything new there."

Each of them logged on to their e-mail accounts.

"The only thing I have is a confirmation from Hal that Mike McCarthy will call the Russian intelligence chief first thing tomorrow," said Scott.

"I have something from Yuli that may be useful," said David. "He says that he thinks the warehouse manager from the original Kazakhstan operation is living in Finland now. He was one of the original suspects in the disappearance of the plutonium. His daughter works at Mihkli Manor. Her name is Sonia Pernen, and that name rings a bell. I'll check my old e-mails, but I think Jerry mentioned her in one of his e-mails."

"Good," said Scott. "We at least have something we can follow up on tomorrow. I've been worried we were running out of leads to work."

David Greenberg and Inspector Thor Roskil motored to Mihkli Manor the next morning and met with the hotel manager. They asked to meet with Sonia Pernen, the Manor's restaurant manager. Ms. Pernen came to meet with David and Inspector Roskil in one of the hotel's small conference rooms. She was a striking woman—beautiful in a quiet way. David watched the lines of her shapely figure as she took a seat. Her pale blue, silk blouse fit perfectly and drew his eyes.

The inspector began the questioning.

"Good morning, Ms. Pernen. Thank you for meeting with us. I am Inspector Roskil from the Finnish Ministry of Justice and this is David Greenberg, an American in government service. You will no doubt recall the killing that took place in one of the hotel's rooms a few days ago, and you may know that room had originally been booked by an American citizen. That man is a colleague of Mr. Greenberg; they work together. We are still investigating that killing and hope you will answer a few questions for us."

"I will be happy to answer your questions, but I know nothing of the killing. I was not on the premises when it occurred."

The inspector continued, "I understand you were not here at the time of the killing. Our questions have to do with the American who has disappeared. His name is Jerry Paul. Do you recall him?"

"No, I'm afraid not. I am not involved with the registered hotel guests directly. I manage the restaurant which is a separate business operation. I am unaware most of the time whether one of our restaurant customers is a hotel guest."

"I see," said the Inspector. "But do you recall the American, Mr. Paul? According to his hotel charges, he had dinner at the restaurant on two successive nights, including the night before the killing."

"No, I do not remember him," said Ms. Pernen.

"May I ask a question?" said David, addressing the inspector.

"Certainly," said Inspector Roskil.

"Mr. Paul, the American guest, had been trying to locate a Russian gentleman who may have dined at the hotel a few days before Mr. Paul had dinner at your restaurant. He may have asked if you could help him locate the Russian. Does that sound familiar?"

Ms. Pernen hesitated for several seconds, looked at Inspector Roskil uncertainly, and finally responded. "I do recall now. It was probably Mr. Paul who asked me if one or two Russian gentlemen had lunch in the restaurant two or three days earlier. I checked our reservation book and could not identify anyone matching Mr. Paul's description. I did not make the connection when answering the inspector's earlier question."

David continued. "Did Mr. Paul dine alone?"

"Yes, I believe he did."

"Did you notice Mr. Paul speak with anyone or meet with anyone in the lobby?" asked David.

"I did not notice," said Ms. Pernen with finality.

"Thank you Ms. Pernen," said Inspector Roskil. "I have a few more questions on another matter if you do not mind."

"I'll try to answer," she said.

"Am I correct that you are the daughter of Pavel Nosenko?"

Sonia Pernen stiffened noticeably. "Yes, but what has any of this to do with my father?"

"Probably nothing," answered the Inspector. "Am I correct that your father now lives in the area?"

"I think he does, but we are estranged."

"Can you tell us how to contact him?" asked the inspector.

"No, I cannot. As I've told you, we are estranged."

"Do you know where he lives? Is he employed?" Inspector Roskil continued insistently.

"I'm sorry, I just do not know anything of his circumstances," said Ms. Pernen.

"Have you seen your father recently?" pressed the inspector.

"No, I have not," said Ms. Pernen, offering no further explanation.

"Thank you for your time, Ms. Pernen. Do you have additional questions for Ms. Pernen?" the inspector said to David.

"No, I do not," said David. "I, too, thank you for your time, Ms. Pernen."

David and the inspector left the hotel, went to their car, and left the hotel parking lot. The inspector turned backed toward Helsinki, drove about a quarter mile, and took a sudden U-turn back toward the hotel. He turned into a gravel road across from the hotel parking lot, parked the car, and turned the engine off. The inspector did not say anything to David; he dialed his cell phone and spoke a few sentences to someone on the other end.

David spoke, "She is a beautiful woman, but I sense she was not truthful."

"I agree," said the inspector. "Especially regarding her father, she avoided my questions."

In another five minutes, a red Fiat sports car left the hotel parking lot and turned onto the road going away from Helsinki. The Inspector waited about five seconds and pulled out to follow the Fiat.

"That's her in the red Fiat," said the inspector as he steadily increased the speed of the car. "I don't know where she's going, but I think our questions have upset or frightened her."

"It seems so," said David.

They were driving on a two-lane, winding rural road. The inspector pushed the speedometer to 125 KPH in pursuit of the Fiat. David gripped the handle over his head as they rounded the curves. The large deciduous trees along the road were losing their leaves and their red, yellow, and brown leaves swirled around the car as they raced along. After driving for ten minutes at this speed, the inspector slowed, pulled into the driveway of a large house on the right, and turned the engine off.

"I think certain Ms. Pernen has turned off this road before this point. I am going to turn back toward Helsinki. I will drive more slowly and would appreciate it if you would make notes of the crossroads and other places where Ms. Pernen might have turned off. We'll be lucky if we are able to spot her car, but I think that is unlikely. If we note the places where she may have turned off, we can come back later and do a systematic search."

"I'll be glad to note the turnoffs. If you can give me the kilometer distances between each, that will help too."

"When we get back to my office, I will call the hotel to see if she has returned to work," said the inspector.

David noted about six crossroads and another eight places where the Fiat may have left the roadway. They were back in Inspector Roskil's office in less than an hour. Inspector Roskil telephoned Mihkli Manor; Ms. Pernen had not returned to work.

Jerry became aware of some movement on his upper lip and wetness on his back. He struggled to clear his mind but instinctively kept his eyes closed and did not move. He listened intently. There were distant sounds of traffic—not steady traffic movement—a vehicle sound every few seconds. He was lying on his back on moist ground. He brushed an insect from his lip, opened his eyes, and gazed up at tall trees almost bare of their leaves. It was full daylight—he guessed late morning. His body seemed free of injury—a little sore and stiff, but his arms, legs, head, and fingers moved freely and without pain. He sat up. His head throbbed. He had been lying in tall weeds in a heavily wooded area. He saw a narrow footpath a few feet in front of him. The suitcase he had brought to Mihkli Manor was a few feet to his right.

Jerry got to his feet and looked around. He saw a break in the underbrush and trees about twenty feet to his left, but nothing but woods in the other directions. He picked up his suitcase, walked along the path and quickly came to a paved two-lane road. A small passenger sedan whizzed by just as he reached the road, startling him. The shoulder of the road was narrow. He stood off the road as far as the woods would allow. Two passenger cars came by in quick succession. He turned and walked in the direction of the traffic flow.

Jerry tired quickly. He had walked less than a mile and had to stop to rest. He wondered if it was the suitcase but the suitcase was not heavy. He unzipped it; his laptop was gone. He saw only his own clothes and a belt he did not recognize. He was short of breath but forced himself to walk on. In a few minutes he came to a low stone wall, put his suitcase on the ground and hoisted himself onto the wall. He began to reconstruct his recent experience. He remembered The Voice, the room where he was confined, the interrogation, the pills. The pills probably explained his breathlessness. Suddenly he remembered the shape standing over his bed, the muffled shot, his own gun, the sound of the man's body hitting the hotel room floor. The memory shocked him and he felt a burst of adrenaline.

Jerry's mind shifted into a problem-solving mode. He hopped off the wall and stood on the side of the road facing traffic. As each vehicle approached, he put his thumb out asking for a ride. He had done a lot of hitchhiking around

Philadelphia and New Jersey as a teenager, but now it felt awkward. Ten or twelve cars and small trucks passed without stopping. Finally, a medium-sized refrigerated truck stopped for him. He ran to the passenger door and saw a young man's smiling face looking at him. Jerry put his suitcase on the floor of the cab and climbed up onto the seat.

"Thank you," said Jerry to the driver.

The man responded with a nod of his head, still smiling. It occurred to Jerry that the man may not understand English.

"Do you understand English?"

The man looked somewhat puzzled and shrugged his shoulders. Jerry tried speaking Russian. The man shook his head. Jerry closed the door of the truck and the man drove off.

After a mile or so, Jerry saw a highway sign indicating Espoo was three kilometers ahead. He could not recall where Espoo was relative to Helsinki or Porvoo. In ten minutes, the truck reached Espoo and stopped at a traffic light. Jerry reached over and shook the truck driver's hand, thanked him several times, and got out of the truck. He stood on the sidewalk for a minute deciding what to do. He spotted a police car about a half block away on the other side of the street and walked toward it.

16

Loose Ends

SCOTT REGAN AND DAVID GREENBERG met for a late lunch at a café near the Ministry of Justice in Helsinki. Scott briefed David on his recent conversation with Hal Bolton.

"I've never heard Hal so wound up," said Scott. "He was excited to be directly involved in real case work, but very upset about Kathleen Paul."

"What did Kathleen do to upset him?"

"She showed up at his office. Hal could actually hear her talking to his secretary outside his office door."

"Really! How did she get past security?"

"Damned if I know," said Scott. "But I had a hard time not laughing when he described how she cornered him. Somehow she talked her way past security and presented herself to Hal's secretary. The secretary tried to put her off, but Kathleen simply told her she would wait and sat down on one of the chairs in Hal's reception area. The secretary started to call security, but Hal brought Kathleen into his office. I would have loved to be a fly on the wall during that conversation."

"I'll bet Hal was squirming. He hates confrontation unless he can totally script all the lines—and the final outcome, too," said David.

"Kathleen stayed in there for almost an hour, and Hal had his secretary arrange a room for her at that new Hilton close to the office. I put a call in to Kathleen at the hotel, but she was out. I'll try her again later."

"I can't wait to meet Kathleen Paul," said David.

Scott changed the subject. "Hal also told me about Mike McCarthy's conversation with Russian intelligence. The results are interesting, but confusing. According to Mike, the Russians say they are not working the plutonium case and knew nothing about Sergei's involvement in it. They were aware of his murder, but apparently thought the murder was associated with a robbery. At least that's what their director said."

"That's a surprise," said David. "Remember Yuli's e-mail a day or two ago? According to Yuli, Russian intelligence is involved in the case."

"I remember you told me that," said Scott. "Do we know who Yuli was in touch with in Russian intelligence?"

"No, his plan was to start making inquiries at Yukos. Both Sergei and Yuli work for Yukos. I had assumed he found a contact in Russian intelligence, but I don't know that for sure."

Scott said, "Why don't you send Yuli an e-mail asking for clarification. Let's not tell him yet about the contradictory information from Russian intelligence. It would be good if we could talk to him in person to get a full report on what he is finding. I think he comes to Tallinn on business frequently, doesn't he?"

"Yes, he does come to Tallinn. I'm not sure how often, but I can try to set something up."

"Do that," said Scott. "We have to figure out what's going on—my head is starting to hurt with all the possibilities."

"It is confusing," said David. "I have started a list of the players and questions trying to keep track in my own mind. The list is getting longer; the cast of characters includes Yuli Karpov, Sergei Andromov, the weapons dealer Ivan Savinkov, Sonia Pernen and her father Pavel Nosenko, the unknown dead guy from Jerry's room, and whoever kidnapped Jerry. I think the one we know least about is the weapons dealer Ivan Savinkov who started this whole thing when he asked Sergei Andromov to verify the authenticity of the plutonium."

"Andromov and whoever grabbed Jerry," replied Scott. "I think we should make finding Jerry our highest priority. The longer he stays missing, the more worrisome it is. I anticipate that Hal will be showing new interest in Jerry now that he has to deal with Kathleen Paul. Do you have suggestions for intensifying the search for Jerry?"

"Yes, I think we should focus on Sonia Pernen and her father. I believe they are central to this whole business. At the same time I think we should try to locate the arms dealer Savinkov and put him under surveillance."

"I agree with those priorities," said Scott. "I'm not sure it's a separate line of inquiry, but I think identifying the purchaser of the plutonium is a high priority, too."

"Right," said David. "I was thinking the weapons dealer will lead us to them, but if we can figure out how to identify them in another way, that would be great."

"There's one more player, or one more *possible* player," said Scott. "Yukos Oil. Sergei worked for Yukos, and Yuli still works for Yukos. And we know that a number of former Russian intelligence officials moved from Russian government service to Yukos in recent years. We should explore what role, if any, Yukos has in this whole deal."

"Good point," said David. "I have another suggestion. I think we now have some confidence that the missing plutonium is in this area."

"I agree," said Scott.

"I think we should alert our science people to that, and I think we're going to need more detection equipment."

"Good thinking," said Scott. "Let's make an action plan. You contact Yuli. Tell him Jerry's still missing and we have a lot of questions for him. Try to get him to come to Tallinn or somewhere we can meet with him in person. And try to get the Finnish police to step up the effort to find Jerry. Do you think the Finns feel Sonia Pernen and her father are important?"

"Yes, I do," said David. "They are very interested in Sonia, her father, and Jerry. In their minds, Jerry is a killer, and they will have to be convinced that he acted in self-defense."

"Okay," said Scott. "While you're working those angles, I'm going to talk to Hal and update him. And I'm going to involve some more of our assets at CIA headquarters and in Moscow to gather information about the weapons dealer Savinkov and Yukos Oil. Hopefully we can get a surveillance started on Savinkov. And I'll ask Hal to get us some nuclear expertise, too. Let's go back to the embassy and get to work."

Roy DeSantis had set up a small conference room at the Helsinki Embassy as a workplace for Scott and David. They had separate desks, computer stations, and phone lines. They had been working less than an hour when Roy burst into the room.

"They found Jerry! He turned up at a police station in Espoo, and they are in the process of transporting him to the Ministry of Justice in Helsinki. He seems to be in good shape—no significant injuries."

There were handshakes and high fives all around, and the noise brought the nearby embassy staff to the conference room. Within a few minutes, staff from other floors in the building were crowding the hallway. Roy made a call to the ambassador and suggested he have an impromptu meeting in the embassy's auditorium. Soon there were sixty or seventy people in the auditorium seats waiting for the ambassador to come to the podium.

The ambassador, Roy, Scott, and David gathered in the ambassador's office to try to get more information from the Finnish Ministry of Justice before meeting with the excited employees. Finally, the ambassador was connected to the Minister of Justice.

"Hello, Mr. Minister. I understand your police have located Mr. Paul. That is wonderful news. We very much appreciate your efforts in finding him. What can you tell me about his condition and the circumstances of finding him?"

The ambassador listened intently for more than a minute. "That is wonderful news. When can we see him?"

The ambassador listened longer this time, the expression on his face growing more serious. "I understand your need to question him, but I would appreciate it if you would grant us the courtesy of having one of his countrymen present during that questioning."

The ambassador listened intently again. "I see," he said. "Thank you for that information. I will get in touch with the Finnish Ministry for Foreign Affairs." The ambassador laid the telephone down and spoke to them.

"Well, they tell me Jerry is fine—in good shape physically and mentally. But they are insisting on exercising their authority to question him privately, given his possible involvement in a murder. They are also going to arrange a physical exam and psychological interview. The Minister tells me it might be two or three days before we can see him."

"Can they do that?" asked Scott.

The ambassador responded, "They should at least let us see him, so to that extent, they may be overstepping their authority. But I am reluctant to play diplomatic hardball right now. They are still smarting a bit about our having begun an espionage operation in their country without their knowledge. At this point, I am inclined to make a call to the Ministry of Foreign Affairs to express our concern and then give them a little time to reach a consensus among themselves. The Foreign Affairs folks will be interested in accommodating us, but they will not want to be heavy-handed with their Justice Ministry people."

"Meanwhile, we wait three days to see Jerry," said Scott.

"I don't think it will come to that," said the ambassador. "I think when I call back in the morning, they will try to find a way to respond positively."

"But meanwhile, we wait," repeated Scott.

"I think that's the prudent thing to do at the moment. It appears that Mr. Paul is safe and unhurt. I don't think that making forceful demands now will bear fruit and could delay things further."

"Okay," said Scott. "I accept your judgment, but please keep after them."

"Rest assured; I will be insistent with the Foreign Affairs Minister."

The ambassador, Scott, David, and Roy went to the conference room and briefed the waiting embassy employees. Some of the excitement was taken out of the air when the ambassador announced there would be a delay in meeting Jerry.

Back in their makeshift office, Scott said to David, "I'm going to call Kathleen and tell her about Jerry. Then I'll call Hal. I want Kathleen to hear the good news from a friendly voice."

"Good idea," said David. "But do you think that will piss Hal off?"

"Probably," said Scott. "But what can he do about it? It's still morning in northern Virginia isn't it? Hopefully she's still at the hotel."

Scott got through to Kathleen's hotel in less than a minute and asked to be connected to Kathleen Paul's room. David heard Scott say "Kathleen?

This is Scott Regan calling from Helsinki. It's good news, Kathleen. We've found Jerry and he's okay."

Scott waited. "It's okay, Kathleen. Take your time. I'm in no rush. I'll just hold on here. I'm sure you have questions."

David could hear sobbing from Kathleen's end, and noticed Scott struggling to keep his own composure. Finally, Scott said, "Yes, he's fine. We haven't seen him and we don't know any details yet. He was found in Espoo—a Finnish town not too far from Helsinki. Apparently, he contacted the local police there, and they contacted the Ministry of Justice in Helsinki. I think I told you the Finnish police have been looking for Jerry, too."

Scott listened for a short time.

"It may be a couple days before we can see him, but we're working on that. The Finnish police want to question him and have him examined by a doctor. But the important thing is that he is safe and unharmed. I wanted to let you know as soon as I could."

Scott listened again and responded, "Come over here? That may not be a good idea Kathleen—at least not for a few days."

"We literally just found out about Jerry moments ago and are trying to get the Finnish authorities to agree to let us see him. Our ambassador has talked to their Foreign Minister, and their Foreign Minister is going to get in touch with the Finnish Minister of Justice. We have a little bit of a diplomatic and turf thing going here."

"I know it's bullshit, Kathleen. But it's real bullshit. We are afraid that putting too much pressure on the Finns right now could be counterproductive. Is anyone there with you? Wonderful. I haven't met your children, but I know from Jerry they are great kids. They're both in their twenties now, aren't they?"

After a brief response from Kathleen, Scott continued, "Kathleen, I would really appreciate it if you would just hold on there for a little while. I promise to keep in touch whenever I have new information and no less than once a day. Like I said, Jerry is fine."

"Thank you, Kathleen. One more thing. I am going to call Hal Bolton as soon as we finish talking. Please act surprised when he calls you."

Scott placed a call to Hal Bolton and waited for Hal's secretary to get him out of a meeting.

"Good morning, Hal. David Greenberg and I are in our temporary office at the Helsinki embassy. Can I put you on the speaker phone so that David can be a part of our discussion?"

"Go ahead," said Hal.

Scott activated the phone's speaker. "We have some very good news, Hal. We have located Jerry. We don't know any details yet, but he is not hurt. The Finnish Justice Ministry is questioning him about the dead man that was found in his hotel room in Porvoo, but they won't let us see him right now. We're hopeful about negotiating something with the Finns tomorrow that will let us see him face to face."

"Do we know where he has been?" asked Hal.

"He was found in Espoo—not far from here—a short time ago, but we do not know anything else at the moment. I will let you know the details as soon as we can get them. There are some other things David and I would like to discuss with you."

"Fine, go ahead" said Hal.

Scott summarized recent developments and told Hal about the plans to focus on Sonia Pernen and her father and to engage some CIA assets in Moscow to develop more information on the weapons dealer and Yukos. Hal agreed to recruit some nuclear expertise to support the operation in Helsinki.

"There is something else," said Scott. "The Russian intelligence chief told Mike McCarthy that they were not working the plutonium case."

"Right," said Hal.

"We got different information from Yuli Karpov. He told David in an e-mail that the Russian Federal Security Service is involved in the case. David is going to try to get Yuli to clarify this and to provide more information. We are going to try to get Yuli to come to Tallinn or Helsinki to meet with us in person. But do you get any sense from Mike about whether the Russian Director was being straight with him?"

"That's interesting. I'll talk to Mike again, but I had the feeling that he thought he had a good rapport with his counterpart in Russia. Mike will be interested to hear about this contradiction."

"Okay," said Scott. "We're going to get moving over here. I'll keep you informed. Are you going to contact Kathleen, Paul?"

"I'll call her as soon as I hang up."

Scott and David attempted without success to get in touch with Inspectors Roskil and Hassi. Apparently they were questioning Jerry and not available. They discussed the possibility of going to Mihkli Manor and the Porvoo Cathedral on their own, but decided in consultation with Roy DeSantis that these actions could cause further conflict with the Finnish authorities. They decided the Finns needed to satisfy themselves about Jerry and his activities, and the Finnish bureaucracies had to make decisions about their own responses. David sent Yuli an e-mail, and Scott did some administrative housekeeping while they waited for more action-oriented opportunities.

Jerry's relief and elation about being alive and free was short-lived. After arriving at police headquarters in Espoo, the initial friendly attitude of the local police quickly disappeared, and he was photographed, fingerprinted, and locked in a cell. His pleas to be permitted to contact the American Embassy were ignored; he was told the Americans had already been notified that he was in custody.

In a few hours, a Finnish Justice Ministry van arrived at the Espoo police station, he was handcuffed, placed in the secure back of the van, and driven, he assumed, to Helsinki. There were no windows in the rear of the van, and when it arrived at its destination, Jerry was removed from the van in an underground garage and taken up two flights of stairs to a windowless cell. There was a three-blade fan in the ceiling moving at a slow speed. The stainless steel bed folded up against the wall; it had a thin mattress. There were stainless toilet and sink and a small desk and chair. The cell was lighted by two low-watt bulbs mounted about six feet up on opposite walls. He had the odd feeling that he was an alien.

Jerry was given a bottle of water and some fresh fruit through a long, narrow opening in the cell door. There did not appear to be other occupied cells near him. It was very quiet. He could hear the hum of what he assumed was the building's heating system but nothing else—no voices, ringing telephones—nothing.

After about two hours, he was taken to an interrogation room and advised by one of the three men in the room that he was under investigation for murder. The men did not identify themselves. The room was about ten feet by twelve feet with a simple wood table about three feet long in the center of the room. There were a half dozen formed plastic chairs, gray in color. The questioning began by dealing with his identity and reasons for being in Helsinki. Jerry withheld nothing initially, acknowledging his employment by the U.S. Counterterrorism Center and his mission in search of the missing plutonium. He told of his reasons for coming to Helsinki and Porvoo and his investigative activities there. He described as best he could remember the intrusion into his room at Mihkli Manor, his killing of the intruder, and his abduction in the parking lot. He described his interrogation, his taking of the drug that rendered him unconscious, regaining consciousness in the woods alongside the road, and his truck ride into Espoo. When the interrogators began probing for specific information about the Springboard case, he told the interrogators he would not discuss the case without first meeting with an American diplomat and a representative of U.S. intelligence.

The interrogators pressed him for the information they were seeking, and threatened him with continued incarceration and indictment for murder. Jerry held firm. After several hours, the interrogators abruptly left the room without comment. In a few minutes, two uniformed officers entered the room and escorted him back to his cell without speaking. He found more water; a sheet, blanket, and pillow on the narrow bed; and a tray of cold food.

In about two more hours, the light in his cell was extinguished. Within a few minutes, Jerry fell asleep exhausted.

After what seemed like a long deep sleep, Jerry was awoken by the opening of his cell door. Two different uniformed men entered his cell, waited while he used the toilet and put his shoes on, and took him to the same interrogation room. He assumed the large glass section on one wall hid an observation room on the other side. The same interrogators asked most of the same questions they had asked previously. Jerry answered with the same information and again refused to answer questions about Springboard. The three men left the room wordlessly after about two hours. This time, he was not taken back to his cell.

In about twenty minutes, one of the interrogators entered the room.

"My name is Inspector Roskil of the Finnish Ministry of Justice. We are classifying your killing of the unidentified man in your hotel room as self-defense, and are recommending that our prosecuting attorney not file a case against you. We have also called the American Embassy. They tell us that they will be here to pick you up within the hour. Your suitcase will be returned, but we are keeping your handgun as evidence. Our ballistics examiner tells us that it is the weapon that fired the bullet that killed the man in your room. If there are not further developments in the case, you may request return of the weapon after one year. I have for you a letter from our Justice Ministry. The letter prohibits you from carrying a weapon of any kind in Finland ever again without the express written consent of the Ministry of Justice. Do you understand?"

"I understand," said Jerry. "May I ask—have you identified the man I shot?"

"No, we have not. We believe he is a foreigner, but we have been unable to develop any solid evidence about his identity."

When Jerry asked no further questions, the inspector left the room, leaving the door open. He returned in a few minutes, placed Jerry's suitcase just inside the door and left. In a few more moments, he came back again and asked Jerry to get his suitcase and follow him. In less than a minute, Jerry found himself in the building's main entrance reception area looking at Scott Regan and Roy DeSantis. Scott and Roy shook Jerry's hand without speaking, left the building, and got into the embassy car waiting in the parking lot.

"*Wow!*" said Jerry after he was seated in the back seat next to Scott. "Just like that, I'm a free man. There were moments when I thought it was all over."

Scott reached over and embraced Jerry. "We had our doubts, too. We had no idea what had happened, and there were moments when we feared the worst. Do you feel up to a debriefing right now?"

"Right now I would like a shave, shower, and some clean clothes. Then I want to call Kathleen. After that, I think I can tolerate telling my story."

"So be it," said Scott. "Roy, lets take Jerry over to the Crowne Plaza where David and I are staying and get him a room."

Within twenty minutes, Jerry was under a hot shower in his own hotel room. The others left Jerry's room so that he could talk to Kathleen in private after his shower. When they returned forty minutes later, Jerry was asleep. Scott and Roy left him sleeping and went to the embassy, leaving Jerry a note to call when he woke up.

17

Collaboration

THINGS BEGAN TO MOVE QUICKLY that afternoon. The Director of National Intelligence, Mike McCarthy, wanted to have a telephone conference the next morning with several of his staff and Scott, Jerry, David, and Roy. Hal Bolton would participate. A secure line would be set up at the Helsinki embassy. The call was scheduled for 1100 hours Helsinki time—0600 in Washington. The Finns wanted to have another meeting with the Americans at the Ministry of Justice and planned to invite representatives from the Ministries of Foreign Affairs and Interior. Yuli Karpov was coming to Tallinn the next day and was going to come to Helsinki for a meeting that night. They would meet with Jerry as soon as he awoke, and complete that discussion no matter how long it took so that Jerry's experiences could be part of the National Intelligence

Director's teleconference the next day. Adrenaline effects were noticeable all around.

Jerry slept for only a couple hours, and an embassy car was sent to pick him up. He arrived looking fresh, energetic, and anxious to get to work. He carried a man's trouser belt with him, prompting some quizzical looks. Jerry, Scott, David, and Roy met in the conference room where Scott and David had set up their Helsinki operation.

They began by bringing Jerry up to date on what had happened since his abduction: Yuli's belief that Russian intelligence was involved in the plutonium case, the involvement of Sonia Pernen and her father, the on-again, off-again cooperation with the Finns, the Russian's denial of involvement to Mike McCarthy, and the plans for the next day.

Jerry began his briefing with a surprise announcement. "My wife is coming to Helsinki. She'll arrive the day after tomorrow."

Scott hesitated, but finally said, "Do you think that is a good idea, Jerry?"

"Good idea, bad idea—I don't know. But she *is* coming. I want to stay to finish my work—to recover the plutonium. Kathleen insisted that if I wasn't coming home, she is coming here. She knows our business; she won't intrude on our work. But I know Kathleen; sometimes I can't say no to her, or it wouldn't matter if I did say no, and this is one of those times. And frankly, I am anxious to see her. There were moments a couple days ago when I doubted I'd ever see her again. So she's coming. She will not be asking the agency to help with travel arrangements or pay her airfare; she is coming on her own."

Scott smiled. "God bless her, Jerry. God bless her!"

"Thanks," said Jerry. "Now let me tell you where I've been."

Jerry told the entire story. He had told it several times already: to The Voice, to the Finnish police, so it was a smooth narrative. His three listeners did not interrupt often. David took notes on his laptop. When Jerry had finished, the group's questions focused mainly on The Voice: his manner of speaking, the substance of his questions, his likely affiliation, and his interests.

"I strained my ears to identify his accent, and I've racked my brain trying to understand his interests—to put them in some context. Here are my tentative conclusions. He is not a native English speaker, but his accent is almost imperceptible. It is not British English, but it could be English learned in the U.S. Perhaps he went to high school or college—or both—in the U.S. I don't think it's likely that he could have developed such good English without having lived in an American English-speaking environment for some time."

"Did he use any American colloquialisms or slang?" asked David.

"I can't recall any," said Jerry.

Roy asked, "Could you guess what interests he had or what government or group he is allied with?"

"Not exactly," said Jerry. "I did get the sense that he is not a rogue actor like a weapons dealer or member of a terrorist group. He was very logical and systematic in his questioning and in the way that he dealt with me—no angry threats or ideological talk, for example. He could work for a government, but I have a gut feeling that he is not an intelligence operative. I have trouble saying exactly why I think that—except that I did not get a sense of any intelligence tradecraft practices that I am familiar with in the way that he dealt with me."

"Why do you think he didn't kill you?" asked Scott.

"That's a very good question, and I have to say that I thought the pills he gave me were poison, that I was history," said Jerry. "I think his reasons were complicated. He was very careful that I not see him so that I could not identify him visually, although I will never forget his voice and could easily identify that. I also wondered if he wanted to avoid killing an American agent and thus stirring up an aggressive hunt for him. And I suspect too that there was an element of compassion on his part. I got the sense that he was basically a decent guy. But in a sense, it was illogical not to kill me if he wanted to be certain that I could not identify him. I still don't fully understand why I wasn't killed."

"So he may not have been associated with the guy you killed?" asked David.

"I think it's unlikely that he is associated with those who tried to kill me," said Jerry. "One guy came into my room and fired a bullet into my pillow where he thought my head was; the other fed me some sleeping pills to put me to sleep and set me free."

"So you were being stalked by two different guys?" asked Roy.

"That's the logical implication," said Jerry. "But I admit it is confusing and does not help us identify the affiliation and motivation of the two guys."

"One of them simply wanted to eliminate you. The other wanted information from you," observed David.

"Let me change the subject a bit and introduce something else," said Jerry. "Look at this belt. It's the only article of clothing the guy I killed was wearing that had any markings on it. I took it with me when I left the Mihkli Manor room. I am hoping it will give us a clue toward the nationality of the dead man, or at least where he bought his clothes."

Jerry passed the belt to Scott and each of them examined it.

"It looks like it fits about a thirty-two-inch waist and it's real leather."

"The guy who tried to kill me was in good physical condition. He was wiry—he may have been a runner from the look of his physique."

"The markings are not English letters," said David. "Do any of you guys recognize the writing?"

Scott, Roy and David looked closely at the belt. Scott spoke first.

"The lettering is Arabic and look at that symbol on the back of the belt up near the buckle."

"It's a series of elliptical looking characters around a tower or monument of some kind," observed David. "It looks familiar."

"You're right, David," said Roy. "It is familiar. In fact, I think it is the symbol in the center of the Iranian flag. I don't know what it means, but I'm pretty sure it is the Iranian national flag marking. We have a book picturing country's flags in the library upstairs. I'll go check to see if I am right." Roy left the room.

"Now wouldn't that be interesting," said Scott. "If the guy who tried to kill you was an Iranian."

"And what would it mean?" asked Jerry.

"I'm not sure, but we've known for a long time that the Iranians are developing nuclear weapons capability. That's the first thing that comes to my mind," said Scott. "I think we'd better get an expert opinion about the belt. David, check back at headquarters to see if we have someone to verify the origin of the belt? If we have someone who can help, send the belt overnight."

"Okay," said David. "And remember what the Finnish DNA expert said about the ancestors of the dead man; his ancient ancestors came from the Middle East."

Roy returned from the embassy's library.

"That marking on the belt is the symbol from the Iranian flag. I photocopied it."

He passed the copy to the others. The room was quiet as they each considered the implications of an Iranian assassin.

The teleconference between Washington and Helsinki began on time the next morning at 1100 hours Helsinki time. Director McCarthy spoke first.

"We do not have cameras for this meeting, so let me introduce those around the table here at headquarters. Hal Bolton, Director of the National Counterterrorism Center is here; as is Charles Sparks of the CIA's Science and Technology Center; Meg Kupchak, one of our Russia experts; and one of my deputies, Chip Webb. Who is around the table over there?"

"There are four of us: me; Scott Regan of the Counterterrorism Center; Roy DeSantis, CIA chief at the Helsinki embassy; David Greenberg, a

Counterterrorism Center staffer; and Jerry Paul, recently come back to life. I think you know Jerry has been over here in Estonia and Finland trying to locate the missing Plutonium-239."

"I can't tell you how happy I am personally that you are safe and back in the game, Jerry," said Hal. "You should have seen this place the day before yesterday when we got word that you had turned up safe and sound. I never saw so many smiling faces in our hallways. I think all work stopped. I had begun to worry that we were going to have to add another gold star to those already on the wall in the CIA lobby at Langley. It's great to have you back."

"Thank you, sir," said Jerry.

"Okay, let's get down to business," said the Director. "I know of a few things that we have to talk about, and you guys probably have some things on your minds, too. I want to talk first about my conversations with the Russian Director of Intelligence and the apparent contradiction concerning the Russian's involvement in the project we call Springboard. I want to discuss your request for some nuclear expertise over there, and I want to hear your assessment of the case and what we should do next. Do you have issues you would like to discuss, too?"

Scott replied, "There are a few things we have learned that we want to brief you and the others about. Also, the Finns have asked us to come to the Ministry of Justice for a meeting this afternoon. We've met with them once before and it worked out okay, but this time they have invited the Ministries of Foreign Affairs and the Interior, so I am not sure what is up. They were a little put out that we were working Springboard over here without their knowledge, and of course they were very unhappy about the guy Jerry killed.

The Justice Ministry police held Jerry for more than a day, questioned him extensively, and would not let us see him. They did not mistreat him and released him with no charges, but I don't know how sensitive diplomatically things are with the Finns.

"I guess you'll have to wait and see what comes up in your meeting with them. Seems to me, they should be very anxious to find the weapons-grade nuclear material that might be in their backyard. But if it gets complicated diplomatically, I can probably help and get the State Department involved if that makes sense.

"We seemed to be working together pretty well for a little while, but when Jerry turned up, I think they needed to satisfy themselves that he was legitimate and had killed the mystery man in self defense. Hopefully the air will clear up again."

"Good," said the Director. "Don't get too concerned with diplomacy. It makes you risk averse, and I want you to stay aggressive. Let Hal know if you need any help from me. Now let me tell you about my two conversations with the Russians."

The Director described how his Russian counterpart had said confidently during their first conversation that he had no knowledge of any involvement on their part in the search for the plutonium. In fact, he seemed a little miffed that we had not gotten them involved in the search.

Mike McCarthy said, "Now I know the Russians are not above misleading or lying to me, but my sense from that first conversation is that the whole thing was news to him.

"Our second conversation was very different. The Russian Director's conversation was more guarded, and he seemed to be looking for information about the case from me—especially about Yukos Oil. I did not have the sense that he was misleading me; I got the feeling that he was in the dark, like he did not know what the hell was going on. He did promise to look into things further and get back in touch with me. Frankly, I will be surprised if he does call me back. I think he was embarrassed. In a sense, I might have been telling him about things that were going on in his own house that he did not know about."

Meg Kupchak said, "Things have really changed in Russia in recent years. When the KGB was running intelligence during the Soviet years, they were tightly organized and highly disciplined. Since the breakup and the development of a substantial private sector, the power structure is fractured and difficult to assess. Former Soviet government and intelligence officials have become the corporate bosses. They associate regularly with current government officials. Power and profits are intermingled between the public and profit sectors."

Scott interrupted, "The U.S. has a lot of government-private sector cooperation, too. How comparable are the Russians and the U. S. in public-private relations?"

"Russia and the U.S. are very different in that way. In our country, we have lots of movement between the public and private spheres, but there is a clear bold line separating the two. In Russia today, it's difficult to know who is pulling what levers. It is a unique and difficult intelligence problem for us, and we're still learning how to deal with it."

"That is a very good summary, ladies and gentlemen," said the Director. "One thing it means is that we cannot count on the Russians for good information and cooperation on Springboard. We will go our own way and develop our own information."

"We have one Russian asset," said Jerry. "Yuli Karpov, former Soviet nuclear weapons expert and current nuclear physicist with Yukos oil, has been helping us. He is the one who alerted me initially to the reemergence of the Plutonium-239, and he has been helping in the search for it. He is coming to meet with us in Helsinki tomorrow. So far, he has insisted on keeping his involvement secret from Yukos, and my guess is that he will want to keep it that way. But he may provide a window into Yukos' involvement or noninvolvement."

"That's great," said the Director. "Meg is also going to put our current CIA assets in Russia to work as well. Between Mr. Karpov and our own guys, we should develop some useful information."

"There is another line of inquiry that our people in Russia might help with," said Scott. "We believe the Russian weapons dealer Ivan Savinkov has a role in the plutonium deal. As best we can tell, he is attempting to buy the plutonium from the current owner. He no doubt plans to sell it to someone else. We don't know if he already has a customer or whether he plans to find one after he buys the plutonium. Anything our people in Moscow can find out about Savinkov could be helpful. Knowing where he is now and where he has traveled recently will be particularly useful."

"We'll get to work on that right away," said Meg. "I think we already have a file on him."

"Keep us advised about what you learn from Mr. Karpov," said the Director. "Let's talk about nuclear expertise for a minute. Why do you need nuclear experts over there?"

Scott responded, "Two main reasons, sir: First, if we are correct that the plutonium is in this area, we still have a formidable search job on our hands. We may not be able to narrow the location precisely to a particular spot. Second, when we find the plutonium, we will need technical help in moving it safely."

The Director responded, "As you know, Charles Sparks from our Science and Technology Unit is here at the table. Charles, do you have any suggestions for our folks in Helsinki?"

Charles said, "Jerry and David and I had a meeting a week or two ago about how to find the plutonium. Am I right, Jerry?"

"Yes, I remember," said Jerry. "You briefed us on the use of the gamma-ray detector and its limitations. One current problem is that the Finnish authorities confiscated the gamma-ray detectors you sent earlier, and we may need more than one set of instruments. We are going to mount a full-court press, so to speak. We will probably have multiple teams working in different areas simultaneously. We need at least two sets."

"I'll send you three sets so you have a backup. They will be sent overnight tonight."

Jerry said, "Do you think we should have somebody standing by over here that will be able to take control of the plutonium as soon as we find it?"

"Until now, I have thought not," said Charles. "We can have such a person there within two days when you locate the plutonium. Is that quick enough?"

"I'm beginning to think it may not be," said Jerry. "There is a growing feeling that the plutonium is nearby. I don't think we want to have to wait two days for someone to take charge of it if we find it."

There were nods around the table in Helsinki. Scott spoke up. "I agree with Jerry. It would be preferable to have the nuclear material handling expertise on hand right away."

"Okay," said the Director. "I agree. Charles will get you the nuclear expertise and equipment you need."

"I'll arrange to have at least two nuclear material handling experts over there within two or three days."

"I'd like to raise a new issue," said Scott.

"Go ahead," said the Director.

"We have some preliminary indications that Iranians may be involved in the operation over here."

"Really," said the Director. "That is not good news. What are the preliminary indications?"

"The most recent evidence is the belt of the dead guy who tried to kill Jerry," said Scott. "It was the only piece of clothing the dead man wore that had any markings. Jerry took it with him when he left the hotel after he shot the man. We have just looked at the belt here, and it has Arabic lettering on it and a symbol from the Iranian national flag. We were hoping someone at CIA could take a look at it and translate the lettering."

Charles Sparks replied, "We can handle that. We can certainly translate the lettering, and we can probably tell where the leather came from and where the belt was manufactured. Can you send it to me?"

"I'll send it overnight tonight," said David.

"I don't need to tell you that this is potentially important," said the Director. "I'm also going to alert our Iranian assets to see if they can pick anything up about their possible involvement. Are we about finished here?"

"I think so," said Scott.

"Okay," said the Director. "I think our action plans here are to develop information on Yukos Oil and the arms dealer Savinkov in Russia and to get some nuclear equipment and expertise to you over there. You are going to meet with the Finns, Yuli Karpov, and try to track down the location of the plutonium. You'll send us the belt. Is that about it?"

"I think so," said Scott, as he looked inquiringly at the others around the table. Everyone nodded their heads.

"Let us know how your meeting with the Finns goes and if Yuli has anything interesting for us. Good luck, everyone, and again, great to have you back Jerry."

Jerry, Scott, Roy, and David took an embassy car to the Finnish Ministry of Justice. They were again met in the lobby and escorted up the marble staircase to the same conference room on the second floor. This time, there were only five people waiting at the conference table, including the Minister of Justice who was seated at the head of the table. There was no podium on the table this time. Scott was unsure, but took the smaller group and less formal arrangement as a good sign. His optimism was justified. When they were seated, the Justice Minister began.

"Good afternoon, gentlemen. Thank you for coming. We appreciate your willingness to meet with us on short notice. It is especially good to see you, Mr. Paul. We were worried about you. I do not think our meeting will take much of your time. I imagine you are anxious to get on with your search for the missing plutonium. And frankly, we are anxious as well.

"I have asked representatives of our Ministries of Foreign Affairs and Interior to attend the meeting because this situation involves their areas of responsibility. It will be helpful if Foreign Affairs is kept advised of things—in case diplomatic questions are raised by our efforts. The Interior Ministry has responsibility for nuclear power matters in our country. As you know, Inspectors Roskil and Hassi have been working on the case in recent days. They will continue to do so. Would you like to say anything at this point, Mr. Regan?"

"Just that we appreciate your hospitality, and as you accurately said, we are anxious to locate the nuclear material that we believe is hidden in your country. I can assure you that we will give the highest priority to conducting this search safely and in compliance with your laws and wishes. We spoke this morning with the United States Director of National Intelligence about this case, and he is giving it his close attention. He considers the recovery of the missing Plutonium-239 to be of the highest priority."

"Thank you, Mr. Regan. We also recognize the importance of finding the plutonium. The Baltic has been a fairly peaceful part of the world, and we hope to keep it that way. In that regard, we have decided to make whatever resources you need available to you. Inspectors Roskil and Hassi are being assigned to work with you, and they are authorized to bring in additional people and resources as needed."

"Thank you," said Scott. "That is generous of you."

Inspector Roskil said, "It will be helpful if we can sit down together soon to plan our activities. Our department has continued investigative work on the case in the last few days, but I'm sure you agree that we will work together more effectively if we have some coordination."

"I definitely agree," said Scott. "If your schedule permits, we can have a discussion at the end of this meeting."

"That would be good for us too," said the inspector.

There was further discussion about the risks of radiation exposure from the plutonium and a plan for keeping everyone advised about the progress of the case. A follow-up meeting was tentatively scheduled for the same time a week later. The full meeting was adjourned in less than an hour. The Americans and the Finnish inspectors stayed to plan their activities.

When the ministers left, Inspector Roskil began, "The last time that we worked together, we questioned Sonia Pernen, the Mihkli Manor restaurant manager. David Greenburg and I attempted unsuccessfully to follow her when she left the hotel in a hurry after our interview with her. We have been keeping her under surveillance cautiously—attempting to do so without her knowledge. I do not think we have alerted her, but our surveillance has not developed any new information. She works long hours and does not seem to have a social life apart from her work so far. Our main goal has been to locate her father, Pavel Nosenko, of course, because he may be the direct link to the plutonium."

"Did she come back to work at Mihkli Manor after she fled?" asked David.

"Yes, she did," said the Inspector. "She was back at work for the restaurant's dinner hours the same day. And we have checked all the turnoffs along the road where we followed her, hoping we would discover her destination that day. We had no success."

"Do we know where her father lives?" asked Jerry.

"Yes, we know his official address. It is a small country cottage about twelve kilometers from Mihkli Manor. He apparently lives alone, and as best we can tell, he has not been there recently. We have also been watching Ms. Pernen's home. She lives alone in a year-old cluster of small homes about twenty kilometers from Mihkli Manor. We have not been able to observe anyone but Ms. Pernen at her home in the last few days."

David said, "As I recall, Ms. Pernen said she was estranged from her father and could not tell us anything about his recent activities."

"That is correct," said the inspector. "But we have reason to doubt she and her father are estranged. She has been seen in public with him at least twice that we know of in the last month."

"Is it time to question her again?" asked Jerry. "Another interview might develop new information or it might induce her to contact her father."

"I have been thinking the same thing," said Inspector Roskil. "And this time, I believe our questioning should be more aggressive."

"May I make a suggestion?" asked Jerry.

"By all means," said the inspector.

"I would like to participate in the interrogation—if you are agreeable. I questioned her during my earlier investigation activities and was able to observe her during meals I ate at the Mihkli Manor restaurant. I think she would remember me. My participation might unsettle her."

"That is an excellent idea," said the inspector. "In fact, I think we should have four or five people in the room during questioning to increase the possibility of unhinging Ms. Pernen. I will approach her alone tomorrow and ask to speak with her. But when she enters the room for questioning, we will all be there to greet her."

The usually quiet Inspector Paavo spoke, "Before questioning this time, we will make some preparations to observe her responses. We will have vehicles in place to follow her in case she leaves again and observers near her home and her father's home. We have also gotten legal clearance to listen to her telephone calls and those of her father."

"I like that plan," said Scott.

Yuli arrived at the American embassy in Helsinki in the early evening. Jerry met him at the security checkpoint and brought him to the conference room that Roy had reserved for their meeting. After introductions and handshakes, Yuli spoke.

"I am troubled. As I've told you before, I thought that the Russian intelligence service had become involved in the search for the Plutonium-239. Now, I am not sure. My main source of information at Yukos has been Leonid Popov, who works in the company's security department. I have known him for years. He worked for the KGB until the Soviet Union dissolved and then as the chief personal security guard for Yukos' founder. He is now head of corporate security for Yukos."

"I recognize his name," said Jerry. "Wasn't he one of the KGB security officers during the Kazakhstan operation?"

"Yes, he was. I had forgotten that," answered Yuli. "In any case, I think he has been misleading me. I checked with some former colleagues and have found no indication that current Russian internal security has any knowledge or involvement in attempting to find the plutonium."

"That is consistent with some information we have obtained recently," said Jerry. "One of our sources in Russian intelligence says they are not pursuing the case, or at least they had not been. I would not be surprised to find, however, that there is now an active case on the Russian side. What do you think Popov's involvement means? Do you think it indicates that Yukos itself is involved?"

"I am not sure," said Yuli. "I think Popov is implicated, but I do not know if his involvement is an individual one or on behalf of Yukos."

Scott asked, "Is Yukos involved in nuclear power?"

"I have not known them to have an interest in nuclear power," answered Yuli. "Yukos focuses on oil and gas. I have also discovered something disturbing recently."

"What is that?" asked Jerry.

"I am under surveillance," said Yuli. "Someone has been watching my home, according to my wife. And I detected surveillance at the airport in

Moscow and earlier today in Tallinn. It's beginning to seem like the Soviet days again."

"Do you think you were followed here?" asked Scott.

"I do not think so. Before I left my Tallinn hotel, I sat in a phone booth in the lobby for some time pretending to talk on the phone, but watching the comings and goings carefully. When the lobby was empty, I left and took two different cabs to the ferry. I detected no surveillance on the ferry or on my way here."

"Can you guess why they are watching you and who is responsible?" asked Jerry.

"No. It's confusing. I sense that something has changed for me at Yukos, but I do not understand it except that it must have something to do with Sergei's death and my inquiries about the missing plutonium."

David Greenberg, who had not spoken until now, asked, "Does Yukos do much business with the Iranians?"

The four Americans waited intently for Yuli's response.

"Yes," said Yuli. "But why do you ask that?"

Jerry answered, "We have some indication that Iranians are involved in the case. The man who tried to kill me may have been an Iranian."

Yuli was silent for some time.

"Yukos does a lot of business with Iran. We buy their oil. We help them search for it and provide equipment to extract it. Iranians often visit our offices. Yukos people travel regularly to Iran. Russia and Iran are political allies. But I do not understand how a connection between Yukos, Iran, and the missing plutonium fits together."

"We are not certain there is a connection," said Jerry. "But we know Iran is attempting to build their nuclear weapons capacity, and we know they are frustrated by the limits placed on them by the international community and the International Atomic Energy Agency. It is logical for them to attempt to obtain Plutonium-239. They would advance their atomic weapons-development capability immediately."

The group discussed the case and Yuli's information for another half hour. They decided that Yuli should cautiously continue his effort to find out what connection Yukos might have with the plutonium case. Yuli left the embassy, took a cab to the ferry, and returned to his hotel in Tallinn.

Later that night, Yuli sent an e-mail to Jerry. *I was followed from the Tallinn ferry dock to my hotel this evening.* Before going to bed, Yuli secured the security chain on his door and put the two chairs in the room in front of the door, piled on top of each other. Yuli had no weapon; he slept fitfully.

Kathleen's Finn Air flight was due to arrive at the Helsinki International Airport at 8:45 a.m.. Jerry arrived at the airport to meet her at 8:15, entered the terminal to check the arrivals monitor, and found that her flight had landed early. It took fifteen minutes to find the baggage claim area for Kathleen's flight. As Jerry approached, he looked down the long corridor and, between figures in the moving crowd, he saw her silhouette. She was standing quietly, arms folded loosely across her breasts, waiting for the luggage carrel to begin circling. Involuntarily, he inhaled and quickened his pace. He was about ten feet from her when she sensed him coming and turned. In another second, they embraced silently. It was a long embrace. Jerry could feel the contours of

Kathleen's body and the almost imperceptible trembling that prompted him to tighten his embrace.

They finally released each other and looked at the other's face—still not talking. Silently holding hands, they turned to face the luggage carrel. It was not moving yet. After another silent moment, Jerry felt the need to speak.

"How was the flight?" he asked.

Kathleen laughed out loud. "Be quiet for a little longer. I want to stand here with you for another minute." And after a pause, "I was afraid I would not ever be able to hold your live hand again." In another minute, the luggage carrel began turning abruptly, breaking the spell.

Jerry and Kathleen drove to his hotel. Kathleen had not slept much during the long flight and wanted to shower and sleep for a while. After she was settled, Jerry went to the office at the embassy.

After the Mihkli Manor restaurant lunch hour ended, Jerry, Scott, David, and Roy arrived at the hotel. Inspectors Roskil and Hassi had left earlier and arranged a meeting with Ms. Pernen. They were all seated at a table in one of the hotel's meeting rooms when Inspector Roskil brought Ms. Pernen into the room. For a moment, it looked as if she would turn and flee, but after hesitating, she took a seat at the far end of the rectangular table. Inspector Roskil let the tension build for a full minute before speaking.

"We appreciate your meeting with us," he said.

Ms. Pernen said nothing.

The inspector continued, "Your answers to our questions are important. Our inquiries are about the safety of our citizens, the security of our country, and our relations with other countries. I do not exaggerate." He paused, looking at Ms. Pernen. She remained silent.

Inspector Roskil continued, "As you recall from our last talk, we are interested in locating your father."

He waited.

Finally, Ms. Pernen responded icily, "As I told you before, Inspector, my father and I are estranged. I have not seen or spoken to him recently."

Without speaking, the Inspector passed two photographs to Ms. Pernen and let her examine them. One showed her and her father together at an outdoor market, and the other showed them at a restaurant table engaged in what looked like an animated conversation.

"The pictures show you and your father. Is that correct?"

"Yes."

"Did you notice the dates on the bottom of the pictures?"

Ms. Pernen glanced down at the pictures.

"The dates must be a mistake. I have not seen my father for months."

"We are certain of the dates, Ms. Pernen, and as you notice, they are recent."

Ms. Pernen did not respond.

They continued questioning Sonia Pernen for about forty-five minutes, Inspector Roskil asking most of the questions, but David Greenberg asking occasional questions, too. Jerry said nothing, but he could tell she recognized him. She did not ask the identity of her questioners. The questioners made her state her denials repeatedly. Finally, Inspector Roskil concluded the meeting.

"Ms. Pernen, we know you are not telling us the truth, I assume because you feel you are protecting your father. If you think it is in your father's interest to refuse to answer our questions, you are wrong. I know you are aware of the killing that took place upstairs not too long ago. You may not be aware that another man was murdered in a hotel room in Tallinn a few days before that. We have reason to think the killings are related and reason to believe that your father's life is in danger, too."

Ms. Pernen sat with her head down and did not speak.

The inspector ended the meeting by saying, "I hope you will reconsider your answers to our questions. I could arrest you now for lying to the police, but I am not going to do that. Here is my card. Please call me when you wish to talk."

When she had left the room, Inspector Roskil closed the door.

"We have observers in place that will follow her if Ms. Pernen decides to leave the hotel. If she leaves, we will not lose her this time. We have also gotten the reluctant cooperation of hotel management to monitor the telephone in her office here at the hotel, and I believe we told you that her home phone is being monitored. I have the sense that our conversation with her today, one-sided as it was, will force her to take some action."

Jerry said, "I'll bet that Ms. Pernen feels isolated."

"I agree," said the inspector.

18

Discovery

DAVID GREENBERG WAS THE FIRST one in the embassy office the next morning at six o'clock. He was catching up on his e-mail when the telephone rang. Inspector Roskil was on the other end.

"We've found Sonia Pernen's father. Unfortunately, he's dead, and it appears to be a professional killing."

"Where did it happen?" asked David.

"At his home…just outside Helsinki. His daughter discovered him. He was probably killed less than twenty-four hours ago. She tried to contact him and went to his home when she could not reach him. Our officers have been watching her and followed her there. They were on the scene almost immediately."

"Is it too early to ask about the plutonium?" asked David.

"No, but we're still processing the murder scene. The body has not been removed, but we would like your help. Can you and your colleagues come to help hunt for the plutonium?"

"Definitely," said David. "I'll contact the others, and we will come there. What is the location?"

"I will send a car to your embassy in an hour. He will bring you here."

David contacted Scott and Jerry at their hotel and Roy at his home. They all gathered at the embassy in less than an hour and followed the Ministry of Justice car to a rural setting about fifteen miles outside Helsinki. They turned left off the road into a dirt driveway narrowed by shrubs and trees on both sides. Branches slapped the sides of their car as they circled slowly to the left. After a quarter mile, they came to a clearing. The parking area was already crowded with police vehicles; ten or twelve uniformed officers and technicians busied themselves inside and outside the small stone house. The house looked neglected; shrubs had grown up above the window's ledges. Inspector Roskil stood in the yard talking to a middle-aged man in a business suit. He joined the four Americans as they exited their car.

"We are about ready to remove the body. The medical examiner tells me that things look straightforward to him. Mr. Nosenko was killed by a single bullet to the back of the head. There are no other apparent injuries. He was killed late yesterday afternoon or early last evening. His daughter discovered him about three hours ago. We have taken her into custody; she may be in danger herself. She is distraught, but not hysterical. We plan to question her as soon as we finish here."

Scott asked, "Has the crime scene been informative?"

"Hardly at all," answered the inspector. "There may have been two others with Mr. Nosenko at the time of his murder because there were three coffee cups in the living room where the murder took place. There is no sign of struggle, and the shot that killed Mr. Nosenko was fired from close range as he sat in a stuffed chair across from the couch where the two others apparently sat. We speculate that one of the two made an excuse to go to the kitchen or bathroom, both of which were behind Mr. Nosenko, and then shot him in the back of the head. There is no indication that the killers searched the home or took anything. Mr. Nosenko's wallet was on a counter in the kitchen."

"Has Ms. Pernen provided any information yet?" asked Jerry.

"She was not able to provide any information about her father's killing. She came to check on him when she could not reach him by telephone. Her calls were being monitored and indicate she tried to reach him five or six times last evening. We have not yet questioned her, but when we do, I expect to have a more cooperative witness than in our earlier conversations."

"You were monitoring Mr. Nosenko's phone, too, I think. Did he have any calls recently?" asked Jerry.

"There is no record of a call to or from Mr. Nosenko's phone since we started monitoring it several days ago—except his daughter's unsuccessful calls."

"Have you searched for the plutonium yet?" asked Scott.

"We have searched the house and the grounds immediately adjacent to the house carefully, but have found nothing of note. We were hoping for some help from you on the plutonium search. I had one of our officers bring the instruments that we took from Mihkli Manor here. They are in my car, and you are welcome to use them."

"Excellent," said Scott. "We can start with the house and grounds right now…if it's okay with you."

"As soon as we remove the body and some of the other people and cars leave."

"I'd like to make a suggestion." said Jerry. "If you, Scott, and the inspector agree, I'd like to participate in the interrogation of Ms. Pernen."

"I think that will be helpful," said the inspector.

"I would like to participate, too," said David. "Unless I am needed here."

Scott and Roy waited for the police to finish their work before searching the house and grounds. Inspector Hassi and two uniformed Finnish police officers stayed at the scene to observe and assist. Inspector Roskil, Jerry, and David drove back to the Ministry of Justice in Helsinki.

When they arrived at the inspector's office, the door was closed and a guard was standing outside the door. Sonia Pernen was asleep on the couch in the darkened office. Someone had found her a pillow and blanket. She stirred when they opened the door.

"Ms. Pernen?" the inspector said quietly. She sat up slowly. They waited while she gathered herself. "The ladies room is just around the corner to your right."

She recovered her pocketbook from underneath the couch, rose slowly, and walked to the bathroom. She was gone about twenty minutes and returned looking better. Even in her disheveled grief, she was an attractive woman; her body was lean, but nicely shaped. Her dark hair was thick and sensuous; her green eyes, unlike the rest of her face, had a soft look.

The inspector began, "I am sorry about your father."

She nodded her head. Tears welled up in her eyes. "He was a good man," she said.

"I'm very sorry, Ms. Pernen. I know this is difficult, but can you answer some questions? We are determined to find the person who killed your father."

"I will try to help," she said. "I was trying to help him, but I may only have endangered him."

"How were you trying to help him?" asked the inspector.

"My father was a dedicated Communist all his life. He was crushed when the Soviet Union fell apart—when the Communists lost power. He continued for years to work for the party, even after they stopped paying him. Life has been a struggle for him in recent years."

"What kind of work did he do for the Communist Party?" asked the inspector.

"It was mostly routine, I think. He was not highly educated. In the 1990s, he lived in Russia about 150 kilometers southeast of Moscow. I think he was a local party organizer. He traveled often for a few days at a time. When my mother died a few years ago, I think he lost his enthusiasm for his work. He seemed to work less. It was difficult for me to tell what was going on. I have worked here in Finland for more than ten years. After a visit to him two years ago, I convinced him to sell the small house he owned and move close to me here. He has not been able to find work locally."

"Do you know why he was killed?" Jerry asked.

Sonia Pernen looked at Jerry and David as if noticing for the first time that they were in the room. "No. He had no enemies that I know about. I know that recently he was negotiating some business with a Russian man. He seemed more energized, less sad."

"Do you know what the business negotiations were about? Were they recruiting him? Was he trying to sell them something or to buy something from them?"

Ms. Pernen thought for a minute.

"I think he had something the Russian man wanted. He had very little money, so I can't see that he was going to buy something. I have been helping him a little financially. His pension income is not sufficient. He had only modest savings."

"Did your father have friends or colleagues in the Helsinki area?" asked the inspector.

"I know of no contact with colleagues from the Soviet or recent Russian eras. I think he has made a few casual friends here in Finland. He loves… *loved* flowers. He spent a lot of time tending his flower garden."

"Where is his garden?"

"I'm not sure exactly. The widow of an old friend from Soviet times allows him to have a garden near her house. There is not enough sun at his house. You saw it. There are many large trees that block the sun for most of the day."

"Does his widow friend live near him?" asked Jerry.

"I do not think she lives very close to him, but it is not a long distance either. I do not have her address, but I think I have her name and telephone number at home."

"Do you know the name of the man your father was negotiating with?" asked Jerry.

Ms. Pernen thought for a moment.

"I do not think I ever heard his surname, but I believe his given name is Ivan."

Inspector Roskil stood up from his desk and walked across the room to a window. The others waited as he stared out the window. David tried not to stare at Sonia Pernen.

"Ms. Pernen, I have an important question to ask. Please consider it carefully. Did you have any involvement in the negotiations your father was engaged in? Even in the most superficial way."

She thought for a moment before answering.

"None whatever. I knew nothing about that. In fact, I am not even certain I am correct in saying that my father was negotiating with this Ivan. I got this impression watching them at lunch at my restaurant. I could not hear what they were saying, but they had a long and animated conversation. They seemed to be bargaining."

"Thank you," said the inspector. "There have now been three people killed in connection with the transaction that has apparently been unfolding in our country—a transaction that we believe your father had a major part in. The parties to this transaction are determined to keep it secret. It is my belief that your father and another man were killed to make certain that no details of the transaction could be disclosed."

"Why do you think my father was involved?"

"We have information that I cannot share with you right now. The evidence indicates he had valuable material that he was attempting to sell."

"Does this have anything to do with the missing weapons investigation a long time ago? My father was harassed by the KGB in connection with such a case many years ago."

"That is possible," said Jerry. "I was involved with a joint Soviet and American project in Kazakhstan some years ago. Weapons material went missing during the operation. Did your father work in Kazakhstan in the early 1990s?"

"Yes. But I think it was for a very short time."

"Your father was a suspect because he was in charge of the warehouse where the missing material was stored."

Ms. Pernen looked at Jerry. In a moment, she asked, "Do you think my father was responsible for the missing material?"

"It is possible," said Jerry. "We do have information that suggests he was involved."

Sonia Pernen was silent.

Inspector Roskil said, "I think we need to be cautious, Ms. Pernen, so until we learn more, I am going to assign one of my men to stay with you. We can book a hotel room for you here in Helsinki or, if you prefer, you can go to your home as long as you will agree to have one of my men stay with you."

"Do I have a choice, Inspector?"

"You cannot choose to stay by yourself for the time being."

"I want to stay at my own home."

"That is acceptable," said the inspector. "I have one request. Please give the name and telephone number of your father's widow friend to the policeman as soon as you get home."

"I can do that. How long do you expect that your bodyguard will stay with me?"

"I cannot say precisely, but hopefully it will not be long."

At Pavel Nosenko's home, Scott and Roy began searching the house and grounds with the portable gamma-ray detector. They began on the second floor of the house. Their search was unproductive until they got to the basement. The gamma-ray detector began to react in a small closet in the far corner of the basement. The closet was empty, but the gamma readings were elevated. On the floor of the closet, the outlines of previously stored containers were visible. The area covered by the container outlines was consistent with numerous cylindrically shaped containers. Scott took several digital pictures of the container outlines.

Scott and Roy began searching the grounds around the house. They spent several hours going slowly back and forth being sure to include every inch of the grounds. The Finnish police observed them work. After searching back and forth over straight lines, they changed their search pattern and went over the same areas using a circular pattern. They completed their circular search just as darkness began to make their work difficult.

The results of the search were clear: there was a single hot spot in the basement closet. Scott and Roy felt certain that they had found the former storage location for the plutonium. But the material had been moved, and it could not have been long ago. The gamma ray residue would not have remained for more than a day or two. The Americans drove back to the embassy.

Jerry and David were already at the embassy office. They briefed the others about Sonia Pernen's questioning; Scott reported the results of the plutonium search at the home of Pavel Nosenko. The regular workday was still in progress in Washington, so the group decided to place a call to Hal Bolton at the Counterterrorism Center. He came on the line in a few minutes.

Scott started, "Hi, Hal. We've got some developments to report from here and are wondering if you have anything new for us."

"We do have some information for you," said Hal. "If you guys are in your office, I'll try to catch up with Meg Kupchak and Charles Sparks and have them call you right away."

Scott continued, "We will write all this up for the record, of course, but a discussion with you now will help. We think we have found the location where the missing plutonium was stored at some point, but it's been moved. It's gone. The Russian we suspected was responsible for stealing it in the beginning was killed; his name was Pavel Nosenko. In searching his house, we think we found where the containers of plutonium were stored. We took pictures of the container outlines on the floor of the storage location. We will fax these to Science and Technology to see if they can make anything of them. But I think we should assume for now that the plutonium was stored in Pavel Nosenko's house recently."

"Who killed Nosenko?" asked Hal.

"We don't know, but it looks like a professional job—one shot to the back of the head. We are working with the Finnish Ministry of Justice and have some leads to follow—so we are still hopeful we will find the plutonium. We are more and more convinced that we are on the right track. The plutonium was in this area and hopefully still is."

"There's something I am having trouble understanding," said Hal. "It's obvious whoever is involved in this plutonium deal is deadly serious. They killed the Russian nuclear physicist who they hired to verify the authenticity of the plutonium. They tried to kill Jerry, and now they've killed the guy who apparently had the plutonium. But then Jerry gets kidnapped, interrogated, and let go. We must have different groups involved. Otherwise, letting Jerry go does not make sense."

"We agree," said Scott. "We've talked about this. There are multiple interests at stake; we just don't know who they are yet."

"Meg Kupchak has some interesting information for you that is consistent with your belief," said Hal. "Do you need anything else from me?"

"No," said Scott. "I know you will keep the case high on everyone's priority list back there. Information from the Russian division and the Science and Technology folks are important for us."

"Okay," said Hal. "Let me hang up and try to get Meg and Charles to call you with their information."

The phone rang at the Helsinki embassy Springboard office ten minutes after they ended their call with Hal Bolton. It was Meg Kupchak.

"Hello, guys," said Meg. "Who is around the table over there?"

Scott told her and she continued.

"I have gotten information that I think is relevant for your work, but still can't give you much in the way of specifics."

"We're still trying to understand things, too," said Scott.

Meg continued, "First, the weapons dealer Ivan Savinkov; he has been trafficking in weapons for years. He has a lot of customers. He's done deals in Africa, South America, and extensively in Yugoslavia in the 1990s. Lately, he seems to be focusing on the Mideast—especially in Lebanon and the Palestinian territories. We think he is a principal supplier of weapons to Hezbollah and Hamas. The Hezbollah and Hamas connections are particularly interesting given your suspicion about an Iranian connection. The Iranians are the single most important supporters of these groups; they get plenty of weapons and money from Iran."

"Those groups are mainly a threat to Israel and Mideast stability, right?" said Jerry.

"They are clearly a threat to Israel and Lebanon and the stability of the region. But we have recent information that they plan to operate outside the region as well. This is a new development."

"That is worrisome," said Jerry. "We don't need another Al Qaeda-like organization threatening us and our allies."

"We're paying very close attention. But let me get back to Ivan. I know you are interested in where he is right now," said Meg. "We have been unable to establish that. It is not unusual for him to go under the radar for periods of time. He does that frequently. It probably means he is not in Russia, but he could be anywhere."

"Jerry asked, "How solid is your information that Savinkov is doing a lot of recent business with Hezbollah and Hamas?"

"It's solid," said Meg. "We have it from multiple sources. Our own folks in Russia and Lebanon confirm it, and the Israelis, who keep very close tabs on these groups, tell us the same thing."

When the phone line from Helsinki was quiet for a few seconds, Meg continued, "Now let me say some things about Russian intelligence and Yukos. I'm going to give you information that may sound disjointed, but that's where we are. The Russian intelligence director told our director that they were not involved in the current plutonium search, but he may have said that out of ignorance. He may not be aware of everything his folks are doing."

"Director McCarthy said the Russian director sounded a little uncertain during the second conversation he had with him. But do you have information that the Russians are in fact involved in the plutonium deal?" asked Jerry.

"I believe so. Yes," said Meg. "Although it does get a little confusing here. We have two sources into Russian intelligence, and they both picked up recent activity in the Baltic concerning nuclear material. This is likely the same situation you guys are working."

"What's the confusion?" asked Jerry.

"First, let me tell you about Yukos; then you'll have a better understanding. We have very specific confirmation from a source within Yukos that they are involved in the plutonium matter. We are confident that this information refers to the same missing plutonium you are hunting because the activity dates and locations match your own activities. We are not as certain about the Russian intelligence activity. It makes sense that they are working the same missing plutonium case as you are working. It's just that our information about Russian intelligence is not precise. Have I confused you?"

"A little," said Jerry. "Yukos is definitely working the case we call Springboard; the Russians may or may not be."

Meg answered, "Well, I would state it more definitely. I think the Russians are almost certainly working the case. We haven't understood their reasons for doing so and their goals. It's also possible that those involved are doing so unofficially for their own self-interest."

Scott spoke up. "Do we understand why Yukos is involved?"

"We're suspect that Yukos is involved in the sale, either to get control of the plutonium for themselves or as middlemen for the Iranians."

"Let me add another wrinkle, Meg," said Jerry. "Do you know that Yuli Karpov, former Soviet nuclear physicist and current physicist for Yukos, is the one who initially alerted us to the availability of the plutonium?"

"Yes, I was briefed about him."

"Yuli is continuing to help us, and the last time he met with us, he told of being under surveillance."

"That doesn't surprise me," said Meg. "I'd guess it's his own employer who is tracking his activities. I suggest you advise him to be very cautious."

"So it sounds like you believe Yukos is the important player and that Russian intelligence is peripherally involved," said Jerry.

"Yes," said Meg. I have a hunch the Russian's motivation is simply to stay informed, or maybe they tacitly approve of Yukos' activities and are allowing Yukos to act as their surrogates. Or as I've said, it could be rogue Russians who are involved."

"Very interesting," said Jerry. "That could explain why I was not killed. It was Russian Intelligence, not Yukos, that abducted and questioned me and then let me go. Russian intelligence would be reluctant to kill an American agent."

The four Americans continued their discussion at the Helsinki embassy after the Meg Kupchak call. There was a new urgency given the information Meg had provided about Iran and the Iranian-backed terrorist groups. They decided that their own search activities would not be affected by the Russian Intelligence-Yukos uncertainty. Their major problem was that they did not have specific information about locations to search for the plutonium. They discussed ways that they might develop leads to identify possible search locations. Jerry suggested that they warn Yuli that he was at risk. David sent Yuli a short e-mail: ***KEEP YOUR HEAD DOWN.***

Charles Sparks from CIA Science and Technology called just as the group was getting ready to leave for their hotel. He had two reports for them. The belt had been made in a small leather goods factory south of Teheran. The photos of the outlines from the floor of the closet where the gamma ray residue was detected were consistent with the shape of nuclear material storage containers.

Jerry got to his hotel room and found Kathleen in bed watching television. He went to the bed, sat down, and embraced her.

"It is wonderful to have you to come home to," he said.

"I'm glad to be here, but I have begun to wonder whether I should have come. Perhaps my impatience and willfulness have gotten you and me into an awkward situation."

"Are you uncomfortable here?" Jerry asked.

"It's not that. I am bored. I do not want to leave until you've finished this business, but I am too distracted to go sightseeing and too impatient to simply sit and wait for you to come back to the hotel."

Jerry took her hand.

"I'm sorry, Kathleen, and I can't give you a good sense of how long my work will continue. There are still a lot of unknowns here."

"Let's not worry about it right now. Tell me how things are going."

Jerry told her about Pavel Nosenko's murder and his daughter's distress.

"Poor Sonia," said Kathleen when he had finished. "She sounds so sad and alone."

"I feel badly for her, too," said Jerry. "I believe her when she says she had no knowledge of her father's activities. I think she was helping him because she loves him and he seemed to be unhappy and struggling."

"Do you think she's in danger?" asked Kathleen.

"She might be. It's clear that those who are after the plutonium will kill if it suits their interests. I don't think Sonia Pernen has any information that would be useful or a threat to them, but they could think otherwise."

"That's not good," said Kathleen.

"On the lighter side, I think David Greenberg is developing a personal interest in Sonia."

"A romantic interest?" asked Kathleen.

"I think so. He has commented on her attractiveness and his demeanor during our questioning of her was revealing."

"That could be complicated," said Kathleen.

"It could be, but at least it doesn't seem that she's a Russian spy."

"I guess it's nice there are positive emotions mixed in with the bad stuff."

"I'm going to get a shower and get in bed with you. Can you stay awake a little longer?"

"Certainly, hurry up," she said.

Jerry took a quick shower and got into bed beside Kathleen in a darkened room. She had removed her nightgown. They came together without speaking. Kathleen was active and Jerry soon found himself on his back understanding he should relax and enjoy the ride. They had a wonderful trip.

Jerry, Scott, David, and Roy gathered at the embassy office at seven o'clock the next morning. They were discussing a plan to search additional areas with the nuclear detection equipment when the phone rang. It was Inspector Roskil. He had gotten the name and address of the location where Pavel Nosenko kept his flower garden, and he was going there. He asked the Americans to come along. Jerry and David decided to go with him and Inspector Hassi. The inspectors picked them up a half hour later.

In only five minutes, they were outside the city limits of Helsinki. Within ten minutes, they were through the near suburbs and into the countryside. They drove along a two-lane road lined with a mixture of tall deciduous and evergreen trees. The leaves were almost completely gone from the deciduous trees. The morning was cloudy, giving the countryside a wintry appearance. The evergreens looked to Jerry like those in the forests of northern California and the Pacific Northwest. It was thickly forested on both sides of the road. Traffic was light going in their direction, but heavy coming into Helsinki.

Inspector Hassi drove and Inspector Roskil briefed Jerry and David. The widow on whose land Pavel Nosenko kept his flower garden would be at home and show them the flower garden a short distance from her house. Sonia Pernen was giving her minder a difficult time. A woman relieved the male assigned to her originally, but Ms. Pernen insisted that she be allowed to leave her home. She was incensed that they would not allow her to go to work. She wanted to leave to make arrangements for her father's funeral. She was angry and frustrated. Occasionally, she would retreat to her bedroom and her minder could hear her crying.

Jerry had an idea, which he kept to himself for the time being. It might help both Sonia and Kathleen if they were together. Sonia could use a friendly and sympathetic woman companion who did not have to say no to her. Kathleen needed something to do and could provide emotional support to Sonia. Jerry decided he would call to discuss it with Kathleen as soon as he had the chance.

They drove for about thirty-five minutes. The terrain became hilly. Jerry estimated they had traveled about twenty-five kilometers when they entered a small town with a post office and retail establishments along both sides of the road. A short distance after they left the town, Inspector Hassi turned left at a paved crossroads and, in less than a kilometer, turned right into a gravel road. They drove up a slight hill and soon came to a clearing with three structures: a house, a barn, and a silo. It had obviously been a working farm, but now showed signs of lack of use and neglect. There was no sign of activity and rusted farm equipment lay alongside the barn. The door to the house opened as they were getting out of the car.

An elderly woman came a few steps into the yard and waited for the men to approach. The woman was short and slightly stooped, but still looked strong and vigorous. Inspector Roskil introduced them to the woman.

"Do you mind if we take a look at Mr. Nosenko's garden?"

"First tell me what happened to the poor man."

"Someone killed him, Mrs. Kondrashev. We are looking for the killer, but we have little information to help us. Do you have any idea why someone would kill Mr. Nosenko?"

"My word, no! He was a nice man, a gentle man, a quiet man. I think he was lonely, but I have no idea why anyone would kill him."

"We hope to discover who killed him and why," said Inspector Roskil. "Can you direct us to Mr. Nosenko's garden?"

"It's right up there behind the barn. Why all the interest in his garden? The other men you sent were just here last evening."

"What other men? We did not send anyone else here," said the inspector with alarm.

"Well, they showed me police identification."

"How many men were there?" asked Inspector Roskil.

"There were three of them. They had one of those vans with no windows on the sides."

"Did they remove anything from the garden?"

"It was getting dark, but yes. I could see them putting boxes into the van. I thought they had dug up some of the flowers."

The two inspectors, Jerry, and David hurried to the garden behind the barn. As they expected a section of the garden had been dug up—a rectangular area about six feet by eight feet, and three feet deep. The excavated hole was empty. Jerry and David brought their detection equipment to the excavated area. They got gamma readings. The two inspectors questioned Mrs. Kondrashev closely. They got descriptions of the three men. The only one who spoke used Russian. The van was dark gray, but she did not notice the license plate. The men were gone from her farm before nine o'clock. They had to use their headlights when they left because it was dark.

Before they left Mrs. Kondrashev's farm, Inspector Roskil called headquarters to put out a countrywide alert for the police to stop and inspect all gray vans. Inspector Roskil instructed his office to begin compiling a list from the national registry of all vans registered in Finland. He had started contacting all car rental agencies in the country. A ferry was scheduled to leave Helsinki for Tallinn within the hour. Inspector Roskil contacted the Finnish marine authorities and ordered the ferry to remain at the dock. The Finnish Justice Ministry contacted the Estonian authorities and alerted them. Within the hour, the police and transportation systems of Finland and Estonia were looking for the gray van. Within two hours, the authorities in both countries recognized the need for additional radiation detection equipment across their countries and began enlisting the help of their government and academic scientists to procure the equipment.

The inspectors, Jerry, and David went from Mrs. Kondrashev's farm to the Helsinki ferry facility. With the help of the ferry's security force, they searched every vehicle and interviewed every passenger. There were no suspicious vehicles or individuals.

On the ride from the ferry back to the embassy office, Jerry listened to Inspector Roskil's side of his conversation with one of his security people. It seemed apparent that they continued to have difficulty with Sonia. When they arrived at the American embassy, Jerry spoke privately with Inspector Roskil about having Kathleen go to see Ms. Pernen and perhaps stay with her. The inspector was skeptical but agreed that Jerry should ask Kathleen whether she was interested in talking to Ms. Pernen. The more he thought about it, Jerry was convinced it would help Sonia, Kathleen, and the Finnish authorities if Kathleen were to get involved.

When he got to the embassy office, Jerry called Kathleen and discussed Sonia's situation. As he expected, Kathleen thought it was a wonderful idea that she try to comfort Sonia and was delighted to have something to do. Jerry called Inspector Roskil and arranged a meeting with him at the Finnish Justice Ministry. By the end of that meeting, the inspector was enthusiastic about Kathleen meeting with Sonia. Inspector Hassi took Kathleen to her hotel where she packed a small bag. The inspector then drove her to Sonia's house.

Later that evening, Jerry got a telephone call from a very pleased Inspector Roskil.

"I just got a call from my man at Sonia Pernen's home."

"How are things going?" asked Jerry.

"Sonia and your wife are playing cards and laughing."

"That's great," said Jerry. "I guess I'll be sleeping alone tonight."

"I'm afraid so," said the inspector. "I'm very grateful."

"You owe me one," said Jerry.

Coordinating the hunt for the plutonium quickly became a major headache. The hunt involved federal police in Finland and Estonia; transportation authorities in both countries had to be engaged; nuclear testing equipment had to be collected and distributed; the Finnish Interior Department wanted to be kept informed because of the nuclear risk; local police departments in numerous cities and towns of the two countries became directly involved; both Finland and Estonia had long coastlines along the Gulf of Finland that had to be monitored; the U.S. diplomatic embassy and the U.S. National Counterterrorism Center staff were participating. Inspector Roskil's head hurt.

An early decision was made to concentrate resources on locating the gray van that Mrs. Kondrashev had described. Contacts with automobile dealers revealed that five gray vans were purchased in the two countries in the previous week. After investigation, the police discovered that all were purchased by legitimate local businesses or tradesmen. Interviews with the owners eliminated any suspicions. Eight gray vans were leased at rental agencies in the several days before Pavel Nosenko's murder. Over the next two days, six of the vans were located. Three had been returned to the rental agencies and bore no evidence of having transported nuclear material. The other three were still on the road and found to be involved in legitimate activities. With difficulty, it was discovered that one of the vans had been rented by three young people. They were traveling around Estonia and sleeping in the van at night. The eighth rented van could not be found.

One of the hardest parts of the search was to check and monitor the boats and boat traffic along the Gulf. There were numerous marinas up and down the coast with hundreds of pleasure craft. Lots of tug boats and barges operated in the area. There were a few large commercial fishing operations and a lot of small fishing boats. The individual fishermen were the most difficult to deal with. They were hostile to the investigators and did not easily tolerate answering questions and having their vessels searched. At one commercial fish processing location, the police returned to their car to find it filled with the entrails of dead fish. It took almost a week, but the authorities were reasonably satisfied that the plutonium had not been moved out of the area by boat.

Starting on the second day, the police began being questioned about their visible and aggressive police activities. Word that the search involved radioactive material became known. Reporters began to question authorities. The police tried to keep specifics of the case obscure and to sidestep questions, but the effort was futile. Soon, television reporters were talking on camera about missing nuclear material. The police chiefs and mayors of Tallinn and Helsinki were forced to hold news conferences. Several police and politicians' staff members had to be assigned to respond to questions from the public and the media. Fortunately, no one had yet made the connection to nuclear weapons, terrorism, and the involvement of U.S intelligence.

Helsinki's school district began to talk about possibly closing the schools until the "radioactive" material was recovered. Inspector Roskil spent half a day in meetings with school officials and teachers assuring them there was little danger.

Initially, the authorities were unhappy about the publicity. It complicated their work and no doubt had alerted those in possession of the plutonium. But after a few days, the authorities understood there was an advantage to the public awareness. The police began to get reports about suspicious people and activities.

There were some amusing occurrences. The police went to a suburban residential community in response to reports of a suspicious, strangely attired person roaming the neighborhood. They found a former mental patient in a backyard with a metal detector looking for "the bomb." He had a metal bucket over his head with large eye holes cut into the metal.

Two pieces of information were intriguing. A gas station owner along the northern Gulf of Finland coast reported a gray van bought gas from him late on the night that Pavel Nosenko's garden was dug up. He remembered the van and its driver because he had already closed for the night when the van driver prevailed on him to reopen because he was about to run out of gas. A second report from a dairy farmer in the same vicinity described having seen a gray van parked off the road barely visible under trees that bordered one of the fields where his cows grazed. Additional Finnish Ministry of Justice resources were moved to the southeast of the country. Local police agencies were alerted to continue looking for the gray van and suspicious activities.

Jerry, Scott, David, and Roy participated in the search activities. They split into two teams. Jerry and David worked together, and Scott and Roy teamed up. They spent long days checking the new and rented vans for evidence of having transported the plutonium. When the van phase was completed, the Americans worked with the local and marine security authorities checking pleasure boats, tugboats, barges, and fishing boats for evidence that the vessels had been used to move the plutonium. They too had to deal with hostile fishermen and tugboat captains, but fortunately were not attacked with fish entrails. They found no evidence of the plutonium being moved by boat and, as time passed, they worried that the plutonium had already been moved out of the area.

For several days, the Americans did not get any useful information from Washington, and they did not try to contact Yuli in Russia for fear of endangering him. Finally, Meg Kupchak gave them some information that raised their hopes and redirected their search. The U.S. intelligence network in Russia had gotten information about Ivan Savinkov. Savinkov had recently traveled from Moscow to St. Petersburg, but almost immediately made arrangements to go from St. Petersburg to Vyborg, Russia. Vyborg was very close to southeast Finland, just across the Gulf of Finland. In fact, the city had been a part of Finland until 1944.

The CIA had intensified their efforts to get more information about Yukos' activities. The CIA was collecting information from Western companies and individuals doing business with Yukos as well as through their intelligence network. So far, there was no direct evidence that the company was attempting to procure nuclear material or to broker such a transaction. The name Leonid Popov emerged as a Yukos official whose role was unclear, but whose name seemed to come up whenever there was questionable activity. He was not a company officer, but he appeared to have considerable influence over the firm's activities. Popov had been a KGB officer and had a reputation for ruthlessness. Currently, he was traveling somewhere. Jerry and the others remembered Yuli's reference to Popov. They wondered if he was in Vyborg or Finland in connection with the plutonium transaction.

Jerry contacted Inspector Roskil immediately after Meg Kupchak's intelligence briefing and passed the information on to him about Ivan Savinkov and Leonid Popov. The inspector was easily able to get pictures of both from his country's files. Given their long, bitter, and violent history with the Russians, the Finns paid close attention to notable Russians, especially those who might represent a threat. The inspector had the quality of the pictures enhanced and had hundreds of copies made.

There were now several pieces of information that made the southeast Finland area along the Gulf of Finland the focus of the plutonium search: the two sightings of a gray van, the presence of Ivan Savinkov a short boat ride from the Finnish coast in Vyborg Russia, and the suspicion that Leonid Popov might already be nearby or on his way. Inspector Roskil knew the area well, having vacationed there with his family as a child. The missing plutonium could be taken across the Gulf of Finland to Russia easily by boat.

For investigative purposes, the Finnish authorities decided they would assume that there would be an attempt to move the plutonium in this way.

A plan was developed to set up temporary operating centers in Kotka and Hamina on the Gulf of Finland. Kotka is a town of 50,000 and has a busy container port. Hamina is an old town about half the size of Kotka that has a lively commerce with Russia. Jerry and David operated out of Kotka, and Scott and Roy worked from Hamina. The search operations were housed in existing local law enforcement posts in these towns. Arrangements for overnight stay for the Americans and Finnish inspectors were made in a bed and breakfast in Kotka.

The Kotka operation was just getting set up in a maritime security building near the waterfront when reports started coming in from local police and citizens about suspicious vehicles and people. The nuclear monitoring equipment was still in the trunk of the car when Jerry and David got their first request to check an old boat storage shed. There was no evidence of nuclear material being stored in the shed. There was a steady stream of similar requests.

As usual, the population of this area of Finland was fairly stable at this time of year. Vacationers and pleasure boaters were back at school or work. So when the word spread that the police were interested in unusual activity and unknown individuals, a steady stream of leads came to the attention of the police. The two American teams concentrated on testing various locations for evidence of nuclear material. They hopped on and off countless medium and small boats and discovered what messy places bilges are. They found the equipment that supports fishing and maritime activities is rarely stored neatly. They spent hours navigating around fishing net spools, rusty anchors, and piles of thick rope. At the end of each day, they were tired and dirty.

The Finnish Ministry of Justice and local law enforcement people focused on checking out the "people" leads and looking for the missing van. The Finnish maritime police closely monitored ship and boat traffic and the onshore activities of sailors and the few pleasure boaters who were still active at this time of year. Everyone stayed steadily busy, but after the second day, things began to slow down, and pessimism began to seep into everyone's attitude.

19

Recovery

JERRY AND DAVID WERE SITTING idly in their small makeshift office late on the third day. The "office" was a former storage room that showed the remnants of it's former use. Metal cables and rope were draped over large hooks screwed into the wood walls. Empty oil drums and boxes used to store fish in the holds of fishing trawlers were scattered around. There was a single metal table that wobbled due to a bent leg. The fish storage boxes were used as chairs.

Jerry's cell phone rang; it was Inspector Roskil.

"We have an interesting lead," he said.

Jerry's pulse quickened. "Great! What's up?"

"We might have found the place where our fugitives are hiding."

"Wonderful. Is it nearby?"

"Not too far from you, but stay where you are. We will come there to develop a plan. Meanwhile, the place is under surveillance, and there is no indication that the targets know they are being watched. We'll be there in fifteen minutes."

Inspectors Roskil and Hassi and two other officers arrived ten minutes later. They all crowded into the small room, standing or sitting on fishing boxes.

Inspector Roskil began, "Our local police got a report of an unfamiliar man buying groceries from a local market on the outskirts of Kotka, so they checked it out. The man spoke with a Russian accent. He bought a large grocery order and paid in cash. The man drove an old faded blue Volvo with a local license plate. The police began checking the area yesterday, and this morning they found the car at a house on a rural road outside town."

"Is the gray van visible?" Jerry asked.

"No. They did not investigate the house up close, but got in touch with the registered owner. The owner rented his property to a Russian man about a month ago. The man gave him three months rent and asked if he could wait thirty days before signing a one- or two-year lease. The man said he was starting a business to distribute containers shipped to the port of Kotka throughout Finland and Estonia. He planned to move his family in a month or so."

"Is there a garage at the location?" asked Jerry.

"There is an outbuilding on the property. The outbuilding was used in years past as an automobile repair shop. The van could easily be stored in this building."

"Do we know whether others are staying on the property?" asked Jerry.

"We think so, but we have not found a witness who has seen anyone but the man who bought the groceries."

"Do we know this man's name?"

"Yes, we have a name, but we suspect the man used a forged passport. The owner of the property copied down the man's name and number from his Russian passport, but it does not check out. He did not enter Finland within the past ninety days using that passport. He probably used another passport when he came into the country, or he entered the country illegally."

"It does sound promising," said Jerry. "He may be the one who dug up the plutonium and drove the gray van. I am sure you have a plan. I hope we can help."

"We have an evolving plan, and yes, we want your help. We will assume for now that the plutonium is stored at this rented property, so we will need your testing equipment and knowledge about how to handle the plutonium. We also need to know whether the material is dangerous or under what circumstances it is dangerous. This will influence how we handle the situation."

Jerry answered, "If the plutonium remains undisturbed in the containers, it is not dangerous—provided exposure to it is not protracted. But the material could become dangerous in two ways. The most unlikely scenario is that a triggering device to cause a chain reaction could set off a nuclear explosion. This would be catastrophic of course, but I see no reason to think this is a possibility for several reasons. Bringing about a chain reaction requires sophisticated expertise and has technological requirements that I don't think exist at the site. In addition, there is every reason to think that the goal of these people is to get the plutonium out of your country and into the hands of people who want to make nuclear weapons elsewhere."

"How else might the plutonium be dangerous?" asked the Inspector.

"Regular explosives could be used to explode the plutonium without causing a chain reaction. This would not result in a nuclear explosion with catastrophic blast and radiation effects, but it would be disastrous in other ways. I am sure you have heard the term 'dirty bomb.'"

"I have," said Inspector Roskil.

"A subatomic explosion could spread dangerous nuclear material into the air and could contaminate a large geographical area. Depending on wind patterns and the effectiveness of the explosion, it could kill a lot of people and sicken many more. In addition, it would be difficult and expensive to clean up. It would be a public health and public relations disaster."

"Okay," said the inspector. "We need a plan to recover the plutonium that prevents those who have it from exploding it in some way."

"I agree," said Jerry. "I'm going to check with our people back in the U.S. I believe there are a couple of experts in the handing of nuclear material on their way over here. This has been our plan since the beginning. Our job is to find and secure the plutonium, and scientific specialists will then move it to secure storage in the U.S."

"I'll need formal approval from my government before I can allow you to take this material, but I do not anticipate a problem. I think we will want to be rid of the plutonium as quickly as possible."

Inspector Roskil's cell phone rang and he answered. He listened for some time and then said to the caller, "Call in extra men and vehicles. Do not worry about being observed by the people at the house. Pull three or four vehicles into and across the entrance to the property. If you do not already have them, bring automatic weapons to the scene. Make sure you have at least twenty-five people there. Under no circumstances allow any vehicle or person to leave the scene. You have permission to fire your weapons. I will be there in about twenty minutes."

The inspector said, "Two men arrived at the house we are watching a few minutes ago; they drove a Mercedes sedan. They are now inside the house. I am concerned that the plan is for these men to take delivery of the plutonium."

"We should assume that is the plan," said Jerry.

The six men left in two cars. David and Jerry followed the inspector's vehicle. Jerry called Scott along the way and gave him a report. They arrived at the scene in about fifteen minutes—after having to stop to identify themselves at a police blockade of the road about a quarter mile away. Jerry counted thirteen vehicles and thirty-one officers in the area.

Jerry began carefully to survey the area. There was a curved driveway onto the property little wider than a car. The area along the road in front of the property was heavily wooded. There were tall trees and thick shrubbery about eight feet high. The shrubbery looked similar to the wax myrtle that proliferated on the southeast North Carolina coast. There was a lot of it in Jerry's backyard at home. He loved its appearance and its effectiveness as a windbreak and property divider. But it was a fast grower and dense. A man could not walk through this shrubbery without cutting away branches to open the way.

Jerry paid attention to trees. He had worked for a tree removal and trimming service the summer between high school and college and developed a permanent interest in them. The trees on this property were a mixture of evergreens and hardwoods. The leaves were gone from the hardwoods, making it possible to see the house and outbuilding. If it proved useful, the lower branches of the hardwoods would support a man's weight.

Because the driveway was curved to the left away from the main house, it was not possible to look down the driveway to observe the house. But standing to the side, he could tell that it was a two-story stucco house with a gabled roof. The stucco had not been maintained and had faded to gray. Streaks of black dirt marred the stucco surface every few feet. There were two double windows and a door on the first floor in front of the house facing the road and three single windows along the second floor. Jerry guessed the rectangular building was about thirty-six feet along the front and about twenty feet deep. No lights or people were observable in the house. The blue Volvo and black Mercedes sat quietly side-by-side in the yard.

The former automobile repair shop on the property was about a hundred feet to the left of the house. It was a long narrow building; Jerry guessed forty feet long and twelve feet wide. There were two single windows along the length of the garage about eight feet from each end and a sliding door at the middle. The building was metal. It looked as if it had been trucked to the site and assembled there. The garage building looked deserted. Binoculars revealed there was no lock on the door.

Jerry joined Inspector Roskil and several police supervisors who were having an animated conversation about how to ensure that no one left the house. They were concerned that the rear of the property might provide an escape route. It was heavily wooded back there. It was decided that a perimeter of armed officers would be set up behind the house about a thousand feet back. It would be daylight for another six hours. Three large searchlights were being brought to the scene in preparation for darkness; one searchlight would be set up to light the rear perimeter.

The police began to discuss how they would communicate with the occupants of the house. The occupants had to be aware of the activity around their property. Some of it was clearly visible from the house, and the police made no attempt to conceal their presence after the Mercedes arrived. There was no visible movement in the house. The police had determined that the house had a telephone connected to the hard wiring. The service had been discontinued months earlier, but the police arranged for the telephone company to reactivate the line. The phone company provided equipment to ring the telephone in the house and speak to whoever answered. They rang the line several times, but no one answered.

There was a small rural fire station about a mile north of the target house, so the police set up a command post there. At a meeting Inspectors Roskil and Hassi, Jerry, Scott, David, and two ranking local police officers discussed strategy and tactics. Caution was required because of the plutonium. They would avoid the use of force until they got a better idea about the location of the plutonium on the property. They also hoped to make an assessment of whether there was a risk of a nuclear explosion at the location. After Jerry explained the difficulty of preparing a chain-reaction event, it was agreed that their operating assumption would be that a chain reaction explosion was unlikely to be a risk. The group agreed that for the time being they would assume that a "dirty bomb" scenario was a possibility. This could occur if the group at the house had explosives.

They decided that the first priority would be to determine whether the plutonium was in the garage. If it was in the garage, it could be secured and the police could be aggressive in their approach against the house and its occupants. It was assumed that the people in the house were armed and that they would use their weapons if the house were approached directly. The back side of the garage could be approached safely because it was shielded from the house by the building itself. Darkness would provide additional protection. They sent for acetylene equipment to cut through the rear garage wall and decided to wait until dark to begin this work.

Jerry looked around at the assembly of people. Inspector Roskil was busy deploying the police. Police vehicles were arranged in a semicircle around the front of the property. A dozen officers with semiautomatic weapons and sniper rifles with scopes were stationed behind the vehicles. All of the police had either night-vision scopes on their weapons or stand-alone night-vision instruments. Ten men had already been deployed in the woods behind the house. Scott and Inspector Hassi were making sure the searchlights and communications equipment were working.

Jerry looked for David. He thought this was probably David's first real action with live weapons and wondered how he was doing. He found David kneeling behind one of the police vehicles, already in body armor, checking and sighting an AK-47. He had a "game face" and looked ready to charge the house. Jerry smiled and stopped worrying about David.

When the sun dropped fully below the horizon, it was very dark. There were no streetlights along the road and no lights inside the house. They did not turn the searchlights on immediately to give Jerry and the acetylene torch crew the opportunity to reach the back of the garage. The searchlights were then turned on, flooding the house with bright light. When they started cutting through the metal wall of the garage, there was gunfire toward the garage from the upper windows of the house. Almost immediately, there was a volley of firing at the house from the police. The gunfire from the house stopped.

Within a few minutes, a section of the rear garage wall had been removed, and Jerry entered with a flashlight and the handheld gamma detector to look for the plutonium. The gray van was in the garage, but it was empty. It took only a few minutes to search the remainder of the garage. The plutonium containers were not there, and there was no indication of gamma radiation.

Jerry, Scott, Inspector Roskil, and several other police officers had a cramped meeting in the back of one of the police vans. They discussed options and agreed they would move aggressively against the house. Inspector Hassi came to join the meeting and announced:

"The people inside the house finally answered the telephone."

"What are they saying?" asked Jerry.

"They are threatening to set off a nuclear bomb unless they are given safe passage out of the country."

"Are they willing to go and leave the plutonium?" asked Inspector Roskil.

"No. They want to leave with their vehicles and what they call their 'belongings.' They want an escort up the coast to an area above Hamina where they will be picked up by boat. They have generously offered to leave their vehicles when they board the boat."

"We could agree and simply subdue or kill them when they leave the house," said Inspector Roskil. "The men in the house may not understand it yet, but they will not be permitted to leave the country with or without the plutonium."

Jerry and Scott listened as the Finns planned their next activities. As the lengthy discussion about alternatives went on, a sense of certainty and confidence grew. A consensus developed that it was not likely that the group had explosives to cause the dirty bomb explosion. Making a dirty bomb would not have been part of their planning which envisioned a secret operation that would not come to the attention of authorities. It's clear the plan was to move the plutonium out of Finland. The Finns further decided that the sooner they took action, the better. The discussion then turned to how to gain entry to the house and capture or kill those inside. The Americans argued it would be helpful to keep those in the house alive for later questioning. The Finns acknowledged this might be helpful—but for them, it was clearly not a priority.

It took an hour to prepare the assault. At 0244 hours, the assault began. The Finnish police began firing at all the house's windows and kept a steady barrage going. At the same time, three pairs of men in protective military equipment rushed the house. One man in each pair planted explosives on the two downstairs windows and the door. The detonations blew the windows into the house, creating gaping holes. The door splintered into several large pieces. Immediately, the second man in each of the three teams rushed to the openings and threw tear gas canisters into the house. None of the six Finnish policemen was wounded.

The police lines at the front and rear of the house began advancing, weapons firing. The three Americans joined them. There was gunfire from the upstairs windows. Two policemen were wounded. Within thirty seconds, the firing from the house stopped, and after a minute the police stopped firing. Crouching, Jerry and Inspector Roskil entered the door opening, each carrying their AK-47 automatic weapons. The explosions had blown away most of the downstairs front wall. There were two dead men where the windows had been. One dead man did not look badly injured, but the right side of the other's body had been blown away. His head was intact, but his right shoulder, arm, and rib cage were gone.

They heard a moan from the rear of the house. They slowly entered the kitchen and found a wounded, half-conscious man lying on the floor. His head and face were bloody from a scalp wound and his left hand was mangled. But if he did not have internal injuries, it appeared he would survive.

Jerry left the inspector with the wounded man and started slowly up the stairs to the second floor. At the top of the stairs, he could see there were four bedrooms in the rectangular design: two bedrooms facing the front of the house on either side of the staircase and two facing the rear. The bathroom was straight ahead between the two rear bedrooms. Jerry moved cautiously to his right. The right rear bedroom was empty. A dead man lay underneath the window in the front bedroom. He had been shot in the right eye, and most of that side of his skull was gone.

Jerry started down the hall to the other bedrooms. Again, the rear bedroom was empty. Looking cautiously into the front bedroom, he could see a man's legs on the floor on the other side of a bed. The position of the man's legs told Jerry he was lying on his back. Jerry entered the room slowly. The sound of gunfire reached his ears a split second after he felt a thump on his right leg. He collapsed to the floor. His first sensation was confusion, but then he saw the man stand up and begin to raise his weapon. Jerry fired first, and the man spun around and fell to the floor. Jerry tried to lift himself, but could not. He heard footsteps on the stairs just before he passed out.

Jerry's next sensation was being moved. It hurt a lot and he passed out again. Some time later, he awoke on white sheet in the back of an emergency vehicle. Two women in uniforms were leaning over his lower body. He had an IV in his arm. He felt like he had just finished a strong gin and tonic.

One of the women turned and looked at him.

"Hello," she said. "How do you feel?"

"I feel fine," he answered.

"Do you have any pain?" she asked.

"My leg aches," he said.

"No wonder," she said. "You were shot in the right thigh. It looks ugly, but I think you are going to be okay. I don't think the bullet hit bone, and we've got the bleeding under control. You'll be on crutches for a while though."

"Are my friends nearby?"

"I think I can find them," she said. "Do you want to talk to them?"

"I'd like to know what's going on," Jerry said.

"Okay. I'll try to get someone."

In a few minutes, Scott and David were at the rear door of the emergency vehicle.

"Hello, Tiger," said Scott. "How do you feel?"

"Not too bad. My leg aches and I'm a little woozy. I guess they gave me some pain medicine."

"I'm sure they did," said Scott. "You were bleeding a lot. They say the bullet nicked your femoral artery. We were afraid the worst happened, but David got to you quickly and started to control the bleeding."

"Only the good die young, my mother used to say," said Jerry. "What's happening with the plutonium?"

"The containers of plutonium were found in the kitchen pantry along with Savinkov. The plutonium appeared to be intact and the total weight was within 1.5 kilograms of the amount that we thought missing. The CIA scientists who are going to arrange transport are not here yet, but they should arrive within twenty-four hours. We've decided not to move the containers, but to guard them carefully until the disposal team arrives."

"What a relief!" said Jerry. "How about the men in the house; did any of them survive?"

"There were three dead men inside the house. One of them is Popov. He was traveling using his own passport. The others had no identification. The wounded man in the kitchen is a Russian who claims he was just the driver and gofer; his injuries are not life-threatening. The weapons dealer is not hurt. The guy who shot you is alive, but your shot hit him in the left shoulder. He'll live, but he's facing extensive surgery and a long recovery."

Jerry said, "So, we have three live captives, but the one who would probably have been the most informative if he talked—Popov—is dead."

"Popov may have given us important information," responded Scott. "But the weapons dealer and the guy who shot you may give us a lot of information."

"I hope I get to question them," said Jerry.

20

In Hospital

JERRY WAS MOVED TO A Helsinki hospital. Scans verified that the bullet that passed through his thigh had simply grazed his femur and did minimal damage to the bone. A surgeon performed a procedure to clean the wound and repair damaged blood vessels. Jerry was resting, heavily sedated in a private room within five hours of his arrival at the hospital. When he opened his eyes about noon, he saw Kathleen sitting beside his bedside, a serious look on her face. She did not notice Jerry looking at her for a few moments. When she did, she stood quickly and knocked over the chair she had been sitting in.

"You should be careful not to disturb a sick man," he said.

With a smile on her face, but force in her grip, she reached across the bed and pinched both his cheeks. Then they embraced.

"You can't be trusted," she said.

Jerry looked at her with feigned hurt feelings. "But, baby, I was just doing my duty."

"Don't give me that crap. What were you doing stalking terrorists you knew were armed to the teeth?"

Jerry shrugged. "I really thought it was safe. The house had been bombed, tear-gassed, and riddled with high-caliber bullets."

"Really, Jerry. If you had gotten shot in the chest or head, I would be making funeral arrangements right now. You have to start thinking about me and our children."

"I really can't imagine ever being in a similar risky situation again."

"I hope you are right," Kathleen said.

"Have you talked to the doctor?" Jerry asked.

"Yes. You were very lucky. Not only because you were shot in the leg, but the bullet did not hit your thigh bone. You will be on crutches for a while, and you will have to rehab your leg to build it back up. You'll have a nasty scar."

"Have they said how long I will be in the hospital?"

"I think you can probably leave in several days if you do what you are told. Are you having any pain?"

"Yes. The leg is throbbing like hell."

"I'll tell the nurse. You are allowed to have pain medication right now."

"Good. I'll take some. I'm a pain-sissy."

A nurse came into the room in a few minutes and gave Jerry two pills. Jerry asked Kathleen about the captured terrorists, but she could not answer his questions. They talked about plans for going home, but Jerry soon became drowsy. A few minutes later, he went to sleep.

Jerry awoke several hours later. It was dark and Kathleen was not at his bedside. He rang for the nurse and found that Kathleen had gone back to the hotel for the night. He got more pain medication and soon went back to sleep.

Noise in the hallway woke Jerry early the next morning. His leg was still throbbing, but he decided to wait before taking more pain medication. A male nurse came into his room with a basin of water, soap, washcloth, towel, and a fresh hospital gown.

"Would you like help with your bath, sir?"

Jerry thought for a few moments. "No. I think I can do that myself."

"Good," said the nurse. "I'll come back in a half an hour to get you out of bed. The doctor left orders that you sit in the chair this morning. This afternoon we'll practice with your crutches."

Jerry struggled to wash himself—twisting and contorting awkwardly in the bed. When he finished and got his fresh gown on, the bed was wet, he was exhausted, and his leg hurt. The nurse came in a few minutes later and helped him get into the adjustable chair beside his bed. When he got settled, he took more pain medicine. He was dozing in the chair an hour later when Kathleen spoke to him.

"Good morning, Mr. Paul."

He opened his eyes to find Kathleen's face only a few inches from his own. He reached up and drew her face to his. "How wonderful to wake up like that," he said.

Kathleen smiled—one of her real smiles. "What kind of a night did you have?"

"Not bad. I woke up once and took a pain pill and went right back to sleep. I found out this morning though that I do not know how to take a bath in bed with a bad leg. I had water everywhere and aggravated my leg in the process."

"I'll bet," said Kathleen. "I wish I had been here to see it. Has anyone talked to you about a treatment plan yet?"

"They're going to have me practice on crutches this afternoon, but I haven't seen a doctor yet."

"If I'm not here when she comes in, ask her how soon you can travel. I've started thinking about going home and I'm not leaving without you."

"Do you know anything about the plutonium and the terrorists?" he asked.

"Just what you know. Three are dead and I heard the nuclear material guys from the U.S have arrived. Scott and David are coming to see you this afternoon. I'm sure they can give you details."

"Good. I've been wondering about some things—especially who the six guys are."

"Your part of the case is completed, right?" asked Kathleen. "Your job was to find the plutonium and that's done."

"Yes, but the case is not over yet. There is a lot left to learn."

Kathleen was silent for a moment. "I want us to go home as soon as possible," she said.

"I'm with you there," said Jerry. "The sooner the better."

They sat quietly for a few moments. Jerry broke the silence.

"I forgot to ask. How is Sonia doing?"

"Pretty well, I think. She is still very sad about her father's death, but she's gone back to work. I spoke to her last evening."

"Thank you for helping with Sonia. Inspector Roskil was grateful. I hear you and Sonia hit it off nicely."

"We did. She is a very nice smart woman, very attractive too. It was fun to spend some time with her and I think it helped her. She feels very alone. She has relatives in Russia, but none in Finland. She is a quiet private person, so I don't think she has many friends here—at least none she wanted to confide in about her father's murder. I was a sympathetic shoulder she could cry on. I might like to have her come to visit us someday."

"That would be nice."

"David Greenberg has been cute. Every time I see him, he asks about Sonia."

"Has he seen her since we recovered the plutonium?"

"No. I think he'd like to ask, but I have not helped. I'm not sure Sonia would like to meet him."

"You might have an opportunity to play Cupid."

"I'm not sure I want to."

Jerry had been practicing in the hallway with his crutches and was resting in his chair when Scott and David came into the room.

"Well, I guess he's going to make it," said Scott, looking at David.

"He looks pretty good to me," said David. "Shall we take him with us?"

Jerry smiled. "It's hard to kill an old man," he said. "I've been up walking around with these sticks," he said, pointing to the crutches.

"That's great," said Scott. "They were terrible moments before we found you alive."

"I was lucky, wasn't I? But tell me what's been happening."

Scott replied, "The CIA science guys are here and have taken charge of the plutonium. That is a relief. The Finns decided not to move he plutonium, so it has been sitting at that old house. They are guarding it carefully, but we are resting easier now that we have given the responsibility to someone else."

"Are the Finns willing to allow us to simply take it away?" asked Jerry.

"It appears so," said Scott. "Inspector Roskil has not formally said that yet. He is waiting for a decision further up the chain of command—probably from the Interior Minister or maybe even the Prime Minister. They may be considering other options, but the inspector thinks the political and practical implications of keeping the stuff will make them want to be rid of it. I guess they could be looking for something from our government too, but that's something to be dealt with above my pay grade."

David spoke. "Last I spoke to Charles Sparks, he was hoping to arrange for an Air Force plane to come to Helsinki. Sparks and his people will make sure the stuff is properly secured, and the Air Force will fly it out of the country."

"That's what they did originally in Kazakhstan," said Jerry. "A transport plane flew in, loaded up the nuclear weapons and fissile material, and flew it all to Lawrence Livermore."

"I'll rest easier when the plutonium is on its way out of Finland," said Scott.

"Tell me what you know about the living and dead captives," asked Jerry.

Scott answered. "Unfortunately, Popov is dead. He was probably killed in that burst of gunfire from our side when the assault started. I think he was the highest value person among the six. I'll tell you more about him in a few minutes. Two other dead guys we think are Iranians. One was probably killed by the explosives, and the other during one of the gunfire volleys during the siege."

"Are you sure they are Iranians?" asked Jerry.

"Pretty sure," said Scott. "There is one Iranian man still alive; the one you shot. At least we *think* he is Iranian. So far he won't talk, but the two Russians who survived say he is Iranian. One of the surviving Russians is Savinkov. He is the talkative one. He wants to make a deal with us. Our problem with him is likely to be figuring how much of what he tells us is true and how much is crap. I guess it's no surprise given what business he is in, but he seems like a pathological liar-wheeler dealer to me."

"How about the other Russian?" asked Jerry.

"He seems to have been a worker bee. He is talking, but unless he is very shrewd, I don't think he knows much. He may not have been much more than the van driver. I could be wrong, but it seems to me that Popov was the boss and the brains, the Iranians were the killers and the ultimate buyers of the plutonium, Savinkov was the dealmaker and money man, and the van driver was the gofer who did what he was told and didn't ask questions. I could be wrong about one or more of those judgments, but that's the way it looks to me now. Some of my reasons for those thoughts come from Yuli."

"Oh, you've heard from Yuli?" asked Jerry.

David said, "Yuli was trying to get in touch with us right when things were coming to a head. But we were occupied and not able to speak to him until yesterday. He has been nosing around Yukos and developing some information."

"Useful information, too," said Scott.

David continued, "It seems Yukos—or at least Popov—was very involved in the plutonium deal. There's a lot we don't understand, but the political and economic ties between Yukos and some Iranian factions seem well developed. We have no direct evidence yet, but the Kuds Force might be the Iran connection. They sometimes operate independently of the Iranian government, have a radical Islamic agenda, and give support to terrorist groups."

"You know, I've wondered if the Kuds Force was involved," said Jerry. "It makes sense that they would try to get their hands on the plutonium. They are the Iranian army unit that considers their major role to be guardians of the Islamic Revolution. They are more radical than their government and would love to have an independent nuclear capability."

Scott said, "The Iranian who will not talk does seem like a radical type. He is disciplined and stoic. There has not been a single word out of his mouth. I would not be surprised to find out that he is connected to Kuds."

"Where is this guy?" asked Jerry.

"He's right here in this hospital, under heavy guard. His wound is worse than yours. They had to try to rebuild his shoulder. We're probably going to move him to Guantanamo as soon as he can travel—if the Finns will allow it."

"What did Yuli tell you exactly?" asked Jerry.

Scott answered, "He found someone at Yukos, he would not say who, that told him about the close Yukos-Iranian connection. This person also confirmed that it was the Yukos security people who were watching him. He also told us what we now know ourselves, that Popov was involved in the plutonium deal."

"Does he know Popov was killed?"

"We told him about Popov's death. At the time we were talking with Yuli, word about Popov's death was not known at Yukos, at least as far as Yuli could tell. Yuli is worried about his own safety and that of his family. He asked about the possibility of asylum in the U.S. I told him about your injury and that I would check about asylum. What do you think about the asylum idea, Jerry?"

"If he is worried, I think we should take it seriously and try to arrange asylum. If it was not for Yuli, we would not have known about the plutonium. He performed a valuable service for us. Yuli is a traditional Russian with deep roots and love for Russia. If he is considering leaving his country, the threat to him and his wife must be real."

"I'm sure you're right," said Scott. "I have already brought the subject up with Hal Bolton. He did not seem sympathetic, but I will raise the issue again. If I have to go over Hal's head, I will."

"I think we owe him," said Jerry.

Jerry was dozing early that evening when Kathleen visited, but he heard her enter the room.

"Hi, baby," he said as she approached his bed.

She bent and kissed him. "How are you feeling?"

"Okay. My leg hurts, but I think it's a little better."

"I spoke to the doctor," she said.

"Good news, I hope," he said.

"Pretty good news, I think," said Kathleen. "She would like you to stay in the hospital two more days to make sure there are no complications, to give you a chance to practice on your crutches, and to learn some physical therapy exercises that you will have to do to build your leg back up. You have lost a lot of muscle in your thigh. It could be you'll have a permanent limp, but that will be determined by the success of your rehabilitation."

"I can tolerate two more days," Jerry responded. "Will I be able to travel home after that?"

"It depends on your progress, but probably yes—if we can find a nonstop flight. We will probably have to buy you an extra seat or two on the plane so that you can elevate your leg during the trip."

"I hope she will give me some pain medication, too," he said.

"She will, but she also said you need to be careful about the pain medication, and start to wean yourself after you get home. You are also going to have to continue rehabbing your leg for a while. Apparently it was a big bullet that went through your thigh, so there is significant muscle loss. She plans to talk to you tomorrow morning about the plan."

"That all sounds good to me," said Jerry. "It will be nice to get home. I miss the waterway."

Scott came to visit Jerry at the hospital late the next morning. He looked tired and was all business.

"Things have fallen into place pretty well. Apparently there were negotiations going on all day yesterday between the Finnish Ministries, our Helsinki embassy, and Washington. The State Department and our Director's office were involved. The Finns have agreed to let us take the plutonium. An Air Force plane will come in early tomorrow and fly it out of here. The Finns wanted to keep the two Russians and the Iranian to prosecute here, but we were able to negotiate taking the Iranian and Savinkov. The Russian van driver stays here and will probably end up in prison for a while. Between you and me, Savinkov and the Iranian are going to Guantanamo for interrogation. The Finns may not know that—or at least they don't want to acknowledge it publicly."

"That sounds good," said Jerry.

"I think it cost us," said Scott. "I believe we are paying all the cost of the Finn's operations."

"What about Yuli's asylum?" asked Jerry.

Scott looked uncomfortable. "I have not been able to get Hal to agree to that. I'm sorry, Jerry. I hope when I get back to Washington, I will be able to get Hal to reconsider. Or barring that, figure a way to get around him. I have an idea to get someone else to make the case directly to the National Director. It is something we need to do. I agree with you that we would not have found this plutonium without Yuli."

"Waiting until you can arrange something in Washington may be too late, Scott. Yuli's in danger right now."

"I know. David and I are flying back home tomorrow, and I promise I will get to work on asylum for Yuli as soon as I get home."

"How did David leave it with Yuli? Is he going to contact us, or are we supposed to get in touch with him?"

"He is going to contact David by e-mail."

"Would you have David let me know as soon as he hears from Yuli? I'm going to see if there is any way to help while you are working on things in Washington. Maybe we can help get him and his wife out of Russia at least."

"Okay. I'll let you know as soon as we hear from him. You are going to be here for a few more days, aren't you?"

"Yes, the doctor wants me to stay in the hospital two more days. No departure arrangements have been made yet, but I'd like to be on an airplane headed home within three days."

"When you feel up to it, I'd like you to come to Washington to help us do a final report on this episode."

"I'll be happy to do that. Do you know anything about interrogation plans for Savinkov and the Iranian?"

"I don't think there is a plan yet, but I know we will want to get all the information we can from them. There's still a lot we don't know about this episode. I'm especially intrigued with the Iranian connection."

"The Iranian piece is important, and there are a lot of loose ends to tie up. It will help our future plans and activities a lot if we can determine what the relationships are between Russian intelligence, Yukos, and the Iranians. One piece of the puzzle will be to figure out who questioned me and did not kill me. I don't think it was Yukos or the arms dealer or the Iranians."

"That is still confusing, but I'm betting it was the Russian Federal Security Service," said Scott.

"I would like to participate in the interrogations, Scott. I have a long history with the case, my Russian is fluent, and I think I am a pretty good interrogator. Can you support that?"

"Absolutely, I can," said Scott. "I think it is a great idea. I hope I can convince Hal that it is a good idea, too—although I'm sure he will insist on having one of our active people work with you."

"Good. I'll probably need two or three weeks to recover, but after that, I'll be raring to go. I've been working this case for many years. I want to see it to the end."

"I'll try to make it happen," said Scott.

"By the way, please don't say anything to Kathleen about this. It's going to take her a little time to agree for me to work on the case anymore."

"Mum's the word," said Scott.

Kathleen came to visit Jerry around dinnertime. She looked concerned.

"I got a call from Yuli," she said. "I don't know how he knew how to reach me, but I picked up the phone in my room expecting to hear your voice and it was Yuli. He is worried. You may already know this, but both he and his wife are being watched. He didn't explain why, but he thinks his life is in danger. Were you aware of that?"

"Yes. Scott and David told me. Yuli had been in touch with them hoping the U.S. will help him get out of Russia. He must really feel threatened; Yuli is not an alarmist."

"Things must be bad if he wants to leave Russia," said Kathleen.

"I think the threat is real. Did he ask you to do anything?"

"He asked me to talk to you and ask you to do anything you can to get help for him. He thinks the CIA may be dragging its feet and not taking him seriously."

"He's right about that. My old nemesis Hal Bolton is resisting doing anything to help Yuli. Scott Regan is working on it, but it's going to take some time."

"Is there anything we can do?"

"I'm not sure," said Jerry. "Did Yuli say anything about a plan to leave Russia?"

"No. I think he is hoping we can help with that—that the CIA can arrange it."

Jerry was quiet for a minute. "This is new territory for Yuli. He has not worked in intelligence. He has basically been a scientist for the Russian government and now for Yukos. He doesn't know tradecraft."

"Could we help him get out of Russia?"

"I don't think you and I can help with that. We could probably find a way to help if he can get out of the country. Let me think about this."

Jerry spent an hour considering what he might do to get Yuli and his wife out of harm's way in Russia. He called Roy DeSantis at the Helsinki embassy to learn more about getting into Finland surreptitiously. He asked Roy to talk to his CIA counterpart in Moscow to find out how Yuli and his wife might get out of Russia without being stopped. He called Scott in Washington to tell him what he was doing.

"I can't just sit here without trying to help Yuli."

"I understand," said Scott. "I'll keep working on this end, too. I think what you are trying to do is a great idea. If we can get him out of immediate danger in Russia, it will give us some time to work the bureaucracy over here for a formal arrangement. Do you think Yuli wants to leave Russia permanently?"

"He sounds desperate right now. I don't know how he will feel after he's gone for a while. Both he and his wife have deep Russian roots. Their son is working in Hong Kong, but I think his daughter and at least one grandchild live in Russia. Leaving the daughter and grandchildren would be hard—especially for his wife."

"He has a pretty good job, too, doesn't he?" asked Scott. "Yes, but it is with Yukos, and that seems to be the problem. He is well educated and experienced, so I think we could get him a good job in the U.S. if he wants to stay."

"Okay," said Scott. "I'm going to assume that we will work on getting a full package for him here: relocation to the U.S., a transitional place to live, a temporary financial stipend, finding a job for him, and relocation to a permanent home here. We'll wait to see if any permanent financial stipend is reasonable."

"Good," said Jerry. "I'll work on getting him out of Russia and finding a temporary place for him to stay."

"Let's keep in touch," said Scott.

Jerry responded, "You know, this could all blow over for Yuli. I can imagine the Russian government intervening at Yukos and cleaning up whatever is going on there. Yuli could end up looking like a hero when the dust settles. But for now, we have to act as if it is necessary to extract him and find him a permanent situation in the U.S."

When Jerry ended his conversation with Scott, he looked over at Kathleen. She had been sitting by his bed watching him talk to Roy and Scott.

"I've been enjoying watching you work," she said with a smile. "I always wondered what you were doing when you were a spy."

"I'm sure you noticed I was not disguised, and had no dagger in my hand."

"I did notice that. As you were talking, I had an idea."

"Oh oh," he said, smiling.

"Seriously, if we can get Yuli and his wife to Finland, I'll bet Sonia would give them a temporary place to stay. In fact I think she would be excited to contribute."

"That is a great idea! We'll have to figure how to get them here."

Roy DeSantis called Jerry to discuss what he found out about getting Yuli and his wife out of Russia.

"I talked to our people in Moscow about extracting our friends. The good news is that it is not nearly as difficult as it was under the Soviets. The bad news is that the Yukos people are just as efficient as the KGB was. In fact, a lot of former-KGB folks work for Yukos."

"Were you able to find out anything new about Yukos and the plutonium deal?" asked Jerry.

"Not much. Some Yukos folks were up to their eyeballs in the deal, but we still can't tell if it was sanctioned by the company. Popov's death has roiled things there. Things are buzzing—internal management meetings, a board meeting for tomorrow, a lot of back and forth between Yukos and Russian intelligence."

"Are they still watching Yuli?"

"I think so," said Roy. "But I think things are confused, too. I don't think they will decide to do anything drastic at least for a few days. Our guys in Moscow think the Yukos people are scrambling at the moment and thus would be unlikely to order Yuli arrested or eliminated for the moment."

"So we might have an opportunity to make a move. Or Yuli might have an opportunity to leave town. Can our people help him?"

"Probably, but they have two conditions: Yuli and his wife have to make the initial move out of town. Our folks suggest they arrange a vacation to St. Petersburg—make very visible arrangements to go there, book a hotel, buy some sightseeing tickets, tickets to the ballet, etc. The other condition is that we have a firm arrangement on this side from the Finns. They suggest a fast boat pickup and ride across the northern Gulf of Finland. Our people can get them from St. Petersburg to a rendezvous point on the coast for a pickup."

"We can probably work with those conditions," said Jerry. "Do you have any ideas about how to get them from the Russian side over to Finland?"

"Nothing specific," said Roy. "I do think that Inspector Roskil might be willing to help. I think he would be sympathetic to a request from you."

Jerry thought for a few seconds.

"I think you're right. That's a good idea. I'll bet he would help us set something up. And he almost surely knows where to send a boat across the Gulf. I'll call him to see if I'm right about his willingness to help."

"Do we have a way to contact Yuli and have a private conversation?"

"We'll have to wait for him to contact us, but I think he will do that soon."

Jerry called Inspector Roskil. "Hello, Inspector. This is Jerry Paul."

"Hello, Jerry. Good to hear from you. How are you doing?"

"Pretty well. My leg still hurts, but there's no bone damage. I'll make a full recovery, be getting out of the hospital in the next day or two, and heading home to North Carolina a day or two after that."

"That's wonderful news. I hope you'll come back and visit us on a pleasure trip."

"I'd love to do that. You have a beautiful country. I'm calling you now in the hope that you can help me with a problem."

"I'll try."

"I don't think you met him, but a Russian physicist named Yuli Karpov was essential in our effort to find the plutonium. I have known Mr. Karpov for many years. He is the man who alerted us that the plutonium was being offered for sale. He also helped to locate the plutonium by giving us information about the people involved in the transaction. Mr. Karpov is in danger because of the assistance he provided to us. We think his life is at risk."

"Is he in Finland?" asked the inspector.

"No, he is in Russia, but we are trying to help him and his wife escape the country. In Washington, Scott Regan is trying to arrange long term asylum in the U.S., but it is taking some time to get the formal approvals. We are optimistic about arranging permanent asylum in the U.S. so that any stay in your country would be for a short period —until we can finalize arrangements in the U.S."

"How would you like me to help?"

"We need your advice about a plan being considered. The plan is to bring Mr. Karpov across the northern Gulf of Finland by small boat from Russia to your country. I do not know if this is a sensible or feasible plan."

"That could work," said the inspector. I could arrange to have our marine services ignore entry if the boat is a Finnish one. I do not know if it would be difficult on the Russian side."

"This plan is in the formative stage. The idea is that Mr. and Mrs. Karpov would travel to St. Petersburg pretending to be on a vacation. Then the U.S. CIA would assist in getting them to a boat on the Russian coast. I do not know if they have a specific location identified on the Russian coast for a pickup."

"I would like to help your Russian friend, but I have to check some things first. I do not know how dangerous it would be for a Finnish boat to approach the Russian coast to extract Russians fleeing their country. I must also check to be sure no ministries or local authorities have a problem with such an action."

"I understand," said Jerry. "Can you estimate how long it might take you?"

"If I can reach the right people, I will probably let you know within a day. How long would the Karpovs stay in Finland, and where would they stay while they are here?"

"I think their stay will be less than a month. We have not checked with Sonia Pernen yet, but my wife thinks she would be willing to provide a temporary place for them to stay. If Ms. Pernen is not able to do so, I will personally help financially."

"I think your wife is correct about Ms. Pernen, and that would be a good solution from our point of view."

"Do you think we should check with Ms. Pernen now—while you are checking things?"

"Yes, I would do that," said the inspector. I will check things out and call you tomorrow."

"I appreciate this very much, Inspector."

When Kathleen next visited Jerry, she had made a plan for their trip home and had gotten Sonia's enthusiastic agreement to house the Karpovs if they came to Finland.

"David Greenberg has been a big help. He got the agency to agree to pay for three seats on the airplane for you so that you can stretch your leg out during the flight. The agency agreed to pay my fare home, too. From the time we leave Helsinki until we walk in our front door will be less than thirty-six hours, and ten or twelve of these hours will be in a hotel room in Charlotte resting and sleeping."

"Nice work," said Jerry. "I have really come to like David and appreciate his work. He was a pleasure to work with when we were hunting for the plutonium."

"David has gotten Sonia's telephone—ostensibly because he may need it to contact Yuli if he and his wife get there."

"So Sonia was okay with David having her number?"

"Yes. And in her understated way, I think she was interested in hearing from David. How is your leg doing?"

"Much better. I have been out and about on my crutches a lot, and I'm doing those leg exercises they gave me several times a day. I can feel the leg getting stronger. They put a smaller bandage on the leg too. That has made it a little easier to get around."

"Are you still taking the pain medication?"

"I'm taking less. I take it at night to help me to sleep, but I've cut down during the day."

"Great," said Kathleen. "Sounds like you are on the mend. Any word from Inspector Roskil?"

"Not yet. But I'm sure I will hear this afternoon."

Final arrangements worked well. On the flight from Helsinki, Jerry and Kathleen had a six-seat row to themselves in the rear of the plane. After they were airborne, Jerry took some pain medication. Kathleen sat in the aisle seat across from Jerry's row. She dozed between food and drink servings. Jerry slept under a blanket for six hours straight. They were home right on schedule. They enjoyed their first night at home in their own bed just a day and a half after they left Finland.

On the same day that Jerry and Kathleen left Helsinki, Yuli and Anna Karpov traveled with a CIA escort from St. Petersburg to the northern Gulf of Finland. They boarded a Finnish speedboat on a moonless night. They sped across the gulf and were in Vyborg in less than a half hour. The Finnish Ministry of Justice met them and took them to Sonia's home. Sonia was waiting to serve them hot soup and tea. They slept soundly that night in a large bed in her guest room.

21

At Home

ON HIS SECOND DAY AT home, Jerry began rehabbing his leg. He could not walk without his crutches, but he did his strengthening exercises several times that day. Jerry was in a hurry to discard his crutches and strengthen his leg so that he could participate in the interrogation of the Russian weapons dealer and the Iranian. He had not yet spoken to Kathleen about this. Scott told him that it would be several weeks before the serious interrogation would begin, so Jerry figured he had time to win Kathleen's approval for his participation.

For the first time since he finished his basketball career at Drexel, Jerry imposed a demanding conditioning regime on himself. He started at 8:00 a.m. with leg strengthening exercises; at noon, he rode his stationary bike; at 2:00 p.m., he did several isometric exercises they had taught him at the hospital; and at 8:00 p.m., he repeated the morning strength routine. Initially, all the exercises were painful, and his right thigh muscles were so weak that his entire leg would quiver under the strain. After a few days, he could sustain most of the strength exercises for thirty seconds. In a week, he added two-pound weights to his right ankle to increase the difficulty of the exercises. He began walking without the crutches, and in ten days he took the crutches to the basement and stored them.

Jerry adhered to the three-times-a-day regime, and in two weeks he was walking without a noticeable limp. His right thigh was still thinner than his left, but it was much stronger. He began walking outside, and a month into his program he was walking two miles a day and had cut back his exercise routine to twice a day. His strength and stamina continued to improve. He began planning his approach to the interrogation. After five weeks, he sent an e-mail to Scott saying simply: *I'M READY.*

Jerry waited until late afternoon of the day he e-mailed Scott, and asked Kathleen to sit down for a talk.

"I am not sure the agency will approve, but I would like to participate in the interrogation of the terrorists we caught in Finland."

Kathleen was silent.

He continued, "Bringing the plutonium case to a conclusion is important to me, and I think I can get useful information for the country. I know more about the case than anyone, so I am the logical choice. There is a good chance that the interrogation of the weapons dealer and the Iranian will provide insights about the weapons trade among terrorists."

"I had a feeling you were not ready to let go of this case, Jerry, and it worries me."

"I understand. If I conduct the interrogation, it will take me away from home for a while. But the work will not be dangerous, and the potential payoff for terrorism prevention is high."

"How is your leg doing?" asked Kathleen.

"It's really coming along well. The pain is gone; the crutches are gone; my limp is almost undetectable. I take pain medication only on nights when I have trouble sleeping, and then it's just over-the-counter stuff."

"I'm not happy about it, Jerry, but I know you need to finish your work on this case, and I believe it's important for the country. I have one request: when the interrogation has reached its potential, please come right home. Let others do the cleanup work."

"Okay. I'll do that. In fact, I'll be happy to do that. I think I can enjoy retirement after I wrap this case. I feel like it's time and I'm ready to do some serious fishing. It will probably be about the time the fishing gets good in the Inlet."

A few days after Jerry and Kathleen talked about the interrogation, Scott called. He asked Jerry to go to the Guantanamo Bay Naval Base where the Russian weapons dealer and the Iranian Kuds soldier were being held. Jerry arrived at the base less than twenty-four hours later. He was struck by the beauty of the base's surroundings. Guantanamo is at the southeast end of Cuba and is surrounded by a large harbor. As his navy transport plane banked for landing, the bright blue water of the bay and the rugged mountains rising from the shoreline looked like a picture he would enjoy having on his wall at home. As the plane leveled out for landing, he could see the box-shaped, military-style buildings scattered around the base.

The prisoners had arrived at Guantanamo two weeks earlier. They were placed in an isolated section separated from each other. Except for their solitary confinement, they were treated well. They were given some choice in food and reading material. The Russian requested and received financial newspapers and cigarettes. He was given two newspapers daily—after the papers were stripped of political and terrorism news and editorials. He was allowed six cigarettes a day. The Iranian requested a Koran and books on U.S. history. The prisoners were allowed out of their cells for an hour in the morning and another hour in the afternoon. The Russian smoked his cigarettes and walked a little during his times outside his cell. The Iranian did calisthenics and yoga.

Two interrogators had begun questioning the men. Tom Cunningham was a fluent Russian speaker who had worked as a CIA operative in Moscow and on several Eastern European assignments. Frank Longview was a retired diplomat who spoke Farsi and was an expert in Iranian history and culture. Both prisoners spoke English, but the Iranian would only respond to questions asked in his own language, and he remained mostly silent even when questioned in Farsi.

Jerry reviewed the videotapes and observation notes compiled on the interrogations. He carefully planned the first few days of his interrogation of each man. The plan for the arms dealer was to avoid the difficult issues at the outset. Jerry watched several days of Cunningham's questioning of the Russian from an observation room behind the glass wall The Russian arms dealer was clearly lying and dissembling. In a single four-hour session, Savinkov reported being both married and divorced, having won Soviet military medals and never being in the military, and claimed to suffer from delusions. There were amusing moments. One day, the man claimed to believe he was at Disneyland.

Review of the Iranian's interrogation was not helpful, except to demonstrate that it would be a challenge to get any useful information from him.

22

Interrogation

JERRY BEGAN TO QUESTION THE Russian. The man responded to all questions, but it was a challenge to know when he was answering truthfully. Some of his answers were verifiable through agency records or by checking with the Moscow CIA bureau. A pattern emerged. He was truthful in describing his employment up to the time of the Soviet breakup at the end of 1991. The information he provided about his activities since then was questionable. Jerry decided that none of the information the Russian gave for the last decade and a half could be relied upon. But it was possible, using agency records and reports of CIA and State Department officers, to document the dates of some activities. The Israeli intelligence service also had a file on him that they shared with the Americans, identifying a number of international trips he had taken during that period.

Jerry spent hours collating information the Russian arms dealer gave during the interrogations with information gathered from other sources. He compiled a list of inconsistencies. Jerry then questioned the Russian repeatedly about the events on the inconsistency list. He was careful not to say explicitly that he doubted the information being provided, but as Jerry's questioning went on over several sessions, the Russian became noticeably uncomfortable. At that point, Jerry broke off the interrogation. The next day, he ordered that no cigarettes or reading material be given to the Russian, and he was not questioned by anyone for three days. He was given no time outside his cell. His agitation grew during that time; he did not finish his meals.

On the fourth day, Jerry started interrogating the Russian immediately after breakfast. The man looked haggard and distracted.

Jerry began, "Mr. Savinkov, you have been lying to us. I have decided to disregard everything you have told us about yourself and your activities since December 31, 1991. So, we are going to start over again—beginning on January 1, 1992. Do you remember that day?"

Savinkov looked dumfounded. He stared at Jerry. Jerry waited. The Russian said nothing. After five minutes of silence, Jerry called the guard and left the room. The Russian was taken back to his cell. The guards reported that the Russian was agitated and did not sleep much that night.

Jerry had the Russian brought to the interrogation room early the next morning.

"Do you recall where you were and what you did on January 1, 1992?"

"How can I possibly remember what I did on a day so many years ago?"

"How old were you then?" Jerry asked.

The Russian stared at Jerry. After a long minute he answered, "I was in my early forties."

"Where were you living?"

"I was living in Moscow."

"Where were you working?"

"I was an economist for the Soviet Finance Ministry."

"How long did you continue in that position?"

"I continued working at the Finance Ministry until the fall of 1992. I was not paid after June of that year."

"Where did you work after you left the Finance Ministry?"

"I was not able to find regular work. My wife's parents had a farm in a rural community west of Moscow. I helped on the farm and with the marketing of the crops. I tried to start a beekeeping business, but it was difficult. I could not make enough money to sustain me and my family so I gave that up."

"What did you do after the beekeeping?"

"I went back to Moscow to look for a job, but it was difficult. It was 1994 and things were still in turmoil. I found some part-time work, but I could not find a regular job."

"Is that when you got into the weapons business?"

The Russian looked at Jerry silently. He had begun to regain his composure. Finally, he answered.

"Before we go any further, I must have assurances. And to ease our discussion, may I know your name?"

"Call me Harry," said Jerry.

"Okay, Harry. I believe you are going to ask me questions that, if I answer truthfully, will require me to betray colleagues and business partners and will endanger me. I cannot do that without certain guarantees."

Jerry answered, "I am sorry, Mr. Savinkov, but there can be no guarantees until after you have demonstrated that you will provide truthful and useful information. After you have given us useful and truthful information and I have verified the information, we may discuss arrangements that will assist you."

"Those conditions are unfair, Harry."

"You are in an unfortunate position, Mr. Savinkov. You were attempting to sell nuclear material to our enemy. If you had succeeded, my country and its people would have been at serious risk. I will not give you assurances until you have demonstrated your value to us."

"You are asking me to sacrifice my life and get nothing in return. I will not do that."

"That is your choice, Mr. Savinkov. But you should be aware of my demands. Here are the conditions you must meet before there can be any consideration of your needs. I want to know all the details of your attempt to arrange the sale of the plutonium that we recovered from the property outside Helsinki. After you provide this information and I verify its accuracy, I will discuss your safety and compensation."

"I don't know much about the plutonium exchange. I was simply a facilitator."

"You may be aware that we have agents in Russia who have been giving us information. I should also tell you that I have a long background on the plutonium case. I have been actively involved in the case since the plutonium went missing in Kazakhstan in 1993. You would be wasting your time if you tried to mislead me."

Jerry paused, but the Russian sat staring at the wall and said nothing.

Jerry continued, "If we decide to make any commitment to you, it will be determined by additional useful information you provide to us about your business. In other words, your compensation will be determined by the value of the information you provide about your weapons-dealing business, your supply sources, and your customers. The only value of the information you provide about the current plutonium business is to get you into a negotiation with me. You will build value for yourself by the information you provide about other weapons transactions, governments, and clients in connection with other transactions. Do you have any questions?"

Savinkov looked distressed again. "You make unfair demands, Harry."

"Perhaps," said Jerry. "But *you* put millions of my countrymen in danger of being killed by nuclear weapons. Considering that, my demands are modest."

The Russian was silent.

Jerry waited a few minutes and said, "Do you want some time to think about my offer?"

The Russian nodded. Jerry called the guard who took Savinkov back to his cell.

Jerry studied the videotapes of the Iranian's interrogation. Frank and Tom had been unable to get the Iranian to discuss any aspect of the plutonium operation. At times, the man would remain silent for long periods. It was also difficult to read his facial expressions and body language. His self-discipline had not wavered. Frank Longview was a patient man, but his patience began to shift to frustration tinged with anger. Whenever issues of his identity, background, affiliation, or activities were the subject, the Iranian would remain silent. Longview tried persuasion, cajoling, threats, ridicule, and bribery. He included Frank Cunningham in the interrogation at times, and at other times Cunningham conducted the questioning without him. They increased the daily frequency of the questioning and skipped questioning on other days. Nothing penetrated the Iranian's disciplined silence regarding substantive information. For the most recent three days, they had taken his reading material from him and eliminated his time outside his cell.

Jerry continued to watch the videotapes of the Iranian's interrogation, but he had not yet participated. He began to plan his own approach to the interrogation, and after discussion with Cunningham and Longview, he formulated his approach. He would try to recruit the man as an agent. At first this seemed absurd, even to Jerry, but he gradually came to believe it might succeed. The Iranian obviously had strong beliefs and values. He would not otherwise be capable of sustaining the discipline he had shown. The man was willing to discuss the governments and policies of his own country and others, including the U.S. Jerry decided he would first engage him in a discussion of Iranian-U.S. relations, taking care to be flexible and open-minded. He would acknowledge Iran's long history and contributions to world history and culture. He would admit U.S. mistakes and failures in connection with Iran. He would not initially challenge the man's beliefs. He would be patient and try gradually to build an intellectual camaraderie with the man. If things were going well after a few sessions, he would return the man's Koran and books. Jerry began to think of the challenge as a political seduction.

Jerry was already sitting at the table in the interrogation room on the day he began meeting with the Iranian. It was the first time the man had seen Jerry. Jerry smiled and spoke in English.

"Life is full of surprises, isn't it?"

The Iranian did not respond.

Jerry continued, "I will be meeting with you from now on. You have worn your previous interrogators out. They refuse to question you any further."

The man did not speak.

"You have convinced us that you will not share useful intelligence with us. And I will frankly admit that we do not know what we will do with you. I will tell you with certainty that you will not be tortured—at least not as long as I have anything to say about it. I asked to speak with you because I think you may be willing to have a discussion about Iran and the United States."

The Iranian looked directly at Jerry for the first time.

Jerry continued, "I have watched videotapes of your questioning by my colleagues and it is clear that you are an intelligent and articulate man who can enlighten me and my government about the reasoning behind your government's policies and actions. In the long run, it could benefit both our countries if we understand each other."

Jerry stopped talking and waited. The Iranian remained silent.

After a few minutes, Jerry continued, "I have been doing some reading about your country's recent elections. Would you like to know the results?"

Still no response. Jerry waited a few more minutes and left the room.

Jerry contacted David Greenberg in Washington and had him fax news articles from Iranian newspapers about the recent elections, and several articles from American publications analyzing and interpreting the election results. He had the articles given to the Iranian captive. He waited a full day and again was in the room when the Iranian was brought into the interrogation room.

"Good morning," said Jerry. "Would you like to talk today?"

"Thank you for the articles about my country. But your journalists misunderstand what the election results mean."

"I would like to hear how your interpretation differs from those in the articles."

"There is a persistent historical misunderstanding of my country by your own. The U.S. allows its hopes to cloud its judgment. Even though we consistently elect conservative, anti-American leaders, and in spite of Iranians' clear acceptance of Islamic principles by our government, you emphasize the minority liberal opposition."

"Do we exaggerate the liberal opposition in Iran?" asked Jerry.

"Clearly you do. There are differing political points of view in my country as there are in your country, but almost all of those holding such opinions are loyal and patriotic Iranians. Your country insults mine and impedes the possibility of relations between us by your distorted views. The American hope that Iran's government can be overthrown by internal dissidents is silly."

Jerry did not challenge the Iranian's point. At least he was talking. And Jerry had already gotten one piece of useful information. Although they were 95 percent sure the man was Iranian, they had not been certain of his national affiliation. The man had confirmed this fact.

Jerry continued meeting with the Iranian twice a day for about an hour each time. They had an animated dialogue on most occasions. The discussion was not always political. The man was a soccer player and interested in the international football competition. Occasionally, they discussed soccer news that Jerry secured from the Internet. During one session, the Iranian gave Jerry a tutorial on the relationship between the Koran's teaching and politics. After a few days, Jerry began to challenge some of the man's political opinions. The man appeared to enjoy the debate. After several more days, Jerry had the man's Koran and books returned to him. The Iranian did not acknowledge this gesture at the next meeting with Jerry.

Jerry was pleased at the progress he was making with the Iranian and, by the middle of the second week, he began to consider how he would begin to exert pressure for information. He decided on a straightforward approach.

At their next meeting, he began by asking, "Are you a member of the Kuds Force?"

The Iranian smiled.

"You have been very patient. I wondered how long it would be until you began to question me about the elephant in the room."

Jerry smiled too.

"I am hopeful that you and I can arrange an exchange."

"Ah, you are ambitious. I appreciate your honesty. But you are bound to be disappointed. I will die before I betray my country—especially to a representative of the American government."

"I do not expect you to betray your country," said Jerry. "I am hopeful that we can reach an accommodation that will benefit both our countries."

"May I ask you a question?" asked the Iranian.

"Go ahead."

"What part of the American government do you work for?"

"I am a contract employee of the National Counterterrorism Center."

"So you are an intelligence officer."

"I am working in that capacity, yes."

"Our countries are enemies, and I am a loyal soldier of the Islamic Republic of Iran. I will not betray my country."

"I agree that our countries interests are currently at odds with each other. But I do not view Iran as an enemy of the U.S. In fact, I believe that we can find common ground and that we should attempt to do so because it would serve both our countries' interests."

"In general, I agree with you—but there is no equality between you and me in current circumstances. You have all the power, but I will not submit to that power."

"I agree that you are currently in a disadvantaged position. But I have something to offer you."

"What do you have to offer me?"

"Your freedom. But I want something in exchange."

"What do you want?"

"I want information about your operation to obtain the plutonium."

"I cannot help you."

"I am sorry to hear that," said Jerry. "I hope you will give it further thought."

The Iranian man did not reply.

Jerry signaled for the guard and left the room.

Jerry decided to stop meeting with the Iranian, but he permitted him to keep the Koran, to receive other reading material, and to allow time away from his cell. He believed that the Iranian had come to enjoy their discussions and that discontinuing their daily meetings might make the man more receptive to providing information. A hiatus in their meetings would also allow Jerry to concentrate on his interrogation of the Russian weapons dealer. He sensed that the Russian would be anxious to arrange a deal, so Jerry decided to try to make that happen.

Jerry had Savinkov brought to the interrogation room, but he waited forty-five minutes before entering the room himself.

Savinkov spoke before Jerry sat down.

"I will give you the information you want if you arrange permanent asylum in the United States for me and my family and a generous income."

"So you want a blank check, Mr. Savinkov?"

"No. I simply want your guarantee that I will be relocated and adequately compensated for the valuable information I will give you."

"There will be no guarantees at this time, Mr. Savinkov. You have yet to earn anything. Have you forgotten the arrangement I outlined for you the other day?"

"That arrangement is unfair and requires me to provide information with no assurances."

"You should consider the initial information your penalty for putting my country at risk of nuclear attack. Now, unless you agree to give me all the details about the plutonium transaction right now, I will leave to conduct more productive business. If I leave, I will not return until you give your unconditional guarantee that you will tell me everything you know about the plutonium, and all the people and groups involved."

Savinkov dropped his head sighed deeply.

"I cannot trust you, Harry."

Jerry said nothing.

Savinkov spoke again, "Please tell me at least whether you are receptive to the arrangement I request—relocation to your country and a generous income."

"If I am convinced that you disclose all the information you have, I will do my best to locate you in a new country with an adequate income."

"You replace my specification of relocation to the U.S. and a generous income with your own words."

"The decision about your future status is not mine alone. But I will do my best for you if you cooperate fully. I can imagine that my superiors would not want you living in the U.S. and the amount of any income we provide will require considering the value of the information you provide and your new living arrangements."

"Okay, Harry. You drive a hard bargain and, I am at a severe disadvantage. I will tell you about the plutonium."

During several hours of questioning over the next couple days, Savinkov gave Jerry most of the information he hoped to get. The Russian was uncertain about the origin of the plutonium, but Jerry was not surprised by that. It appeared that Savinkov was outside the government at the time the plutonium was diverted from Kazakhstan, and the material was hidden and out of circulation for many years. Savinkov became aware of the availability of the plutonium when a business contact at Yukos asked him to make inquiries among his customers about their interest in purchasing the plutonium. He had arranged weapons purchases and transfers to Iranian clients in the past and was aware of their nuclear ambitions, so he contacted them first. He got an immediate positive response. The Iranians requested an exclusive and secret arrangement and offered fifty million dollars for all of the one hundred kilograms of plutonium.

At this point in the transaction, Savinkov said he did not know where the plutonium was or who else was involved. He later discovered that the man who contacted him initially was representing a small number of individuals from Yukos and the Russian security services. Savinkov identified four men by name, one of whom was Popov. Jerry was not familiar with the other three names.

Savinkov also confirmed that Sergei Andromov was not a part of the plutonium sale itself; he was hired simply to verify the authenticity of the plutonium. Yuli Karpov was not a part of the plutonium conspiracy either. He was viewed as a threat and was to be killed because of his attempts to uncover information. After the plutonium was delivered to the Iranians, Savinkov was to receive 15 percent of the sale proceeds, or seven and a half million dollars.

As the plutonium operation unfolded, the Iranians demanded that they be included in all the arrangements. Savinkov described how the operation took on a dark and dangerous character as the Iranians insisted on controlling the process. Karpov was murdered, they attempted to kill Jerry (Savinkov did not know it was Jerry who was questioning him), Pavel Nosenko was killed, and the order was given to kill Yuli Karpov. Savinkov began to think that the Iranians might kill him as well—so he had a plan to go into hiding as soon as the deal was completed. He felt safe until the money was disbursed because he was handling that aspect of the operation.

After each interrogation session with Savinkov, Jerry spent almost as much time writing a summary of the results as he did in the actual questioning. He sent reports to Scott Regan and David Greenberg daily, and asked that they check whatever information from Savinkov they could verify from agency records and active and former field officers. Much of the information checked out—at least on a superficial level. It was usually impossible to verify the detailed operational activities Savinkov identified, but it was often possible to determine whether the information was consistent with their visible activities—such as public appearances and travel schedules.

Jerry was particularly interested in the Iranians' involvement in the plutonium deal, especially the decision makers and their roles in the Iranian government. Savinkov was not very helpful in this regard, and Jerry gradually came to accept that the Russian was not withholding information. The Iranians successfully shielded this information from him. He never knew who the upper-level Iranian decision makers were. Others involved in the plutonium deal may know more about the Iran's participants and their motives and strategy, but Savinkov did not. He served a middleman's role. He handled logistics and financial transactions and shielded others from the more visible aspects of the deal, but he was not a principal. He was not in the room when important decisions were made. The information he provided was useful but did not provide detailed intelligence about Iran's plans and goals.

As the interrogation proceeded, Savinkov's intelligence value became clear. He did not have information about Iran's plans, but Jerry did get the names of individuals in the Russian security service and confirmation that Russian intelligence and Yukos officials were collaborating. These were important advances for the Americans and provided a foundation for developing additional intelligence findings.

After the third day of his interrogation, Savinkov insisted on discussing his compensation.

"I have provided all the information you require. I will not talk further until you fulfill your obligation. I want to know when I will be released, where I will go, and how much my compensation will be."

"Okay," said Jerry. "I will inquire about a compensation package for you—contingent on additional information. It might be several days before I can provide specifics, but I will communicate with my superiors in Washington."

Jerry was glad for a break from interrogating the Russian; he wanted to shift his focus back to the Iranian.

Jerry wrote a detailed memo to Scott Regan summarizing the results of Savinkov's interrogation to date and his expectations of the value of additional information. He emphasized Savinkov's contribution so far and projected further positive benefits. He recommended U.S.-arranged resettlement away from Russia and noted Savinkov's desire to live in the U.S. Jerry did not support U.S. residency. He did recommend a generous financial arrangement: a $100,000 initial lump-sum resettlement payment and $75,000 per year for his lifetime.

Jerry was surprised to get an answer from Scott about the Savinkov package just two days later. Resettlement to a European country would be arranged. The amounts Jerry recommended for resettlement and an annual stipend were approved. The U.S would pay $100,000 at resettlement and would purchase a private insurance annuity of $6,250 monthly for Savinkov's lifetime. The government included two provisions. The arrangement was contingent on Jerry certifying that Savinkov had fully cooperated throughout the interrogation, and the monthly stipend would be cancelled in the event Savinkov was prosecuted for illegal activities in his new country or if the U.S. obtained reliable information that he was engaged in illegal activities.

Jerry met with Savinkov to inform him of the approved U.S. government support for him. The Russian complained about not being relocated to the U.S and about the monthly income level. But his complaints seemed halfhearted to Jerry. After a short discussion, Savinkov agreed to the offer. Further questioning about his weapons dealing would begin in two days. Jerry suggested that Savinkov begin to make notes about the weapons-trade transactions he had arranged in preparation for their discussions.

It had been several days since Jerry had spoken to the Iranian who gave no indication that he would break his silence. For the first time, Jerry went directly to the man's cell.

"I have stopped by to let you know I will be leaving in a few days."

"Where are you going?"

"To my home. My work here is almost concluded. I will continue my retirement."

"What will happen to me?"

"I do not know. Others will decide. I will make no recommendation."

The Iranian looked silently at Jerry.

When the man said nothing further, Jerry left. He hoped the Iranian's continued isolation and uncertainty about his future would motivate him to begin talking, but Jerry was not optimistic.

Jerry asked David Greenberg to gather all the information he could about Ivan Savinkov. He wanted to have some benchmark information to compare the man's known activities to what the Russian told him during the interrogation. He expected Savinkov to make at least one attempt to avoid fully disclosing his activities and contacts.

Jerry began Savinkov's interrogation about his weapons-dealing career. Initially, he focused on the man's early days in the business: how he got started, the kinds of weapons he sold, who his early customers were, and what government officials were involved. He encountered no resistance from Savinkov at this stage. In his early years in the weapons business, he usually bought and sold small lots of handheld weapons. Typically, the weapons had been stolen by military personnel from their own country's supply, or Savinkov purchased small lots of older weapons from militaries that had upgraded.

His early customers were usually small groups of guerillas or terrorists. He did business almost everywhere—from South American drug cartels to the Irish Republican Army. His profits were modest in the early years. The man had an excellent memory and provided a large number of names to Jerry.

Savinkov's business picked up in the late 1990s, and his customer base gradually narrowed to North Africa, the Mideast, and South Asia. The sophistication of the weapons he sold and the dollar volume of his transactions increased. He learned how to conduct semi-official transactions without attracting attention. Often, such deals involved a government that wished to supply weapons to non-governmental groups, where the supplier of the weapons wanted the transaction kept secret. The financial size of his transactions grew, but the amounts that he had to finance and pay in bribes grew as well.

The interrogation was going very well, and Jerry was confident he was getting accurate information. Savinkov was naming individuals and groups. On occasions when Jerry was able to verify the Russian's information with information gathered by David Greenberg, he was reassured. The interrogation hit a snag, however, when Jerry asked Savinkov for the names of the financial institutions he used.

"I need the names of the banks you used."

"I used a lot of different banks."

"I want their names."

"I can't recall what banks I used for the different deals I made. You can get a list of Russia's major banks. I used them all at one time or another."

"Did you use any foreign banks?" asked Jerry.

"No."

"I know that is a lie, Mr. Savinkov."

"I may have used a non-Russian bank occasionally for the transfer of funds, but it was just for transfer, and I cannot recall names."

"Did you ever use Swiss financial institutions?"

"Never!"

"How about precious-metals dealers?" asked Jerry.

"No," said Savinkov, a little less forcefully.

Without speaking, Jerry gathered up his notes and left the room.

The next day, Savinkov asked to see Jerry and was brought to the interrogation room.

"I lied yesterday about my financial transactions."

"I know," said Jerry.

"I made a list of deals where I could remember what foreign banks were involved in the arrangements. The names of the banks are included. However, I will not provide information about my personal accounts. This is not information you need—unless you want to try to seize my accounts."

Jerry took the list.

"You are not living up to your end of the bargain," said Jerry. "But I will assess the list and talk to Washington. If this information checks out and is acceptable, I will let you know."

Jerry left the room.

After discussions with Scott Regan and others at the Counterterrorism Center, the Americans decided not to insist that Savinkov provide information about his personal finances. The information the Russian provided about foreign bank transactions checked out to the extent that it could be verified— and provided a wealth of information about eighteen different transactions.

The disagreement about providing financial information confirmed one of Jerry's beliefs about Savinkov's easy acceptance of the American's initial financial offer. Savinkov did not hold out for a larger settlement because he had wealth of his own—probably in multiple numbered Swiss bank accounts.

American officials in Washington were happy with the intelligence Jerry was getting from Savinkov. The analysts at CIA and the Counterterrorism Center were using a recently developed state-of-the-art analysis technique with the information. Jerry did not understand the technique very well; it was called "network analysis." The technique detected patterns between people, locations, activities, and calendar time. It had become a commonly used sociological method and had recently been adopted by U.S. intelligence analysts.

The patterns detected were informative and provided new directions for investigation. Based on the information Jerry was getting and the network analysis, new American intelligence initiatives were begun in Palestine, Afghanistan, and Yemen. Previously unknown terrorist operatives were identified and put under surveillance. Savinkov's information would have a substantial intelligence payoff.

After a full week of long daily interrogations of Savinkov, Jerry declared a two-day holiday. He wanted to assess where he was and discuss the next and probably final phase of the interrogation with Washington. He was also frustrated by his failure to make progress with the Iranian and wanted to try again.

Jerry was puzzling about how to approach the Iranian's further interrogation when he got a call from Scott Regan.

"How is the interrogation of our Iranian going?" asked Scott.

"It has gone nowhere. The man is glad to discuss world politics and U.S. abuses of various countries and groups, but he shuts down whenever his identity, activities, or Iran is the topic."

"Well, it may not make much difference," said Scott.

"Why do you say that?"

"Iran has grabbed one of our guys, and they want to trade him for their guy."

"Oh shit! Really? How did they get our guy?"

"We think it was a setup. Our chief of station in Jordan went to meet with what he thought was a potential new agent. The Iranians or their agents abducted him outside the hotel where the meeting was to take place. We lost contact with him, and his car was found in the hotel garage. Two days later, our State Department people in Amman got a call with an exchange offer. They want to trade our guy for the Iranian you are questioning."

"Damn," said Jerry. "What is the thinking at National Intelligence?"

"I think we are inclined to agree to the exchange, but the Director wants a report on your progress with the Iranian and your assessment of his value to us."

"I have gotten almost nothing from the Iranian. He's a tough cookie. And frankly, I haven't seen any cracks in his determination. We haven't tried harsh treatment, but I have a hunch that wouldn't work either. I'm not sure this guy would talk if we pulled his fingernails out one at a time."

"So I guess that means giving him up would not be a big loss?"

"I'd like the opportunity to work on him a little longer, but if I cannot get him talking, he is worthless to us. Do you think the Iranians grabbed our guy explicitly for the purpose of an exchange?"

"Yes, that's our guess," said Scott.

"So I guess we'll make a deal then," said Jerry.

"I think so," said Scott

"But I probably have at least a couple more days to work on him, right?"

"Yes, and if you can get him talking, we can probably stretch things out a little."

"I'll get back to work on him," said Jerry.

Jerry considered altering his approach to the interrogation of the Iranian. He decided originally on the reasoned, respectful approach after observing the man during many hours of questioning by Frank Longview. That approach still seemed best to him whenever he considered more harsh treatment. He had tried isolating the man and depriving him of his reading material without effect.

When Jerry told the man he was leaving Guantanamo, he had hoped the Iranian's anxiety would be increased with an uncertain future. But if he was feeling more anxious, it had not loosened his tongue. Jerry was unwilling to resort to physical torture, but he had been considering using harsher physical conditions like total darkness and extreme temperature changes. But with the abduction of the American officer in Jordan and the likely trade of the American for the Iranian, there was not the time for a new approach. He decided to start talking to the man again.

Jerry was waiting when the Iranian was brought to the interrogation room.

"I thought you were leaving," he said.

"I am," said Jerry. "This will be our last meeting."

"Will I stay here?"

"I don't know," said Jerry. "Someone other than me will decide what happens to you."

"I have appreciated the respect you have shown me," said the Iranian.

"Your circumstances are harsh enough without me making them worse," answered Jerry.

"Don't you hate me?"

"No. I hate your ideology and what you attempted to do to my country. I could kill you without hesitation on the battlefield, but I do not hate you personally."

"I doubt my next handler will be so reasonable."

"You may be right about that," said Jerry.

Neither one of them spoke for a few minutes.

Jerry spoke again. "I was hopeful that you would give me your true identity and affiliation for our records before I leave."

"Why would I do that?"

"It may be in your interest to do so. Do you think your government knows you are here? Both of your comrades were killed, and the Russian Savinkov is here at this facility. Who would tell your government you are alive? My government could do so, but you have given me no reason to do so."

"It is not important," said the man.

"Do you have a family?" asked Jerry

The man was silent. Jerry waited a few minutes before speaking.

"I am going to make an offer to you. It will be the only offer I make, and I will not modify it in any way. If you provide me with your real name, place and date of birth, your rank or position and affiliation in Iran, I will deliver one message to someone you designate in your country."

The man remained silent.

Jerry got up and said, "I will give you twenty-four hours to consider my offer. If I do not hear from you, we have spoken for the last time."

Jerry left the room.

Jerry's calculation was that if the man accepted his offer, it would be useful to have the information the man provided about himself—and correspondence he wrote would give further information about him and perhaps others. The personally identifying information—along with the man's fingerprints and DNA which had already been gathered—might be useful in connection with the U.S.-Iranian exchange that was being negotiated. He thought it was the best he could do under the circumstances.

The Iranian requested to see Jerry the next day.

When they were seated, he said, "I have written a letter to my family. They live in Hamdam in the west of Iran. I have included their address. If I give you the information you request, will you see that my family gets this letter?"

"Yes, I will do that."

"My name is Mohammed Zahedi. I was born on April 7, 1970. I am an intelligence officer in the Kuds Force. My recent assignment was to bring the plutonium material back to my country."

"Do you have an identifying Kuds Force number?" asked Jerry.

"Yes, I will write down the Farsi version for you."

Jerry had Frank Longview translate the Iranian's letter written in Farsi. It was a personal letter to his wife and children. Then Jerry got in touch with Scott Regan in Washington to give him the information he had gotten from the Iranian. They agreed it had limited intelligence value, but Jerry thought Mohammed Zahedi might be an intelligence asset in the future. Negotiations to trade Zahedi for the American officer were apparently on track. Jerry started making plans to go home and called Kathleen to give her the news.

Over the next two days, Jerry had final planning meetings with his fellow interrogators, wrote final summary reports of the interrogations, and made travel arrangements to North Carolina. He stopped by to say goodbye to the Russian and the Iranian. The Russian spent the farewell time complaining about his living conditions and the time it was taking to arrange his release. The Iranian shook his hand and Jerry hinted to him that his release might be imminent.

As the military transport plane took off from Guantanamo and banked to head north, Jerry looked back at the base and at the island of Cuba stretching to the southeast. The water surrounding the island was a bright blue. He closed his eyes for a few minutes, and when he opened them he looked out the left widow just ahead of his row of seats and saw the continental U.S. waiting. Involuntarily, he smiled and sighed.

23

Epilogue

IT WAS OCTOBER AGAIN. IT had been a year since Yuli Karpov first contacted the agency to warn about the plutonium. Yuli and his wife were recently settled in a four-bedroom home in a northern Virginia suburb. Yuli worked in the research department of a telecommunications conglomerate. His wife Anna was busy implementing a landscaping plan for their new home. They felt safe and satisfied, but hoped someday to go back to live in Russia.

David Greenberg and Sonia Pernen were talking regularly on the telephone. Sonia was planning a visit to the U.S. She planned to stay with the Karpovs, and David was going to show her some of the U.S. capital's highlights. Jerry and Kathleen were going to come to Washington when she was there to spend some time with the Karpovs and Sonia and David.

Jerry was fishing in the Inlet again. The fish were not biting, but this year his mind was at rest. The plutonium was safely stored at Lawrence Livermore, his country was a little safer, and his interrogations were paying intelligence dividends. But a course he had recently taught to new officers of the National Clandestine Service had given him most satisfaction.

Jerry had been home from Guantanamo for less than a week when he got an unexpected call from Scott Regan.

"Before I tell you why I called, I have some news you'll love."

"What is it?" asked Jerry.

"Hal Bolton is retiring. He wants to spend more time with his family."

"Really!" said Jerry. "Is it a voluntary retirement?"

"I don't know the details," said Scott. "But I'm told he was asked to hang it up. You know how negative he can be. The new director is a no-nonsense former military man. He doesn't have much patience for hearing why something he has asked you to do is going to be difficult. He wants you to salute and get to work. He and Hal were just not compatible."

"I think the agency is better off without Hal, and I guess I should feel vindicated," said Jerry. "But I'm surprised at myself. I feel sorry for the poor son of a bitch."

"There's no need to feel sorry for Hal. He's got a bunch of money, and he bought a forty-eight-foot yacht a couple years ago. I think his wife got a nice inheritance. If his ego is bruised, he can soothe it sailing on the Mediterranean."

"Yeah," said Jerry. "He doesn't need my sympathy. Do you know who your new boss is?"

"It's me. They appointed me acting director. They've told me if I do a good job, they'll make me director in about a year if I can get confirmed by the Senate."

"That's wonderful, Scott! I am delighted for you. You deserve it."

"Thanks, Jerry. As you know, a lot depends on the people you have working for you—and that includes you."

"You'll get the full job and be terrific at it."

"Thanks again. But let me tell you the real reason I called. Would you be interested in teaching a short course to the new class of recruits of the National Clandestine Service?"

Jerry was speechless for a moment.

"Are you still there?" asked Scott.

"Yes, I'm here. I'm just stunned. I've never taught anywhere, let alone at The Farm. What would I teach?"

"The training for new clandestine service officers has been undergoing changes with more attention being given to counterterrorism. Your recent success with Springboard got the attention of those designing new training course components. The training for new officers will still emphasize the traditional espionage topics: recruiting agents, conducting and detecting surveillance, establishing false identities, and so forth. But the people designing the curriculum want to integrate authentic case examples with the more generic course material."

"Have they said exactly what they want me to teach?"

"No. My call today is to find out if you are interested in considering the possibility. If you are interested, they will meet with you to discuss specifics.

They don't yet have a firm idea about a case study component; they want to talk to you about possibilities. Good bureaucrats that they are, they wanted me to be sure to tell you that they cannot guarantee you a training role at this point. They'll pay your expenses and consulting fee for meeting with them of course, but they've not made a firm decision to go down this road."

"It's an intriguing idea," said Jerry. "I'll be happy to meet with them, and in the meantime I'll develop some thoughts about how the plutonium case might fit into the training for new clandestine officers."

"Good. Someone will get in touch with you to set up a meeting."

Jerry went to sit on the porch looking out over the waterway. The idea of using the plutonium case to assist the training of new clandestine officers interested him. He quickly got excited about the idea. He went to his desk and began to jot down some ideas. Within minutes, the training potential of the case was apparent to him. There were lessons for teambuilding within the service, working with friendly and hostile foreign governments and individuals, dealing with complex technical matters, using secure communications, and other lessons.

He could even testify to the value of his practice at the firearms facility; he was convinced it saved his life that night at Mihkli Manor. While he was working, Jerry got a call from a secretary at The Farm who arranged for him to meet with the agency's training staff for two days the following week.

By the time Jerry boarded the airplane to Dulles Airport the next week, he was prepared for his meeting. He had gotten out his thirty-year-old training material and integrated those earlier training components with plutonium case details. He had almost fifty pages of material that he thought might fit into the agency's training plans. He had to remind himself to temper his enthusiasm and listen to the agency's own training ideas before he presented his own. He could not be certain his thinking was consistent with that of agency trainers.

Jerry need not have worried. The agency's trainers were as enthusiastic as he was about the teaching value of the plutonium case. Jerry's ideas for integrating the plutonium case into the training regime were consistent with the plan of the trainers. The training staff suggested changes, but they liked his general plan. Jerry and the training staff had a productive give-and-take during their meetings and Jerry left The Farm with a plan for developing a two-day course segment. He would teach his first course in about a month. He was excited and nervous about his first teaching job.

Jerry prepared to teach the new clandestine service recruits so intensely over the next month that Kathleen complained. He worked full time rereading old plutonium case notes, writing lecture material, and developing visuals and handouts for the students. As the teaching date approached, he realized he had too much material for a two-day course. He went through the material and pared it down. When he boarded the plane the day before his course began, he was excited.

Within the first hour on the first day of class, Jerry could tell the clandestine officer trainees were engaged with his material. They continually stopped him with questions and asked him to elaborate. When he gave them bathroom and lunch breaks, they crowded around him with questions. Jerry left the building during the afternoon break on the first day just to escape the students for a few minutes and clear his head. When the time came to end the first day's work, the students wanted to continue.

On the morning of the second day, Jerry divided the class of thirty-eight into ten groups. He had each group develop a plutonium search strategy set in the contemporary global reality. The groups were enthusiastic and competitive. They surprised Jerry by developing a variety of approaches. He was fascinated with the class makeup. There were no females in his training group in the mid-1970s. About a third of the current class was women. There was a diversity of ethnic backgrounds too: African American, Hispanic, and Middle eastern. Three students had an Islamic background. When Jerry ended the final segment on the second day, the students gave him an ovation. He was pleased and moved. His eyes glistened with moisture. He was confident he would be asked to give the course again.

Jerry settled into his seat on the flight back to Wilmington. He was exhausted and exhilarated. He realized that he had been living under a shadow since his involuntary retirement more than two years ago. The shadow was gone.

He began thinking about his recent lack of success in catching fish. First thing in the morning, he planned to go to the fishing tackle supply store a few miles from home. He was going to buy some different rigs and hooks. Maybe he'd try some artificial lures, too. He might even get an extra rod and reel so he would not have to waste time changing gear while he was on the water. He planned to go to the bait store, too. He usually used minnows for bait, but he had heard mullet often worked better. He planned to buy some live mullet.

Jerry fired up his laptop and checked the tide chart for Carolina Beach. High tide would be at 1058 tomorrow morning. He would have plenty of time to get fresh bait and be on the water at his favorite fishing spot before the tide peaked.

Printed in the United States
132868LV00007B/62/P

ML

9 780595 508341